# Hazing
# Meri
# Sugarman

by M. APOSTOLINA

Simon Pulse
New York   London   Toronto   Sydney

"Butterfly" © 1997 Sony/ATV Songs LLC, Rye Songs, Sony/ATV Tunes
LLC, Wallyworld Music. All rights administered by Sony/ATV
Publishing, 8 Music Square West, Nashville, TN 37203. All rights
reserved. Used by Permission.

SIMON PULSE
An imprint of Simon & Schuster Children's Publishing Division
1230 Avenue of the Americas, New York, NY 10020
Copyright © 2006 by M. Apostolina
All rights reserved, including the right of reproduction
in whole or in part in any form.
SIMON PULSE and colophon are registered
trademarks of Simon & Schuster, Inc.
Designed by Tom Daly
The text of this book was set in Weiss.
Manufactured in the United States of America
First Simon Pulse edition January 2006
2  4  6  8  10  9  7  5  3  1
Library of Congress Control Number 2004118416
ISBN-13: 978-1-4169-0610-0
ISBN-10: 1-4169-0610-X

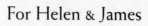

For Helen & James

*With thanks and gratitude*
to David Carlos Martinez, who read the first rough chapter
and told me to keep going; Anjali Ryan, whose encouragement
continues to inspire me; Lori Grapes, who selflessly taught me
how to persevere against impossible odds; Jennifer DeChiara,
whose faith in the outcome sustained me; Julia Richardson,
whose final notes made all the difference; and
Frederick Levy, whose belief in my abilities is
worth more than he knows.

*And, of course,*
to the real "Meri," a very classy gal
who graduated from her college sorority some
time ago and gamely shared a few stories—
but flat-out refused to show
me her pledge book!

# April 15

## Dear Diary:

I had a nightmare last night. It was after midnight in Marietta, Ohio, my hometown, and it felt like I was much younger than I really am—maybe twelve or thirteen. Walking through the town square, I noticed there was a long line of women waiting to get inside The Big Bang, a local male strip joint (you know, the type of place where women go for birthday celebrations or bachelorette parties and things), and I really wanted to go in, but not for any dirty reason. I mean, I've never had a boyfriend before, even though I'm close to graduating high school, and yet I felt strangely compelled to go inside.

So I snuck in. I scurried through the back alley, found an open window, pushed myself through, and landed with a painful thud on the ladies' room floor. It was strange. None of the women there seemed to notice me. I was invisible. Still, I held my head low, and when I stepped into the club, I was assaulted with loud music and a crush of jostling women (and a lot of really handsome cocktail waiters, too) and still no one noticed me. What was I doing here? All the women were beautiful. All the men were beautiful. And me? Okay, I'll be honest. I'm fully aware of the mirror and its cruel reflection of my pudgy face, my bulbous nose, and my upper lip, for which there is only one word: wax. In elementary school I was

1

cast as Nana, the dog in *Peter Pan*. And Miss Tucci, the drama teacher, didn't think I needed all that much makeup when she cast me as the Wicked Witch in *The Wizard of Oz*. Hardy har. I know, poor me. Play the tiny violin. I try not to get down about things like that. I try to be optimistic. I try to believe in the goodness of virtually everyone around me, even if they're making fun of me. It doesn't make the teasing any easier, or make me feel less ugly, or any less of a loser, but it gets me through the day.

But back to my dream. Suddenly the music seemed louder, much louder, the lights brighter, and ponying onto the stage was a stripper in a modified cowboy outfit with a ten-gallon hat that cast a long shadow over his face. Well, I may not be the prettiest girl around, but I have a pulse. This guy was really cute. He started dancing and gyrating and taking off practically all of his clothes, until he was wearing nothing but a jock strap, cowboy boots, and that big ten-gallon hat. By this time I was getting nervous, not because of the guy dancing, but because everyone in the club started melting away, literally, till there was no one left but me and the stripper. Then the music stopped cold. The stripper lit a big, fat cigar, pointed his finger directly at me, and whipped off his hat. My jaw dropped. I couldn't believe it. The stripper was my dad!

Then I woke up and there was Dad coming right at me, along with Mom and my sister, Lisa, all of them singing "Happy Birthday." I gasped and yanked the covers up, and tumbling to the floor was my dog-eared copy of *Come Slowly, My Darling*, with a really handsome matador embracing a peasant girl on the cover.

"Eeeow," chuckled Lisa. "Cindy's reading dirty books again."

Mom shushed her, but you could tell she was holding back a laugh too. See, Lisa may be three years younger than me, but she's very pretty (just like Mom). I'll be blunt about Mom. I'm a disappointment to her. I was her firstborn—and look how I turned out.

In a way, I'm glad Lisa's around. The less attention I get, the better. My dad's another story. He's so nice to me. Once he even took me shopping for my sixteenth birthday in Parkersburg, West Virginia (that's the closest big town nearby), and bought me a genuine gold necklace. It sparkles. And, yes, he's handsome, I admit it. He treats me like a real person, too. Not that he shouldn't—he is my dad, after all—but in my life, that's kind of a novelty. He also gave me the sweetest gift for my birthday this year: this diary.

"For all your happy thoughts," he said, and I could see Lisa making a gagging motion behind him.

I'm not sure how many happy thoughts I have, but I do have a potentially good academic future. I was recently accepted to Rumson River University in North Carolina, just like Dad. That's where Mom and Dad met, in fact. He was the star quarterback, she was head cheerleader. I know, I know, but it's true. Mom has a framed picture of herself from her college days doing a high kick on the football field. It hangs right above her scale in the bathroom. Even I have to admit she looks pretty similar; she hasn't changed at all. Lisa's a cheerleader too, but I kind of doubt she'll get into Rumson U. Her grades suck. But enough about Lisa and my mom. This diary is supposed to be about me. Only I don't know what to say. I'm sitting up in my bed right now writing this—my seventeenth birthday is coming to an end. I should be happy, but I'm not. Sometimes I can't stand myself or anything around me, including my bedroom. A few months ago Lisa and Mom discovered decoupage. They decoupaged all my walls: pink pussycats and rainbows. Yuck. They even decoupaged my phone.

Maybe I'll have a nice dream tonight. I wish you could will yourself to dream about nice things. Maybe I'll dream about Rumson U. I have a feeling things will be different there. It is an institution of higher learning, after all, and I'm majoring in literature. People will be serious there, and I'll meet all kinds of like-minded friends—people who are happy to learn and who don't care about what I look like. Maybe I'll even have a boyfriend. Okay, that's probably stretching it, or tempting the gods, or something like that. I'm such a loser. I think I'd like to dream about nothing tonight. Absolutely nothing. That sounds safe.

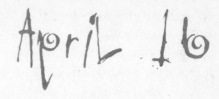

# Dear Diary:

I don't think I can do this diary thing anymore. Why should I? What am I supposed to write about? All the terrible things that happen to me every day? Take today, for example. Bud Finger, this really immature, jerky guy, snuck up behind me at my locker after third period and whispered, "Bud Finger, at your cervix."

I pushed him away and he laughed—with that sputtering, snot-filled laugh he has.

"You're a moo-cow," he added, then he darted down the hall.

Well, that wasn't so bad, I guess, but I had no idea he had stuck a piece of paper on my back that said in big, black Sharpie letters: IF YOU WANT MY ATTENTION, MOO. It took me almost two whole periods to realize why everyone was going, "M-o-o-o-o-o-o," when they saw me. My chemistry teacher, Mrs. Felton, was the one who told me about it. It didn't help that she was stifling a laugh.

At the end of the day I went to my locker, minding my own business (I swear), and I heard soft moaning. I looked over, and two lockers down Julie Murmelstone was making out with Jeff Leigh.

"Jeff. God. You're standing at attention," she cooed.

He grinned. "You know what they say. To fully inflate, blow into the tube."

She coyly squealed and blew a little puff of air at him. Then she turned and saw me. I guess I was gaping. I couldn't move. I was frozen to the spot.

"Aw, lookit. It's little Cindy Bixby. You like to watch? Is that it? Is that what gets you off? Little Miss Priss likes to watch?"

They laughed at me. I don't care what anyone says to me— really, no matter how awful or nasty it is. But being laughed at hurts.

Is that what this diary is going to be? A list of how people make fun of me every day? No, thank you, ma'am. I don't need to look back at this thing years later and relive all the misery. Living it's enough. I'm a good person and I want a good future for myself. If I remain positive, positive things will happen, and people like Bud Finger and Julie Murmelstone won't bug me anymore. I mean, maybe they will, but it won't faze me.

I saw *Carrie* on cable the other night. I didn't identify with that girl. I don't want to hurt anyone. Maybe the trick is to stop thinking about it. And stop writing about it too. I'm sorry, Diary, but I think it's time to put you away. For good. My life is depressing enough.

# August 14

## Dear Diary:

I'm so glad I found you! My room is a complete wreck. I'm packing up for college. There you were under my bed next to my rumpled culottes and my old recorder from third grade. So much has changed. So many good things. I glanced over what I wrote before, and boy, I sure was "down in the dumpity-doo" (Mom always uses that phrase) (in reference to me) (of course). But things turned around as my senior year drew to a close. Goodbye, Chesterfield High.

And guess what? I even went to the prom. Okay, so I went with Bud Finger, but don't draw quick conclusions. See, no one would go with Bud. He asked practically every girl in school, even a couple of the mentally challenged girls from the Special Education program.

"Some of them bitches are tasty," he said, but I guess even mentally challenged girls know better.

Anyway, I was riding the bus home one day and he hit me in the back of the head with a paperback copy of *Forced Heretic 2: Star Wars, The New Jedi Order, Book 16*. (Now you know who reads that junk.) He said it was an accident, and he didn't laugh, so I knew he wanted something. Then he just flat out asked me:

"Wanna go to the prom?"

It took me a moment, but actually not that long. In what

seemed like half a second, I went over all the pros and cons. On the pro side, I hadn't even thought of going to the prom (I didn't even think it was a possibility), so the idea of actually buying a dress and getting a corsage and dancing with all my other class-mates was pretty tempting. On the con side, there was the issue of Bud. I said, "Yes." He grinned stupidly.

"Uh-huh. I figured you'd say that."

Why did I say yes? Well, because even if I'd be going with Bud, I'd still be going. And now I won't be some bitter old lady in a rocking chair in my eighties too embarrassed to tell my grand-children that I never went to my prom. That's too sad. I'm trying so hard not to be sad these days. Usually, I look at every new situation in my life as if disaster is inevitable. It makes me very tense. I guess I lack the confidence of someone like Lisa, for instance. In fact, I don't have any confidence at all. But I'm trying a new trick these days: I'm pretending that I do.

The prom was fun. Bud forgot to bring a corsage, of course, but that was okay. I had a plan. Once we arrived at the school gym, I ditched him. Completely. I spent time with a few girls when they weren't dancing with their boyfriends, and I had a nice chat about my future with Mr. Sherman, my Honors English teacher. Bud kept asking me to dance, and I kept saying no. This was going to be my prom on my terms, and those terms did not include dancing and being groped by Bud. I did dance, though, once. Mr. Sherman very nicely took me to the dance floor when the band played a slightly off-key rendition of "Top of the World" by the Dixie Chicks. In my head, I was mentally crossing items off a list: I went to the prom, I talked with friends, I danced. These are all good things. And even though Bud tried to stick his tongue down my throat when he dropped me off (I bit it really hard), I felt triumphant. Woo hoo!

Who would have thought that I, Cindy Bixby, would have gone to her high school prom?

Things only got better once I graduated. Dad paid for LASIK surgery for my eyes. Wow! I can't tell you how nice it is not to wear glasses (my eyes couldn't take contacts). I feel so much happier. Even prettier.

"You're plain now," observed Lisa. "That's better than before."

Even Mom is treating me nicer, though Lisa thinks it's because I'm leaving, which means she'll have one less "thing" to worry about. But I don't think that's it. Mom made jasmine tea for me the other night and told me all about her days at Rumson U. And get this: Mom was a sorority girl. She was even president of her sorority, Alpha Beta Delta.

"If you want to be popular and meet nice boys, it's important to join a good sorority."

"Then I'll join one!" I enthused.

There was this weird sort of concave pause after I said that, and Mom cupped her mug and stared down at it and seemed to smile a bit.

"Don't you think I should?" I asked.

"My tea is cold," she intoned, then she stepped away to freshen her cup.

If I join a sorority and I become popular, then who knows, maybe I'll meet a handsome football player just like Mom did. I have to laugh. If I'd written down things like this a few months ago (or even thought about them), I'd probably have started to feel sad and imagine all the terrible things that would happen to me if I even tried. But not anymore. This "pretending" thing is working out well. I'm still scared, I still feel ugly (not scary-ugly, but plain, I guess, like Lisa says), and to tell you the truth, I don't know why my attitude has changed. Maybe it's because high school is finally over and I'm packing up. I'm leaving Marietta.

I'm also looking forward to all the hard work at Rumson U. And, yes, I'm looking forward to dating. I think I'm a late bloomer. I think that fits me. Everything good and happy and wonderful that's going to happen to me will happen in college. How's that sound, Diary? See? I can be positive. And if that's stretching it, or tempting the gods, so be it. Cindy Bixby's raring to go!

# August 15

## Dear Diary:

These Greyhound buses sure are cramped. But what a morning I had. Mom, Dad, and Lisa brought me to the bus station in Parkersburg, and I actually thought Dad was going to cry.

"Be careful," he said. "It's a tough world out there."

Mom, on the other hand, was overjoyed. I think she knows I'm a late bloomer too. She seemed so happy to see me off on my big, new adventure.

"I'll e-mail you," I promised.

"No, don't do that," she said, no doubt realizing how busy I'll probably be.

Lisa didn't have anything to say. In fact, she didn't even think it was necessary to see me off at all.

"It's not like you're doing a moon shot," she told me at breakfast.

She also told me that she's reached a decision about her future. Unlike me, she is not going to college after she graduates from high school. Instead, she's going to become a big star like Christina Aguilera. Starting ASAP.

"I'm just as pretty," she said.

I tried to tell her (gently) that maybe she should rethink this. After all, Christina's been at this pop star thing for a very long time, even as far back as *The New Mickey Mouse Club*.

"Same with Britney," she said huffily. "Only Britney's tired. Christina's in it for the long haul. Like me."

Still, I expressed my qualms. Yes, Lisa's just as pretty as Christina, but Christina does sing pretty well.

"Please, it's all computers. That bitch can't sing a note. You watch. In a year or less, I'll be right where she is. Mom's taking me shopping after we drop you off. I'll get the right outfits, I'll cut a demo. Done."

It was hard to argue with her. She seemed so certain. There's a lesson to be learned from Lisa—several, in fact. I wish I had her confidence, but maybe that'll come in time. I remember observing once, in fifth grade, how all the boys and the girls started asking each other out, even going steady; there was no hesitation, no qualms, it was just the natural course of things. So when Peter Gilberti, this really cute guy who wore a retro puka necklace, came up to me on the playground and asked me if I'd like to go out with him, I didn't blink an eye.

"Why, yes, I'd love to, Peter."

He suddenly burst out laughing, and his friends Kate Manning and Jordi Kane leaped out, laughing, slapping five.

"Why, yes, I'd love to, Peter," they chanted in a singsongy tone.

Okay, so that was embarrassing, but it taught me a lesson. See, I'm into this new "pretending" thing now—pretending that I'm confident, that I'm not plain or ugly—and I think I was taking baby steps toward that back in fifth grade, but I just didn't have it down right. One word: practice. In the past few months, I've been rehearsing my pretend confidence around Lisa. At first she was really put off by it, even angry, especially when I told her I'd find the boy of my dreams in college. She couldn't stop laughing. But she sure shut up when she came home from cheerleading practice the next day and saw that I had painted over all the decoupage in my bedroom.

"Me and Mom worked so hard!" she whined.

"Toughie-wuffy," I said, standing firm. "It's my bedroom. And I hate pussycats and rainbows."

Then I slammed the door in her face. True, she wasn't any nicer to me after that—her new nickname for me is "Psycho Bitch"—but she keeps her distance, and she doesn't pick on me anymore (at least not as regularly), and all I had to do was pretend. In my mind I told myself, "Lisa is irrelevant." I don't really believe that, but I've rehearsed it so much that Lisa believes it. That's what counts.

I'm getting sleepy. Only six more hours on this bus and I'll be at Rumson U. I'll write more soon. I think all the packing and all the excitement have finally caught up with me. But I will send Mom an e-mail tonight. I know she'll want to hear that I've arrived okay.

# Apostolina

From: cindybixby <cindybixby@yahoo.com>
Date: 15 August
To: mom <elainebixby@msn.com>
Subject: I Made It!

Hi, Mom!

I finally made it to Rumson!! Unfortunately, my bus was late coming in, so I missed the college shuttle. I had to drag my suitcase and my trunk eight whole blocks just to get to my dorm room, but it gave me time to see the campus a bit, even though it was pretty dark outside.

My roommate doesn't arrive till tomorrow, so I guess I'll wait to unpack until then, just in case she has any preference about which bed or dresser she wants. Either way is fine with me!!

Phew, it's almost midnight and I'm tired!! I'd call to let you know that I'm here, but I know how you hate to hear the phone ringing after ten p.m. Ha!

I'll check my e-mail in a few minutes, though, just to see if you're still up and have written back.

Please give my love to Dad (and Lisa, too). I'm so excited to be here!!!!

Love,
Cindy
xxoo

From: Mail Delivery Subsystem <MAILER DAEMON@outmail6.net>
Date: 15 August
To: <cindybixby@yahoo.com>
Subject: re: I Made It!

—The following addresses had permanent fatal errors—
<elainebixby@msn.com>
(reason: 550 Requested action not taken)
550 5.1.1 <cindybixby@yahoo.com> . . . User e-mail blocked

For some reason Mom's e-mail seems to be on the fritz. What's up with that? Maybe I'll try e-mailing her again tomorrow morning, or better yet, I'll call her. I still can't believe I'm here. My room is kind of cramped, and I'll be sharing it with a roommate, but the curtains are nice (they're white, with pinched pleats) and the small wooden desk has an official "Rumson U." desk blotter. I'm sitting at it right now. I feel so adult! 50 Cent's "What Up Gangsta" is blasting from the next room. The walls must be thin. I really would appreciate it if whoever's playing it would turn it down, but as the old saying goes, "Every party has a pooper," and that pooper is not going to be me. Uh-uh. No way. I am not going to establish my reputation on my very first night by being a bore. First impressions count. They can blast 50 Cent all night long if they want. Really. I honestly don't care.

# August 17

## Dear Diary:

Classes haven't even started, and already my head is spinning. My roommate arrived yesterday. Her name's Patty Camp, and she's from Corpus Christi, Texas, and though I'd describe her as "big," or maybe "heavyset," she was quick to point out that she's fat.

"Just plain fat," she said with a cheery smile. "Why sugarcoat?"

She's a very lively girl, and she's ready to bust a gut—two guts, in fact—in order to find a nice boyfriend and eventually earn her doctorate in psychology. She's already memorized the entire DSM-IV, a clinical handbook of psychological disorders, and when I told her that I didn't care which bed or dresser she wanted to take, she was quick to point out that I was being "indecisive" and might be suffering from a mild depressive disorder.

"Too soon to tell, though. I'll keep an eye out if you want."

Luckily, Patty has already visited RU many times (her older brother went here), so she gave me a tour of the entire campus and helpfully pointed out places of interest, including the library, the sports stadium, even Alpha Beta Delta, my mom's sorority house.

"I think I'm going to try and join them," I said hopefully, and gosh, you should have seen the look on Patty's face—as if I'd just stepped real hard on her toes or something.

"You can't be serious. They're self-important drones, they're

Stepford Wives. Please tell me you're not going to join a sorority. Oh my God, please."

She seemed so desperate, and so sincere, so I said, "Okay," but if I want to meet a nice guy and have lots of friends, and maybe be at least semipopular, why shouldn't I give it a shot? It worked for Mom. And that's how she met Dad. I am trying to put forth a "new me," a more confident me, even if it is just pretend.

Later, I gave Mom a call (just to let her know that I'm okay), but Lisa said she was busy. She also told me about all the "fierce" new outfits Mom bought for her in Parkersburg, but Dad told her she couldn't wear any of them out of the house. Ha-ha for her. Then she read aloud a few song lyrics she's been writing for her first hit single. It's called "Tune My Motor Up." I'd write down the lyrics here, but frankly, I think they're dirty (but not creative-dirty), and I am so not a prude. I really don't think anyone will want to listen to something like that, especially coming from a girl Lisa's age.

"Are you kidding?" she snapped. "The skankier the better. I know what I'm doing."

I did get to talk to Dad (thank God). He was so encouraging. He thinks I should try and join Alpha Beta Delta too. He also reminded me that Mom was president of Alpha Beta Delta, which makes me a "legacy" candidate, which means that they'll have to at least consider me as a pledge, which means that I'll have this huge, major leg-up over all the other candidates. It's like it's meant to be! I always feel better when I talk to Dad. And more hopeful, too.

I'm still unpacking, but it's hard to find places to put things, since Patty's practically turned the entire room into a kitchen pantry. We have Hostess Ho Hos and Mallomars and corn chips and double-butter microwave popcorn and beef jerky and all kinds of cookies and candies, too (basically anything that won't spoil). It was very hard to get to sleep last night because of all the loud crunching sounds. I'd just start to fall asleep, and then I'd hear a plastic package being ripped open—violently—or loud potato chip chewing. At four a.m., I was starting to get a little put out, so I asked her if she could try crunching a little softer, and tomorrow, maybe preopen some of the louder packages before going to bed.

"Sorry." She grinned. "Party in my mouth. But don't worry. I'm, like, so aware of my obsessive-compulsive tendencies. Awareness is the first step."

When I woke up this morning, I was a little surprised by all the garbage on the floor—heaps of empty candy wrappers and chip bags.

"You want help cleaning up?" I asked.

"Don't do that!" she protested. "That's enabling me!"

I'm not quite sure what that means, but I do know that she didn't bother picking any of it up.

I got my class schedule today, and when I was standing in line, I met two guys who live in a dorm room two floors down from Patty and me. Randy O. Templeton introduced himself first (he pointed out that his initials spell ROT, which he thought was really funny). I only talked to him because I felt a little sorry for him. He has an awful lot of pimples all across his face and forehead, a few of which looked like they were ready to pop right then and there (all on their own). He's a journalism major, and his friend and roommate, Nester Damon, who's short and has greasy-looking, corkscrew hair, is majoring in photography. Once they get out of college, they're planning on becoming a news team, which sounds like a fun idea, I guess (for them). Still, I don't think I'll be hanging out too much with these two. Nester kept pestering me with really embarrassing personal questions, like: "Have you ever had a boyfriend?" and "How wide does your mouth open?" and "Is your hymen busted?" Then he chuckled and walked off to go to the bathroom, and Randy elbowed me (kind of hard).

"He likes you. Do you like him?"

I didn't know how to answer that question without offending either him or Nester, so I just shrugged and looked down at the floor, which I noticed was a very pleasant-looking industrial peach.

"Fair warning, though, stay away from his computer. Sticky keyboard. Know what I mean? Get it? Get it?"

Eeeow. Isn't there anyone normal around here? After I left the administrative building, I discovered that I was standing right across the street from Alpha Beta Delta. Well, not directly across, sort of at an angle. It's definitely the prettiest house on campus. In fact, it almost looks like it's been transported from some magic fairy kingdom, but it's right here, right at RU. Wanting a closer look, I stepped from the curb and I was almost mowed down by a pink Volkswagen convertible when it screeched around the corner and swerved into the Alpha Beta Delta driveway. Stepping out of it, I saw this really beautiful girl in a canary yellow Chanel outfit. She was so stylish-looking, so self-possessed—with really long, wavy black hair that she kept running her hands through and flipping back. Then she did something strange. She stepped over to a large poplar tree in front and started talking to it. I couldn't hear what she was saying, but I figured that maybe she was communing with nature, since a lot of movie stars and other glamorous people do that (or for all I know, since the house looked so enchanted, the tree was talking back).

But then another girl fell out of the tree. Literally. She looked kind of pudgy—but not fat—with a wild bush of red hair and freckles, and she was tangled up in all these wires that snaked back up into the tree. The beautiful girl didn't seem too happy about this, and she waved her arms about, screaming, but I still couldn't make out what she was saying. Then she stormed inside and slammed the door. It looked like the pudgy girl was crying, so I figured, what the heck, I should at least go and see if she's okay.

I walked across the street, but I looked both ways (just in case).

"Are you all right?" I asked. "Did you hurt yourself?"

The pudgy girl laughed.

"Naw, I'm okay."

"What are all these wires for?"

Uh-oh. She suddenly got this total panicky look on her face and muttered, kind of stuttering, "C-c-cable modem. DSL."

I didn't want to push it (sometimes people get funny or angry about DSL, because it doesn't always work and they pay a lot of money for it), so I just introduced myself. She did too. Her name's Shanna-Francine, and she's a senior. She's also a sister at Alpha Beta Delta, and I couldn't help it, I had to ask: What's it really like to be a sorority girl and have so many friends and a real social life (and boyfriends, too)? I'm sure I sounded like a complete idiot, but Shanna-Francine just listened. Then she told me about Alpha Beta Delta's upcoming "Smoker," a once-a-year gathering at the house where girls who want to join can come and learn all about Alpha Beta Delta and why it's the best sorority on campus (maybe even in the whole world). She was very excited when she told me this—though even when she's not excited she tends to be very loud, like she's trying to be heard by a deaf person (her eyes are a bit crossed too). I don't think she's terribly bright, but she seems awfully sweet. And get this. Out of nowhere, she offered to be my sponsor, since you can't go to the Smoker meeting unless a sponsor invites you. I couldn't believe my luck. I still can't. Was she teasing me? The Smoker meeting is tomorrow afternoon—and I have a Sponsor! Oh my God, I was so completely happy, and so naturally, I was certain that something horrible was about to happen to me (but it was too cloudy for lightning, I realized, and I'd already managed to avoid being run over, so maybe something horrible would happen to me later). And guess who the pretty-looking girl was who I saw getting out of the pink Volkswagen?

That was Meri Sugarman, the president of Alpha Beta Delta. I should have figured. Meri's a senior, and she's been president every year she's been at Alpha Beta Delta, and everyone knows she's a shoo-in to be president this year too, or at least that's what Shanna-Francine says, and I believe her. I only saw Meri for a few seconds, but there was something so confident about her—but calmly confident, like she doesn't even have to try. She's definitely not pretending (like I am), and maybe if I'm lucky enough to get into Alpha Beta Delta, she can be my mentor, in the sense that I can learn from her. Maybe she'll even be my friend.

When I left Shanna-Francine and walked to Long John Silver's for dinner (there are lots of good restaurants like Long John's real close to the campus), I started crying. But they weren't sad tears, they were happy tears. What if I really get into Alpha Beta Delta? Everyone knows you have friends for life if you join a sorority— and they help you study, and they plan social events together, and all sorts of things. I guess the happy tears were a little sad, too. It's been so long since I've even thought about having friends. I remember in sixth grade once, on the weekend, I was sitting on the stair landing in my house in the late afternoon. No one was home and I just flat-out burst into tears because I couldn't think of a single person to call or do something with. I mean, it's not like I've been rejected my entire life. It's worse. I haven't even been on anyone's radar. But now I have a once-in-a-lifetime chance. If I make it into Alpha Beta Delta, my life will change forever!

By the way, I have to take a sec here to say how much I love-love-love Long John Silver's Chicken Planks. Talk about comfort food (though the Hush Puppies at this particular Long John's are a little greasy). As I finished my dinner, I thought about how nice it was to meet Shanna-Francine, and how fortunate, too. Then I walked back to my dorm and I saw lots of kids going out for the night, all dressed up in cool clothes, gathering in groups. There were some pretty girls who were giggling and talking about boys and blow jobs and Jägermeister, another group of really handsome guys with awesome short haircuts who all seemed to be wearing clothes from Abercrombie & Fitch, and a lot of couples, too, who were holding hands and smiling and even kissing (a few near the park were making out big-time). It made me happy. Soon, I'll be going out at night just like them, maybe with them.

Back at my dorm room, I noticed that Patty hadn't cleaned up her mess from the night before. In fact, it was worse. I was only three steps in when I stepped on a half-empty carton of moo shu pork on the floor (that's just gross). I didn't know where Patty was, but I wasn't about to clean it all up for her. Lisa hoodwinked me into cleaning her room for her on a regular basis when I was in fourth grade—she said she wanted to "learn from my technique." Puh-lease. I'm not going down that road again. Instead, I went over the list of books I have to buy for my classes at the RU bookstore tomorrow and read the opening chapters of *Wuthering Heights*, a book I've read a million zillion times. Maybe I'll buy a small TV for the room, but deep down inside, I'm hoping I won't have to. I'm hoping I'll be living at Alpha Beta Delta soon. Oh my God, that would be so completely amazing if it happens! I better stop thinking about it (and writing about it too) or I'll jinx it.

I fell asleep while reading, but I was woken up by really loud crunching. There was Patty in her bed with a supersize bag of chips and an open tin of cake icing, but before I could say a peep, she shrieked.

"Don't say anything! I won't wake you up tonight. I promise. And I'm cleaning tomorrow. Don't worry."

"I'm not worried," I said.

I do like Patty, but if she thinks she's going to pull a Lisa on me, she's got another think coming. I may be a loser with no friends, but I'm not about to become someone's maid again.

# August 18

## Dear Diary:

The Smoker was unbelievable! Okay, I should back up. Oh my God, I'm just so excited. The day didn't start too well, but it got better and better as it went along. After breakfast I went to the RU Bookstore to buy my textbooks, and I guess I wasn't looking up or something, because when I handed the list to the guy at the window, I almost screamed when I heard, "Bud Finger, at your cervix."

I couldn't believe it—I still can't. There was Bud, standing behind the counter. I didn't even know he was going to RU. He's an earth science major, and get this, he's on Academic Scholarship. What a joke! It was nice to see a familiar face and all, but then I had to remind myself whose face it was, especially when he asked me if I wanted to be his "college bitch." Then he laughed and laughed. Oh, I hate Bud Finger! Why does he have to be here? I hope he doesn't tell anyone we went to the prom together. That would be beyond embarrassing.

It was a little before three o'clock when I went to the RU park near the water tower—that's where Shanna-Francine told me to meet her before the Smoker. A few minutes later she ran up, took one look at me, and blurted out, "Is that what you're wearing?"

God, I'm so stupid. Stupid-stupid-stupid. I didn't even think to get dressed up, and there was Shanna-Francine all decked out with her frizzy red hair pulled up in a bun, and she had a ton of makeup on too. But boy, does she work fast. She opened up her purse and practically attacked me with a steel comb and hairspray, then she put a full face of makeup on me too. I swear, I don't think I've ever worn makeup so thick, and I thought I looked a little bit like a clown when she let me look in her blush mirror, but I figured, heck, she knows what she's doing, she's already in Alpha Beta Delta—and I'm not. From there we walked to Alpha Beta Delta. And something strange happened. As we got closer and closer to the house, I started to get short of breath. My heart was beating so fast I thought it was going to burst out of my body. Was I going to black out? It was like I was afraid of Alpha Beta Delta, which made no sense. I chalked it up to nervousness. There's nothing to be afraid of, I kept telling myself. Alpha Beta Delta is a good place. For God's sake, Mom went there.

I stepped inside—and it felt like I had stepped into a warm pool of water. I was relaxed. Instantly. It almost felt like I belonged (I was invited, so that probably helped). In the living room soft jazz was playing, and all these pretty girls were mingling and chatting. At a side table there was an assortment of spice cakes, carrot cake, finger sandwiches, and teas and coffee. Shanna-Francine gave me a nudge.

"Mingle!" she exclaimed.

Unfortunately, I've never been all that good at mingling. And I tell you, each girl was prettier than the next, and thin, too—and the outfits. Wow. It's like they all stepped out of *In Style*. Then the jazz music abruptly stopped. A hush came over the room. Walking down the stairs—no, gliding, I swear she was gliding—was Meri Sugarman herself, half smiling, flipping back her thick raven hair. We all took a seat and she stepped before us, along with Shanna-Francine and Gloria Daily, Alpha Beta Delta's vice president, a very tall and very thin girl who Shanna-Francine later told me is totally brainy (and hooked on diuretics too, which is really too bad). The silence was deafening, and it seemed to go on forever. Meri just stood there looking at us, still half smiling, like she knew something we didn't (and I'm sure she does). In fact, it was so quiet I could hear the birds outside and the traffic, too, and way off in the distance, a church bell. I thought my throat was going to close up. I was so nervous I couldn't even swallow. Then Meri spoke. Softly. Delicately. Like she was high on a mountain and was speaking only loud enough to be heard by those far, far beneath her. She said, "Katie Couric was a sorority sister."

Then she was silent again. She smiled that special half-smile of hers, letting her powerful words sink in before adding, "So was Sheryl Crow. And Christie Brinkley."

Then she spoke even softer than before, and in very short sentences—kind of like haiku.

"Our symbol is the Crown." And then: "Our flower is the White Carnation." More silence, then: "Our motto? 'Seek the Noblest.'"

I noticed a couple of girls were nodding their heads in silent agreement. We were all spellbound.

"Our purpose? To be known as the best. Pure and simple."

Then she flipped her hair back and giggled—actually giggled—before spinning on her heels and floating away. *Poof.* She was gone. That's all we saw of Meri. But jeez, that was enough. She was so completely perfect. The jazz music kicked back in and Gloria stepped up like a drill sergeant.

"One at a time, in the kitchen. Peek in when it's not your turn, you're outta here. Tell anyone what we're doing in there, you're outta here. Go upstairs and anywhere near Meri, you're outta here. Get it? Good. You first."

She pointed to a girl named Bethany Conova Ponds—probably the prettiest girl in the whole room—and off she went to the kitchen with Gloria and Shanna-Francine. I sat in a corner chair and looked at my hands folded in my lap. I definitely need a manicure. I didn't dare say a word, but I finally looked up and saw that the rest of the girls were perfectly poised and silent. An hour or so must have passed, and by that time, both Bethany and another girl, Lindsay Cunningham, had finished in the kitchen. When they left the house, they both looked a bit rattled, but maybe I was imagining things. After all, my own hands were cold and sweaty, and when Shanna-Francine stepped from the kitchen and blurted out, "Cindy Bixby," it was all I could do to hold back a scream. I accompanied her back to the kitchen, and when I stepped in, I was blinded by a flash of light. I heard *click-whirr, click-whirr.* Gloria was taking my picture. Shanna-Francine closed the door behind me, then Gloria gave me an order.

"Take off your clothes."

"I—I'm sorry?" I stuttered.

Gloria looked impatiently at Shanna-Francine. "I don't have time for this."

Worried that I'd be embarrassing Shanna-Francine if I didn't follow orders, I nervously took off my blouse and skirt.

"Everything," snapped Gloria.

I gulped. Okay, so I've been naked before in front of other girls in gym class at Chesterfield High, but never in someone's kitchen—not even a pretty kitchen like this one—but I did as I was told.

"Step on the scale," ordered Gloria.

I guess I was so completely nervous, because I hadn't even noticed the scale in front of me—one of those big standing scales with counterweights that you see at doctors' offices. I was about to ask where they got it, but Gloria must have anticipated that I was about to say something else, because she suddenly spoke very fast and very impatiently.

"Yes, this is illegal. Yes, you will be disqualified if you object or inform anyone of this or anything else that goes on in this room.

And rest assured, we will find out. The consequences won't be pretty. Am I clear?"

I nodded—so hard I thought my head would fall off—and stepped on the scale. Shanna-Francine balanced the counter-weights and scribbled my weight in her Alpha Beta Delta–embossed spiral pink notebook. Then I stepped off the scale and picked up my clothes.

"Who told you to put your clothes on?" snapped Gloria.

"No one," I gasped.

"That's right. But now I am. Put them on."

Then she looked over at Shanna-Francine's notebook, and I thought her eyes were going to pop out of her head. She looked back at me and said very calmly, "Thanks so much for coming by."

"Wait," blurted Shanna-Francine, who flipped her notebook pages and pointed to something. I'm not sure what it was, but it seemed to make Gloria a little angry.

"Right, okay," she grumbled, slumping in her chair. "Sit down. Here's how it goes. We're going to ask you some questions. Later, Meri and I will go over all the information we've gathered from all of the girls here today and we'll 'Blackball,' which means we'll choose which girls we'll invite to pledge. But being invited to pledge does not mean you've become a part of Alpha Beta Delta. Get it? It only means you've passed the first step."

After that, everything was okay. More than okay. It was great. Shanna-Francine asked me all sorts of fun questions—where I grew up, what my major was, my favorite movie (that was easy, *Moulin Rouge*, because Ewan McGregor is s-o-o-o incredibly cute!), my favorite kind of music (I admitted to liking classical, because Dad listens to it, but I do like some pop music). After a while, even Gloria seemed to be interested, or at least semirelaxed and smiling, especially when they asked me about Lisa, and I told them all about her plans to become the next superslutty Christina Aguilera.

Then I surprised myself when Gloria asked me, "Is there anything you've been through that you regret, or that you would change?"

"The answer is no," I said, shocked by my own words. "Not a thing. I mean, if I'd never gone through what I have, I wouldn't be me. And I like being me, or at least I'm trying to. That's why I want to be a part of Alpha Beta Delta. High school was so hard, and I want a different kind of life for myself in college. I want to be happy."

Shanna-Francine sniffled. Honest, I thought she was going to cry. And Gloria just stared at me, seemingly resigned to something.

"You'll hear from us soon," she said. "And by the way, if you're chosen to pledge, everything that happened in here is confidential. If you're not chosen to pledge, everything that happened in here is confidential. Understand?"

I nodded. Then I meekly mentioned, "My mom was president of Alpha Beta Delta. I think that makes me . . ."

"A legacy candidate?" snapped Gloria. "No, actually, it doesn't. Or it does, but it doesn't matter. Not anymore. One of Meri's first acts as president of Alpha Beta Delta was to revoke the legacy provision, so don't think you're going to squirm in that way. Meri feels that only the best should be accepted, and I quote, 'Bloodline considerations are boring and elitist,' unquote. Get it? You're not boring and elitist, are you? Well? Are you?"

I nervously shook my head.

"Fine. We're done here."

I smiled humbly and stood up.

"Who told you to stand?!" she shrieked.

I yelped—literally—and Gloria chuckled and gave a wave with her hand. "Go on, get out of here."

Shanna-Francine led me out past the living room to the door.

"How do you think it went?" I whispered.

But she didn't say anything. She made a zipping motion over her mouth. But I could tell she was smiling. I gave a last glance to the other girls waiting, then shook Shanna-Francine's hand. And she was still smiling. That's got to be a good sign.

I flew out onto the campus. I was so happy! I felt like I had wings. It felt like the entire world was bursting with happy colors—bright yellow, coral, hot pink, Mediterranean blues and greens. Class starts in a few days, but I don't know how I'll pay attention until I find out if I've been invited to pledge. In fact, I was so happy that I didn't even care (too much) that the dorm room was now even more filled with garbage and papers and half-empty food cartons when I came home. And it didn't even faze me (or at least not too much) when Patty asked, "You went to the prom with Bud Finger?!"

Oh, I hate Bud Finger! Patty met him in the hall a few hours ago. Guess whose dorm room he was on his way to? Randy and Nester's. Big surprise. Okay. I'm not going to let it distract me.

I feel good for once—really good. I'll try and concentrate on that.

# August 18

## Dear Diary:

No word yet from Alpha Beta Delta. I know I shouldn't be depressed, but I am. Classes start tomorrow. I hate myself. Oh, please let them choose me. I wish I smoked, because then I'd have something to do. I'd eat, but I'm not hungry. I woke up at two o'clock in the afternoon today. I couldn't believe how late it was. I have never slept that late in my entire life. I only woke up because Patty was coming back into the room. When I went to the bathroom to wash my face, I noticed that my face soap was gone.

"Oops, sorry about that," she said meekly. "I threw it away. I have this phobia about white soap. Or really any kind of soap or detergent that's white. Totally makes me gag. It's probably sexual, but I'm not sure. You can use my black tar soap if you want."

Maybe it's because I was so groggy, but I surprised even myself when I bluntly asked, "If you can throw away my white soap, why can't you throw away all your piles of garbage?"

Patty started crying. Poor Patty. She told me all about her serious psychological problems. But she was quick to point out that she doesn't need to go to a therapist for help because she's already diagnosed herself with the DSM-IV. She began listing her afflictions—hypertension, borderline personality disorder, panic attacks, all sorts of things—and it actually seemed to make her feel better.

"Awareness is key," she said. "By labeling one's problems, one can better overcome them. Isn't it fascinating that I threw away your white soap, but I can't be bothered to throw away all my garbage yet? Psychologically, I mean."

Honestly, it's not that fascinating to me—I just wish she hadn't thrown away my soap (it was a relatively new bar)—but she sure seemed to think it was, so I just nodded and said, "I'll help you clean up if you want."

She insisted that this was unnecessary, maybe even harmful, reminding me again that I'd be enabling her. But she did give me her DSM-IV.

"I've dog-eared all the pages that list my afflictions," she said buoyantly. "Here. You should read it. I'm a fascinating case."

Why does Patty find her problems fascinating? I don't find mine fascinating at all. I hate them. Maybe I'm the one who needs a therapist. I have so much to learn.

Later, Patty made me an early dinner on her hot plate. "It's a special salad," she said. "It's very healthy for both of us. I call it Patty's Wilted Spinach Salad."

She dumped a large portion of fresh spinach leaves into a pot, then opened a Yuban coffee can.

"Bacon grease!" she exclaimed. "It's the secret ingredient."

She scooped several huge dollops of bacon grease into the pot, put the hot plate on high, stirred it all up, then fried up several bacon slices in a separate pan, chopped them up, added them to the bacon grease and the spinach, and stirred in dried purple onions, canned black beans, and black pepper.

"It's so good, you don't even need dressing," she said, serving me a bowl.

I know Patty thinks this is supposed to be healthy because it's a "salad" and "based in greens," but it just tasted like clumps of hot, fatty grease to me. But I couldn't hurt her feelings. And besides, I don't know anything about food, so for all I know it is healthy. I forced myself to eat spoonful after spoonful until my bowl was empty.

"There's more if you want," she said eagerly.

I told her no, thank you, I was full, and I was. Then she was gone. She suddenly remembered a farmer's market she wanted to check out in nearby Camoville. She asked me if I wanted to go, but I told her to go ahead without me. After she left, I just sat there for a moment. It felt like I couldn't even move. I guess I was feeling sorry for myself. I'm lucky to have a friend like Patty. She accepts me for who I am, and she did make me a healthy lunch based in greens. I stood up. What a klutz. I knocked over the Yuban coffee can, which spewed out this large sludge-pile of bacon grease all over the carpet. Oh my God. Crawling out of the can was a creepy-crawly water bug. I couldn't help it. I ran to the bathroom and threw up in the toilet. All those healthy greens gone to waste. This hasn't been a good day.

What if I don't get into Alpha Beta Delta? Then what? Does that mean college becomes the same as high school? I never once got picked for the debate team. I was always told they had enough reporters for the school newspaper. And Jennifer Goodenow, the president of the pep club, once told me I could help sell bake sale tickets for Spirit Week decorations, but when I reported for duty at the next pep club meeting, she said, "Your name is? You're here for? Whatever I promised, I was very much mistaken. Sorry." I tell you, that was one lousy day.

I wonder how Mom got through this. She might have some good advice for me. Maybe I'll e-mail her before I go to bed. I should probably go to bed early tonight so I can wake up extra early tomorrow morning to make up for all the sleeping I did today. Classes start soon. I'm looking forward to it, though I do think it's silly that we have classes and then we're off four whole days for Labor Day. I've been overhearing lots of students planning parties and outings. Maybe if I'm a pledge by then, I'll get invited to a party too. Maybe more than one! Wouldn't that be awesome?

From: cindybixby <cindybixby@yahoo.com>
Date: 18 August
To: mom <elainebixby@msn.com>
Subject: Good News!

Hi, Mom!

Guess what? I went to the Smoker meeting at Alpha Beta Delta, your old sorority! It was so much fun. I'd tell you all about it, but it is secret (as I'm sure you remember! Ha!).

Now I have to wait and wait and wait to hear if they'll invite me to pledge. Ahhhhhhh! Any advice for a (hopefully) prospective pledge on how to deal with all this pressure?

I miss u (and Dad and Lisa, too),
xxoo
Cindy

*Apostolina*

From: Mail Delivery Subsystem <MAILER DAEMON@outmail6.net>
Date: 18 August
To: <cindybixby@yahoo.com>
Subject: re: Good News!

—The following addresses had permanent fatal errors—
<elainebixby@msn.com>
(reason: 550 Requested action not taken)
550 5.1.1 <cindybixby@yahoo.com> . . . User e-mail blocked

From: <cindybixby@yahoo.com>
Date: 18 August
To: <lisa@lisabixby.com>
Subject: Can You Print This?
Attachments: Good News!

Hi Lisa:

Can you do me a big fave? I can't seem to get my e-mails
through to Mom. Maybe there's a glitch in my account, or
with the Rumson U. server, but who knows? I'm not technical,
and the messages I get back when I try to send her stuff
all read like gibberish.

Could you maybe print out my message and give it to her?
Please?

xxoo
Cindy

From: <lisa@lisabixby.com>
Date: 18 August
To: <cindybixby@yahoo.com>
Subject: re: Can You Print This?

Dear Sis:

I am s-o-o-o not your e-mail bitch.

But I am a nice person. I asked Mom if there was anything
wrong with her account, and she told me, "Absolutely nothing. It's working fine." Anyhoo, I printed out your "Good
News!" thingie and put it on her desk, right next to this
month's issue of British *Vogue*, so I know she'll see it.

You can never thank me enough for this.

Like I Have Time,
Lisa

# August 21

## Dear Diary:

Classes started with a bang. Mr. Charles Scott is my Masterpieces of Western Lit I professor, and he looked very distinguished in his cardigan sweater with dark brown patches on the elbows (just like real writers wear). Luckily, I was prepared, since I'd already finished reading *One Hundred Years of Solitude* and *One Day in the Life of Ivan Denisovich*, and we were only supposed to have read the first one by today (I didn't have anything else to do yesterday). In fact, I practically led the discussion about *One Hundred Years of Solitude*, along with Professor Scott, of course. He was so happy to see that I was able to discuss not just José Buendía, but practically all of his descendants. I heard a few snickers behind me, and after class something felt funny. Then I realized that there was a thick wad of gum stuck in my hair in the back. I guess I could be down about that, but it is a core-curriculum class, which means there are students in there who aren't literature majors.

Riffraff, as Lisa would say.

I bet they won't do that to me when I'm a pledge. If I'm a pledge. Oh God, nothing yet. No news is good news, right?

# August 22

## Dear Diary:

News, news, news! I still don't know if I'm invited to pledge yet, but Shanna-Francine told me all about the Blackballing session with Meri and Gloria when we met, by chance, at Long John Silver's (she likes Chicken Planks too!).

"Oh God, I really shouldn't be telling you this," she blurted, but then she proceeded to tell me everything, or at least it sure felt like she did, and I didn't even have to ask. Here's what happened:

"Okay, let's begin," announced Meri as she went over all the pictures of prospective pledges from the Smoker. "Anyone over one twenty-five, out."

"Wait a minute," blurted Shanna-Francine. "We're not allowing for freshman bloat?"

"Uh-uh, not this year," Meri answered serenely.

See, this is Meri's last year at Alpha Beta Delta, and she wants everything about it to be 100 percent perfect—including the new inductees. She also wants to make sure everyone's predisposed to casting their vote for her once it comes time to elect this year's house president.

"Oh, but why wouldn't they be?" I eagerly asked.

But Meri's a careful and conscientious girl, as Shanna-Francine explained. Then she scrunched up her face.

"Oh God, I really shouldn't be telling you this," she blurted, but I swear I didn't ask her to tell me anything at all. "Remember all those wires I was tangled up in when we first met?"

"For the DSL, right?"

Well, that's what Shanna-Francine thought they were for too, though at the time she had her suspicions.

"Look over here," whispered Meri at the Blackballing session. She pointed to her exquisite antique armoire. "I had it all installed over the summer." Then she swung open the armoire, revealing state-of-the-art DAT surveillance equipment.

"We're bugged?" asked a disbelieving Gloria.

"Mmm-hmm. The entire house. Dean's office and Teacher's Lounge, too, along with selected bathrooms, dorm rooms, fraternities. It's still in the works."

"Wait a sec," blurted Shanna-Francine. "What about outside? All that wiring in the trees. For the DSL."

Meri shook her head.

"You bugged the poplars?" gasped Gloria.

But Meri put them both at ease. It would only be for a little while. Still, before continuing, she instructed Shanna-Francine to make three fat-free mocha cappuccinos with whipped cream and chocolate shavings on Meri's private cappuccino-espresso machine. The whirring of the frothing cup drowned out their voices. She whispered.

"Of course, as your president-elect, I don't know anything about this, and can't know anything about this. I need absolute and complete deniability. Understood?"

Gloria nodded, then they both looked at Shanna-Francine.

"What?!" she blurted, dropping the frothing cup.

As she continued her story, Shanna-Francine gave an involuntary shudder. "Then we went back to the pictures, and we got to yours."

Uh-oh. I should have known what was coming. Meri laughed at my picture. Just laughed.

"There's always one little bow-wow," snickered Gloria, and she reminded Meri that it was Shanna-Francine, not her, who'd invited me to the Smoker.

My heart sank—probably lower than it has in ages. Great. So I'm a "little bow-wow." Fine. I guess that's nothing new. I'm so stupid. Stupid-stupid-stupid. I actually thought I had a chance. I foolishly allowed myself to imagine a better life with friends and fun and a future. I tempted the gods. And I lost. Why can't things go smoothly for me for once? Is this my future? Will I always be fate's pincushion?

I walked home as the sun was setting and considered suicide. Not seriously, just in terms of how people would react, and how sorry they'd be that they were mean to me, and didn't take me seriously, and didn't befriend me or include me in any of their groups and outings. Dad would cry (I know it) and I'm pretty sure Mom would too. I don't know if Lisa would cry, but she'd be awfully upset that I wasn't around any longer to sharpen her claws on. And her triumph as a superslutty Christina Aguilera singer probably wouldn't feel as complete as it would have if I'd been around for her to flaunt it over. But who else? I don't think Bud would really care. And though Shanna-Francine likes me—after all, she did invite me to the Smoker—we aren't close-close. Not yet, anyway. I do think Patty would probably miss me. I think she'd cry, too, and then proceed to diagnose me in terms of the events that led up to my untimely demise. Maybe I'd even become the subject of one of her psychology term papers. I'd be reduced to a case study. And then I'd be forgotten. I shuddered at the thought and felt lonelier than ever. But I didn't cry. Frankly, I think I'm all cried out.

# August 23

## Dear Diary:

No news is good news. Right? Please? Please-please-please?

# August 24

## Dear Diary:

I couldn't even open my dorm room door when I came back from the library today. There's now so much garbage and papers and empty food containers inside the room that I had to shove the door—really, really hard—in order to get it to budge even an inch. I know Patty doesn't want me to "enable" her, but I'm not sure how much longer I can take this. I couldn't even find my bed at first.

Still no news from Alpha Beta Delta.

# August 25

## Dear Diary:

I hate everyone and everything. When I was walking through the main campus square this afternoon, I was suddenly hit in the face by a small, soft, round object.

"Whoa! Money shot! Right in the face!"

I looked up. There was Bud, along with his new best friends, Nester and Randy, doubled over laughing, slapping five. Bud jogged up, picked up the little round thing that had hit me, and smiled stupidly. He does that so well.

"Yo, sorry. We were hacking. And I aimed wrong."

"You were what?"

"Yo, Hacky Sack. Footbag." Then he kicked up the little bag with his foot and bounced it to his other foot on the back side. "That's called the platter serve." Then he kicked it up again and bounced it off his behind. "That's the pooper-shooter. And the money shot's when you hit someone in the face. You know, like in a porno movie when a guy . . ."

"I know what that means, Bud. I'm not an idiot."

"Yo, Cyn. Chill."

"And what's with this 'yo' stuff? Are you from the hood all of a sudden? Bud from the Hood? Ooo. The superscary hood of Marietta, Ohio."

I laughed. I thought that was pretty funny. And Bud was talking weirdly, after all. But I stopped laughing when he leaned in to me and whispered, "I told 'em you gave me a b.j."

"You what?!"

"At the prom. Yo, I'm looking out for you, Cyn. For your rep. Want everyone to think you're a lezzie? Nester likes you, you know. I said you were good. No teeth."

I kicked him in the balls. Hard. He doubled over just like before, only this time he wasn't laughing. And for a split second I thought of my dad—dancing in the strip joint, lighting his big, fat cigar. I whipped around. A guy had just walked past me smoking a cigar. Am I going crazy? I whipped back around. Bud looked ready to explode with anger, and for a second I really thought he might haul off and punch me. He bellowed.

"So that's it, huh? You're a slot-sucker?"

Okay, I'd like to take a moment here to say that I'm just as liberal as the next person, and I'm fairly comfortable with the occasional use of dirty language and crude double entendres, provided the context is appropriate and there's at least a small attempt at humor. However, I did not like being called a lesbian just because I objected to the notion of giving Bud a "b.j.," which is something I would never, ever do in a million years, and I certainly didn't appreciate being called a "slot-sucker," which was more than crude, it was disgusting. By the time I had left the main square and turned the corner to my dorm building, Bud was once more doubled over. This time he fell to the ground and stayed there—because I had kicked him in the balls again (extra-extra hard). I could hear him screaming in the distance.

"I'm filing charges! Yo, I'm taking you to court! I have witnesses!"

*Fine, you do that,* I thought. I'll take my chances in court. It might be fun to be on the witness stand.

"Yo, your Honor, 'sup? I did it. I did it twice. Be lenient, 'kay? I'm Cindy from the Hood. The superscary hood of Marietta, Ohio."

Something like that might even make my college experience worthwhile, since it looks like nothing else will, and it looks like I can forget about Alpha Beta Delta. I know I'm feeling sorry for myself, but it didn't help my self-esteem this morning when I passed Bethany Conova Ponds, one of the prettiest girls at the Smoker, in the Lit Building main hallway. She was very subtle. When she walked past me, she gave a little snort. It was perfect, really. Since it wasn't a full-out snort, an innocent bystander might have thought she was suffering from mild allergies, or maybe a cold, and was just lightly clearing her nasal passages. But I knew better. I knew what that snort was; it was a dig, a way to say, "Guess what? We all had a good laugh when you came to the Smoker, and we're still laughing now." It's amazing how one little snort can ruin the rest of your day. That probably explains why I've been so full of anger. It probably also explains why I had the nerve to kick Bud in the balls (twice), something I'd normally never do (really—I am absolutely not a violent person). Come to think of it, maybe that little snort wasn't such a bad thing. If that's the price for seeing Bud crouching in pain on the ground, maybe it was worth it. Thank you, Bethany. I hate you, but thank you.

# August 26

## Dear Diary:

Okay, I've had it. It looks like Alpha Beta Delta's not going to happen. Fine-fine-fine. But that doesn't mean I have to live in a pigsty. I didn't have classes today, so I spent practically the entire day carrying out huge bags of garbage from the dorm room. Maybe I'm enabling Patty (I know what that means now, and I frankly don't see how being messy can be equated with serious drug addiction and "enabling" the addict, since being messy is just plain inconsiderate), but I really didn't care. Patty cried when she came back tonight and saw the room.

"Oh my God, you really, really didn't have to."

"Um, yes, I did."

"I swear I'll keep it clean from now on. I double swear."

I swallowed, gathered my oats. "You'd better. Because if you don't, I'll move to another dorm room."

That stopped her cold. She just stared at me for a moment, like she was trying to read my face.

"This is good. I need this. I deserve this. This could help me." Then she smiled wistfully, as if the loveliest thought had just popped into her head. "I was a very obstinate little baby, or so I've been told, and when I was two years old, or maybe three—"

I stopped her (kind of boldly). I told her I had my own problems and issues to deal with. Oops. Big mistake.

"Oh, tell me," she gasped. "I can help. I want to help."

Maybe I was just tired from all the cleaning, or maybe I needed to tell someone, so I told her all about the Smoker and my dashed hopes of becoming a sorority sister, and the fact that I had been labeled a "little bow-wow" by Gloria Daily, along with my admiration for Meri Sugarman. Oops. Bigger mistake.

"Meri? Oh my God, you can't be serious. Tell me you're not serious!"

It seems that Patty met Meri once before when she visited her older brother on campus during Alpha Beta Delta's Breast Cancer Charity fund-raiser. She grabbed her DSM-IV, flipped it open.

"Here it is. 'Histrionic Personality Disorder.' HPD. Meri's got it. Look. 'Extreme discomfort in situations in which they are not the center of attention,' 'a grandiose sense of self-importance,' 'exploitation of others to achieve personal goals.' I think she's Borderline, too. And Pathological. This is bad, Cindy. Oh my God, you gotta stay away from her. Promise me you will."

It was easy to tell her that I would. After all, with my hopes of becoming a sorority girl gone, why would Meri have anything to do with me? Somehow, though, my promise prompted Patty to segue once more into a very long discussion of her problems and all of her psychological ailments. I nodded off for a moment, and when I woke up, she was still going strong, discussing her early elementary school years, her rivalry with her sisters, and her absolute certainty that the abuse and neglect inflicted upon her by others had somehow damaged her "core," which was the cause of her many afflictions (which she again noted were "fascinating" in a clinical sense).

Then she ripped open a pack of Hostess Ho Hos. And threw the wrapper on the floor.

# August 27

## Dear Diary:

The phone rang early this morning. It must have been before seven o'clock, because my alarm clock hadn't even gone off yet.

"On behalf of Alpha Beta Delta, I'd like to formally invite you to pledge. Be at the house today at three o'clock. Do not be late."

*Click.* Then a dial tone. I bolted up out of bed. Did I just dream that? Was it a prank call? Patty mumbled from her bed.

"Mmm. Too early for phone calls. Very inconsiderate. Thoughtless of others."

I sat trembling. Okay, it wasn't a dream. It really happened.

"On behalf of Alpha Beta Delta, I'd like to formally invite you to pledge."

In a daze I stepped from the bed—luckily just missing a half-empty tin of nacho cheese dip hurled on the floor—staggered into the bathroom, closed the door, ran the water to wash my face, and caught my bewildered expression in the mirror.

"On behalf of Alpha Beta Delta, I'd like to formally invite you to pledge."

I covered my mouth in shock. This was one of those moments—one of those small, simple moments when you know everything in your life is about to change for the better. Only this time it was happening to me. Me!

For the rest of the morning, I was the target of stares and whispers. And I know why. It was slowly building up inside of me: pure, unadulterated joy. It must have been showing on my face. In fact, I know it was. I couldn't stop smiling. I must have looked like a complete cheeseball. And in Professor Scott's class, out of nowhere, I chuckled. Loudly.

"Is there something about the life of Ivan Denisovich that strikes you as funny, Ms. Bixby?"

"No, sir, not at all," I said, trying to keep a straight face. "It's really so sad. And touching, too."

Then I burst into giggles. I couldn't stop. Students were whispering behind me. Professor Scott was infuriated. Luckily, the class was just ending. Saved by the bell, I guess, though I didn't even hear it. At lunch I ate outside on the school's Great Lawn. Guys were playing Frisbee, a few couples were making out (I've come to realize that couples are very show-offy that way at RU), and at the far end, Bud, Nester, and Randy were hacking (none of them are very good at it, by the way). Everything was the same, but it looked magical, freshly hatched. So this is what it's like to feel good. This is what it's like to have hope. It started raining, just lightly, and most of the people scattered away. But I stayed, allowing the droplets to fall on my head and trickle down my cheeks. I laughed, too. Maybe I was even crying, I'm not sure.

I flew home. I didn't have much time. I took a shower, changed clothes (I made sure to put on something nice this time), grabbed an umbrella, and walked to Alpha Beta Delta. The sky darkened. Thunder rumbled. Rain was pouring heavier than before. Then it happened again, just like before: My heart began racing when I saw the house. A feeling of absolute dread washed over me. Gloria called me a "little bow-wow" at the Blackballing session. And Meri laughed. Was this a setup? Was I about to be ambushed? Why were they asking me to pledge? And then I thought, *So what? Who cares?* No matter what their reasons, at least I get a chance! At least

I can try to show them that I'm worthy, and even though I sort of don't feel like I am (I'm still smarting from Bethany's nasty little snort), I put those thoughts behind me when I stepped into the house.

A lighter suddenly clicked. A big, fat cigar puffed. I recognized the smell immediately: It was a Grand Torpedo Magnum Wrap 54 ring (these are very special cigars, and Dad's favorite, because they've been cured in aged Cognac). What the heck was Dad doing at the Alpha Beta Delta sorority house? Completely confused, I looked up. Angrily stomping down the stairs and puffing a Grand Torpedo, Keith Ryder, RU's supercute star quarterback (I've always found the combination of dark hair and blue eyes so incredibly dreamy).

"Good riddance to you, too," called out Meri from upstairs, though I couldn't see her. I couldn't believe how angry she sounded. "I hope you got what you wanted."

"Oh yeah? How could I?" bellowed Keith, who then loudly proclaimed so that all the gathered pledges could hear, "Hey, you guys know about Meri, don't you? She doesn't have a vagina, it's an ATM swipe."

Everyone gasped, including me. I think one of the girls even squealed. Then Keith charged for the door, and he might have made a very smooth exit if it hadn't been for the fact that I was standing in his way like a ding-dong and fumbling with my umbrella. He crashed right into me. *Ka-boom.* My umbrella popped back open. I shrieked. Then he lifted me in his arms (*He's so strong,* I thought fleetingly), plopped me to the side, and stomped out. I attempted to collapse my umbrella, finally closing it with a snap—revealing Meri standing right before me. I nearly screamed.

"You're forty-two seconds late," she said stonily. "I'm docking you points."

Minutes later in the living room, I gathered with all the pledges, including Bethany, who wouldn't even look at me or meet my eyes. Oh, I hate Bethany. It was deathly quiet as Shanna-Francine and Gloria passed out copies of Alpha Beta Delta's coveted and secret pledge book. It almost felt like it was burning in my hands. Here I was, one of seven lucky girls, and only three among us would be chosen to join the house. Meri stood before us, running her hand through her thick raven hair.

"The demands I make on myself are absolutely fantastic."

Believe me, I don't think there was anyone in the room who didn't believe her.

"I expect perfection. And I get it, on rare occasions—but they're too rare. I expect perfection from all of you, too. That's why you're here. That's why you're going to be tested. Remember our motto?"

"Seek the Noblest!" piped up Bethany.

Oh, what a little suck-up she is. And it didn't work. Ha. Apparently, Meri does not appreciate being interrupted. She jerked her head in Bethany's direction.

"Who just spoke?"

Bethany nervously raised her hand.

"Stand up, Pledge. Position yourself directly before me."

Bethany obeyed. Meri looked her in the eye and whispered softly.

"If I slapped you right now, it would hurt you very deeply. Do you think I should slap you? Do you deserve to be slapped? Think carefully before you answer."

The rest of us in the room sat stock-still. From the corner of my eye, I saw lightning strike the spire of the RU church steeple. Bethany was obviously weighing the ramifications of her answer to Meri's question and no doubt wondering if she was about to be slapped. I'm not a mean person, or a vengeful one, and like I've said, I so don't like violence, but I'll admit I felt a teensy little woo-hoo at the prospect of seeing Bethany slapped. After what seemed like an eternity, Bethany spoke.

"Yes."

"Yes, what?"

"Yes, I deserve to be slapped."

Then she winced, bracing herself. *Oh, slap her,* I thought, *slap her silly.*

"You're right, you do," said Meri, half-smiling. "Sit down. And don't ever interrupt me again."

Bethany sank into the couch. Meri held up a pledge book.

"The opening four chapters. Memorize them. They outline all the rules of conduct you'll be expected to fulfill as pledges. Pledge Week formally starts the day after Labor Day. If I were you, I'd enjoy your freedom while it lasts, because during Pledge Week, we own you. Period. End of sentence. Understand? If you have any questions, don't ask me. You can, if you like, ask Gloria, or Shanna-Francine. However, if your question is deemed stupid or redundant or obvious, you'll be docked points. It's all about points, girls. Those with the most points by the end of Pledge Week will be invited to join Alpha Beta Delta. Some of you will crack under the pressure and elect to disqualify yourselves. If you have doubts about your stamina, I encourage you to disqualify yourself now."

Then she swept out of the room and up the stairs. *Poof.* She was gone. All of us just sat there, unsure of what to do next.

"Okay, you can go now," blurted Shanna-Francine, cheerfully smiling.

When I stepped out of the house, I noticed that the clouds were receding, and shafts of bright sunlight dappled my face. Okay, so I'm not a sister yet, but I have a chance. A real chance! That's more than I had before.

# August 28

## Dear Diary:

Wow! So many rules and regulations! Every moment I had today, I read and reread the opening four chapters of the pledge book. I'll probably read it again before I go to bed. There are so many things I have to remember. The first few rules are fairly simple do's and don'ts, like:

"Rule #6: During Pledge Week, pledges are to remain absolutely silent unless directly addressed by an Alpha Beta Delta sister."

But then it gets more complex:

"Rule #14: During Pledge Week, pledges are required to wear the following uniform: a plain white blouse with Peter Pan collar and leg-of-mutton sleeves; navy blue knife-pleat skirt; plain white cotton panties and bra; plain white hose; black patent-leather one-bar shoes. Points will be deducted for any deviation, uncleanliness, faulty ironing, or loose pleats, with all decisions and deducted points at the discretion of Alpha Beta Delta sisters."

And this one is a doozy:

"Rule #32: During Pledge Week, pledges are required to carry a large, light brown, bottom-fold portfolio briefcase. The contents of the briefcase must contain the following items, as Alpha Beta Delta sisters may at any time ask for them:

Altoids, both mint and cinnamon, along with selected gums and
hard candies (points added or subtracted at discretion of sister
upon inspection of selection).

Pocket shoeshine kit with soft-bristled shoe brush, black polish,
chamois leather buffing cloth.

Pocket manicure set with cuticle pusher, eyebrow tweezers, nail
file and shaper, cuticle scissors and nippers, and toenail scissors.

Makeup supplies (all Chanel unless specified): pressed powder
compact, powder blush compact with mirror, lip brush,
lipliners in nude and rose, lipstick in rose, liquid eyeliner,
lash comb, eyelash curler, small natural sponge.

Hairbrushes: flat-back brush, quill brush with wooden handle,
pitchfork comb, teaser comb.

Smoking supplies: two unopened packs of Marlboro Mediums,
two unopened packs of Salem Light 100s; four
plastic-wrapped, unopened Bic minilighters (pink only).

A selection of DVDs (extra points for new releases not yet
available on market).

A selection of music CDs (points added or subtracted at discretion
of sister upon inspection of selection).

Additional products: Motrin Extra Strength, Neutrogena Sunless
Tanning Spray (Deep), Aveda Oil-Free Hydraderm, Xanax
(.5 only).

Homemade facial masks in plain white eight-ounce containers
in the following varieties made fresh daily: cucumber, lemon,
lettuce, and egg whites beaten with a jigger of rum, all
slightly thickened with baby powder.

There are seventy-two rules and regulations in all, including
one that had me totally stumped at first:

"Rule #66: During Pledge Week, pledges are required to wear a
fresh white carnation at all times. The slightest evidence of pink in

the carnation will result in points subtracted. Carnations must be purchased daily. If even minor wilting is in evidence as the day progresses, the pledge is strongly advised to replace it immediately."

I had to think about that one for a moment. Most of my classes start at eight a.m. There's only one local flower shop that I know of, and it doesn't open until ten a.m. Then I remembered. There is a farmer's market in Camoville, which is about twenty miles or so from campus. Patty's been there (I think that's where she buys her spinach for "Patty's Wilted Spinach Salad"). I called information, found their number, called them, and found out that they open daily at six a.m. Then I went online to look at the bus schedule. It looks like I'll be waking up at four a.m. every morning during Pledge Week and taking a five a.m. bus, which will give me time to get to the market, buy the carnation, and then ride the bus back in order to make it to my first class, though I'll be cutting it close, since it looks like the bus stops at practically every street corner between here and Camoville. Tomorrow's Friday. I should probably make a trial run in the morning just to see how it goes, because come Tuesday morning after Labor Day, I've got to have everything down. Like clockwork.

Oh, I know I can do this! If I don't make it into Alpha Beta Delta, it won't be because I haven't followed the rules. I'll make sure of that.

# August 29

## Dear Diary:

It was still dark when my alarm went off at four a.m. But I practically leaped out of bed. *This is it*, I thought. This was the start of a whole new day—a whole new future! I didn't even mind when I accidentally stepped on a half-eaten microwave tray of cheese and bean enchiladas. Patty mumbled, half-asleep, "Mmm. Alarm too early. Very inconsiderate of others."

After a quick shower, I raced outside and just made the bus. Phew. There was practically no one on it. About an hour later I arrived in Camoville, walked eight blocks to the farmer's market, and quickly spotted the flower stands in the distance. There they were. Fresh white carnations! I was so happy. Then I saw her. Guess who was already there buying several white carnations? It was Bethany. Ugh. She was even in her Alpha Beta Delta uniform already, but I noticed that her blouse had a shawl collar, not a Peter Pan collar, and she also was wearing an opera-length pearl necklace. I don't remember anything about being allowed to wear jewelry, though to be fair it's not Pledge Week yet. Then she sashayed to the corner where her black Jaguar convertible was double-parked and zipped away. Just like that. Easy as pie. She probably rolled out of bed ten minutes ago. I suddenly felt very depressed. Life is so unfair. The nastiest people seem to have it so easy.

Still, the farmer's market turned out to be a total treasure trove. Here's where I can load up on hard candies and Altoids and cigarettes and other supplies each morning, though I'll probably have to start waking up at three a.m. instead of four in order to make the fresh facial masks. I have no idea how busy I'll be once Pledge Week starts, or what they'll have me doing, so I decided to start buying various supplies in bulk right then and there (including four cartons of Marlboro Red and a discount twelve-pack of mint Altoids). Then I hopped back on the bus, carefully timing myself to be sure I'd make it back in time for my eight o'clock class, which I did, but just barely.

The rest of the day went by in a haze. I was so tired. I also noticed that most of the students were leaving campus. Everyone was taking off for three-day vacations, since it's Labor Day weekend. Everyone except me, that is. I'll be alone. As usual. Even Patty's taking off. She's going with a high school girlfriend to a Lobster Festival on Padre Island in Texas. I started to feel sorry for myself again. Boo-hoo. Poor me. But then I remembered that I have lots of wonderful things to do and buy and prepare in order to be ready for the start of Pledge Week on Tuesday, including purchasing my uniform (I should probably buy everything in triplicate, since I won't have time to wash and iron everything each morning). By the time my last class ended at five, I was trashed. Completely. All I wanted to do was go home and sleep. Then a truly horrific thing happened—but not to me, thank goodness. I was walking past the football field when I heard strange noises underneath the bleachers. Curious, I stepped to the side. I couldn't believe what I saw. There was Bethany on the ground with Nester—yes, Nester!—and he had his hand up her skirt. She was moaning and wriggling.

"Oh, yeah. To the left. Up. Stop. Make a circle. Oh, God. That's right, that's . . ."

Then she shrieked with anger—howled, actually—yanked his hand out, and held it up to his face.

"I told you to clip it! You stupid piece of chuck. My thighs cannot be nicked."

"I'm—I'm sorry," murmured Nester.

She bolted up, angrily gathering her purse and jacket.

"Like, I ask you to do one thing for me and you blow it. You lose, bucko. And if you tell anyone we had this little arrangement, you're dead. You hear me? D-e-a-d. I don't know you. I've never known you. When you see me on campus, look away. Just die. Go ahead and die."

She stalked off. And Nester softly cried. I sort of felt sorry for him. And in a way, as amazing as this may sound, I felt sorry for Bethany, too. I mean, is Nester the best she can do? But then again, it did sound like she enjoyed giving him orders, and I have read romance novels where glamorous women like giving orders to "dirty" or "low-class" men, and Nester certainly qualifies for the "dirty" part. It also made me weirdly happy. Bethany's world may be privileged and picture-perfect, but apparently it has a dark side, too. At least I'm not soiling myself behind the bleachers with Nester. Eeeow. Double eeeow. I stepped away carefully—I sure as heck didn't want either one of them to see me—and as I walked across the street, I was almost knocked to the ground when a small, white, floppy-eared mutt jumped right at me.

"Rags! Bad boy. Over here."

Across the street was Keith Ryder, looking superdreamy in Ray-Bans, an RU tank top, and low-hanging jeans that showed off his paisley-print boxers (so cute!), standing in front of a Range Rover with a couple of guy friends (I think they were drinking beer). I'm sure they were all getting ready to go to someplace fun and exciting for the three-day weekend. Rags kept bouncing up and down in front of me, even though Keith kept calling him, so

I thought I'd help out. I took hold of his collar and led him right up to Keith. There I was standing right in front of him. I just wanted to die! And I wanted to be pretty, too, and say something witty and sophisticated. This was Meri's boyfriend, after all—or ex-boyfriend, based on what I'd seen at the pledge meeting, but who knows, maybe they're tempestuous (I bet they are).

"Thanks. 'Preciate it," he said.

He scooted Rags into the Range Rover.

"Sorry about the umbrella," I squealed, a good four octaves higher than I normally speak. Oh, I'm such a jerk.

"The what?"

"At the pledge meeting? My umbrella popped open. I blocked your way. I'm just saying sorry. For, um, you know, for me."

I am such a citizen of Loserville. I'm the mayor. But then he smiled at me—really smiled—and I swear I saw a twinkle in his eye (his left one).

"No prob."

Then he took off with his friends.

"No prob." That's what he said! How completely sweet. And he smiled. And he was looking right at me. He didn't ignore me. Or say something nasty. And his dog was so cute. Rags. I think Rags likes me. I like Rags, too.

# September 1

## Dear Diary:

The weekend has been long, but incredibly productive. I have everything I need for tomorrow. And even though it's kind of depressing being on campus all by myself, I feel good about my future for the first time in a long time. After shopping on Saturday, I called Mom, but she wasn't able to take my call. Still, I did talk to Lisa. Somehow she's convinced Dad to cut a check for eight thousand dollars so she can make a demo of "Tune My Motor Up," even though he thinks it's a dirty song too.

"Oh, Dad, you are s-o-o-o not the target audience," she huffily informed him.

But then again, maybe he is. Lisa recently created her own Web site, "lisabixby.com," in anticipation of her growing fan base. It even has several pictures of Lisa in the slutty clothes Mom bought for her in Parkersburg (in one of them she's posing in front of a men's urinal, which is such a rip-off of Madonna, but Lisa says no one knows who that "ancient bitch" is anymore, so they won't know). Anyway, she's gotten several propositions from a bunch of sixty-year-old men, which is more than creepy, but she doesn't care.

"Like, once my single hits, the pedophiles will be gone. I'm being nice to them, though. They might have kids in my demographic."

I tried to tell her about Alpha Beta Delta, but she didn't seem all that interested—except to ask if she can send me tons of copies of her CD single so the pledges can carry them in their bottom-fold portfolio briefcases (I told her about Rule #32). Pledging is only for a week, and I doubt her single will be done by then—but she'll probably send them anyway.

Today I cleaned out the dorm room. Again. Not as many garbage bags this time, but enough. When I was hurling the last bag in the Dumpster behind the dorm building, I saw Bud. He saw me, too, and he ran. Good. He should keep running. I guess Bud's alone this weekend too. It's too bad that he can't calm down and be a normal person. We could have spent time as friends this weekend. I don't think Bud's a bad person when you get down to it, but he's so determined to be this "playa-gangsta" these days, and he's so not. Oh well. Maybe he'll get over it when he meets a nice girl and gets married. Or maybe he'll be like Mr. Bartow, this creepy married guy who lives in our neighborhood in Marietta and always tries to flirt with the girls playing T-ball in the cul-de-sac. Yuck.

I wish Mom had time to talk to me. She used to give me such good advice when I was a little girl.

"Stop being average," she told me once. She was very concerned at the time that I didn't have as many friends as she did when she was eleven. I think she was also trying to get me used to the idea of "having fun," since I didn't even have a best girlfriend.

"Start small," she instructed. "Ask a girl to go with you on a shopping trip, or swimming, or coffee, or an afternoon at the movies. You'll see. Then you won't be so mopey and boring all the time. No one likes a Gloomy Gus. Not even mommies and daddies."

That's advice I should still follow. Tomorrow is my first day as a pledge. I'm going to be friendly, and fun, and not boring. Maybe

I'll even ask Shanna-Francine or one of the pledges out for coffee or for lunch at Long John's. Maybe I should just pretend that my acceptance into Alpha Beta Delta is a fait accompli. If I really did believe that, then I'd be confident and happy and fun to be around. I should just do it. I'll pretend. So far the pretending thing is working.

From: cindybixby <cindybixby@yahoo.com>
Date: 1 September
To: mom <elainebixby@msn.com>
Subject: Pledge Week Starts Tomorrow!!

Hi, Mom!

I'm sure Lisa and Dad have told you by now that I was
invited to pledge at your old stomping ground! Pledge Week
starts tomorrow morning!!! I'm so excited!!

Any advice on how to get through it all in one piece? I'll
check my e-mail in the morning.

Love,
Cindy
xxxooo

From: Mail Delivery Subsystem <MAILER DAEMON@outmail6.net>
Date: 1 September
To: <cindybixby@yahoo.com>
Subject: re: Pledge Week Starts Tomorrow!!

--The following addresses had permanent fatal errors--
<elainebixby@msn.com>
(reason: 550 Requested action not taken)
550 5.1.1 <cindybixby@yahoo.com> . . . User email blocked

# September 2

## Dear Diary:

Steady as she goes! I looked pretty darn good in my pledge outfit today, and I woke up extra early to make the facial masks and buy my carnation (I'm so glad I did a practice run). When I arrived at my first class, everyone was so much nicer to me. In other words, they actually noticed me. Ha! A few girls even seemed jealous that I was pledging at Alpha Beta Delta and they weren't. When I walked to my second class, my heart almost skipped a beat when I saw Gloria walking toward me. I gulped. *I'm ready,* I told myself. *I'm more than ready.*

"Altoid. Cinnamon," she barked.

No prob. I had them.

"Comb my hair. Use a quill brush. And it better have a wooden handle."

No prob again. I pulled the comb through Gloria's hair.

"That's enough," she snapped. Then she leaned in. "Meeting at the house at three."

"Um, I have a class then."

"Tough shit."

She whirled off.

Okay, so I'd miss a class. Big deal. What was I thinking? Where are my priorities? I hope I don't get points docked for that. After my third class, I went to the Great Lawn to eat lunch and I saw

Gloria again. Oh no. Breathe. But she wasn't coming up to me, she was stomping right up to Bethany, who was all smiles (she'd bought a new blouse with a Peter Pan collar). It looked like they were chatting amiably—like two old friends, which I'm sure they'll be one day. Then Gloria shrieked.

"I see pink!"

"But it's white," gasped Bethany.

"Did I ask you?"

She violently ripped the carnation from Bethany's blouse, threw it to the ground, and—*bam*—stomped on it.

"Get a new one. I'll give you fifteen minutes. And it better not have the teensiest bit of pink in it."

She whirled off. Bethany looked shell-shocked. I guess I should have felt sorry for her, but honest, she has a car, and Jaguars do go fast. If she speeds just a little she should be able to get to the market and back in time. More important, it was a wake-up call for me. If that had been me, and I was given only fifteen minutes to replace my carnation, I'd be in big trouble. I barely inspected my carnation at the market this morning. Note to self: Inspect the carnation carefully before leaving the market.

Come three o'clock, I darted across the campus to Alpha Beta Delta. My heart was pounding. I didn't want to be late. Gasping, I all but barreled inside. I was the first pledge there.

"Five minutes early," said Shanna-Francine, smiling cheerfully. "Good job, Pledge Cindy."

The other pledges arrived a few minutes later, including Bethany. She was wearing a new carnation (I'll bet she inspected it real carefully before she bought it). All of the pledges said hello to me, including a nice girl named Lindsay Cunningham, who I remembered from the Smoker. She's very pretty, and oh my God, she has the clearest skin I've ever seen. It's luminously white.

"SPF 40," she confided. "Every day. And I use an umbrella.

Auntie Christiana died from melanoma. She was a sun whore. I swear, she practically lived on Uncle Stephano's yacht."

Then dead silence. Meri glided forth. After a moment she spoke. Softly.

"Closets should be emptied four times a year. Inspect every item. Seasonal clothes should be cleaned and put into storage. Since you don't know what the hemline will be in the coming months, store every dress with the hemline out."

Silence again. We absorbed her sage words. Her eyes swept past us. Then she pointed at Lindsay.

"You. I'd like to watch a DVD tonight. What's your selection, Pledge?"

Lindsay gulped, reached into her bottom-fold portfolio briefcase, and handed six DVDs to Meri. She inspected them carefully, then casually tossed each of them to the floor after she finished.

"*8 Women*. This is acceptable. It's French. And it stars Catherine Deneuve. *The Matrix Revolutions*. This is borderline. The concept is tired, and Keanu is getting old, but it is fairly pleasant to look at. *Never Been Kissed*. This movie would be entirely unacceptable if it weren't for the fact that it stars Drew Barrymore."

Then she held out the DVD *Far from Heaven*.

"Who can tell me what they think of this movie?"

"Oh, I can," chirped Bethany (like the suck-up she is). "It's completely fabulous. It's, like, this total homage to Douglas Sirk."

"I see," said Meri, her eyes narrowing. "And why would we want to watch that? Why not watch the real thing?"

Then she addressed us all, speaking softly but pointedly.

"This movie is the equivalent of lounge music. If you want to listen to jazz, such as Mingus or Fitzgerald or Parker, you listen to the real thing. You do not listen to a lounge music remix of jazz. Am I clear? This movie is creatively bankrupt. And it should be burned."

She handed the DVD to Shanna-Francine, who dutifully

tossed it into the fireplace and turned on the gas. *Poof. Far from Heaven.* Up in flames.

"Pledge Bethany will be docked seven points for her erroneous opinion. Pledge Lindsay will be given the benefit of the doubt and will only be docked two points."

Her eyes swept past us, then stopped on me. Me! Oh God, I swear it felt like time stopped, especially when she sort of raised an eyebrow. Then she shook her head several times—forcefully, like she was clearing cobwebs—turned to Gloria, and delicately murmured, "Stoli shots."

Gloria stepped away, and when she returned, she set a single shot glass in front of me and filled it with Stoli vodka.

"Well? What are you waiting for?" she barked.

I'd never done a shot of anything before in my life, but I have seen how they do it on TV. Bracing myself for the worst, I knocked it back and swallowed. Ugh. It stung pretty badly and it didn't taste good at all, but I figured what the heck, it didn't kill me.

"Again," whispered Meri.

*Okay, I did it once,* I thought. *I can do it again.* Gloria poured another shot; I knocked it back and swallowed. Yuck again.

"Again," said Meri.

Oh boy. Gloria poured a third shot. Then a fourth. A funny thing happened after the sixth shot or so. It didn't taste so bad anymore. But it did seem like the room was starting to tilt (just slightly), and I thought I heard laughing and giggling, but when I looked up, no one was talking, or at least it didn't seem that way. And when Meri once more whispered, "Again," it almost seemed like she was out of sync—as if she was one of those Japanese actors in a Godzilla movie. Then I heard more giggling, more laughing, and it still didn't look like anyone was moving their mouths. It suddenly dawned on me. I was the one laughing. I was giggling. I suddenly felt levitated. Whoa. Shanna-Francine was picking me up. The room tilted even more. My legs were wobbly. For some reason it struck me as wildly funny. Meri whispered to Shanna-Francine. It didn't quite dawn on me what she was saying, and I'm sort of glad about that.

"Undergarments only," she said. "To the Great Lawn and back."

I exploded with giggles when Shanna-Francine unbuttoned and removed my blouse. Gloria had to hold me up. Before I knew what was happening, I was standing in my bra and panties. I should have been embarrassed, or felt shame, or something, but I didn't. It was the most incredible feeling. I blinked once and I was outside—way far away from the house (how did that happen?) with Shanna-Francine holding me steady (I think). The sun was setting. I heard a few horse whistles and hubba-hubbas. Then we arrived at the Great Lawn. Everyone was there playing Frisbee, holding hands, having so much fun. *Me too*, I squealed inside, *I want to have fun too!* Then I gleefully screamed and ran up to Bud, Nester, and Randy. They were horrified. I swiped that stupid little Hacky Sack and bounced it up and down, not letting it fall once, calling out:

"This is the platter serve! This is the pooper-shooter! And this . . ."

Bam. I hit Bud square in the face.

"That's the money shot!"

I heard a burst of applause from the Abercrombie & Fitch boys. It looked like Bud's jaw dropped clear down to his knees. *Whoosh*. A Frisbee flew right over me. I leaped in the air, caught it. Wow. I've never done that before. Then I threw it out. Leaping in the air and catching it a few yards away was Rags. *Oh, you cute little Rags*, I thought. I ran after him all over the Great Lawn. I guess I ran beyond the Great Lawn, because a few seconds later I heard the screech of tires before me and I fell face forward. Ouch. Cement. The street. And the strange smell of Dad's cigar. And then strong arms picked me up. I could barely focus. I was sputtering with laughter. Then I was laid gently on the ground. Shanna-Francine's face loomed before me. She looked awfully concerned. I turned my head. A guy was walking away from us. There was something about those low-hanging jeans and those cute paisley boxers. It hit me like a bolt of lightning. It was Keith Ryder! I thought, *Does he have more than one pair of paisley boxers, or has he neglected to change them?* Rags bounced up to him, holding the Frisbee. *Oh, you bad little Rags,* I thought. I love Rags. The setting sun was shining brighter. Auntie Christiana died from melanoma. Bethany plays stinky-pinky with Nester Damon. I laughed and laughed, rolling in the grass. Then I stood up. Whoa. How did I get here? I was back at Alpha Beta Delta. All the pledges looked deeply troubled. Gloria refused to give me another shot. Party pooper. Every party has a pooper. Brr. Cold. I was in a shower. Shanna-Francine grinned as she shut the curtain. There were so many nice bath products. I had to try them all. *Would anyone know?* I thought. *Would they mind? Who cares?* I didn't care.

Meri, Gloria, and all the other pledges were gone when I stepped back into the living room. Shanna-Francine was still grinning. She handed me my clothes. The room wasn't tilting quite so much.

"Meeting tomorrow morning at three a.m.," she blurted.

Did I hear that right? I sailed out the door. It was dark.

"I bet you could use a coffee."

I turned around. There was Lindsay, holding an open umbrella above her head. I hiccupped.

"Um-umbrella? The sun's set, Lindsay."

"I know, but the moon's especially bright tonight."

I think Lindsay and I are going to become best girlfriends. She drove me to this really cool café (in her Porsche Boxster S—ha! take that, Bethany), and it seemed like we talked about everything. Lindsay's from a very wealthy family. It turns out that Auntie

Christiana was actually Princess Christiana of Northumberland. Can you imagine? Lindsay's royalty. Wow! And get this. She was interested in hearing about my upbringing and my life too. Honest. When I told her I was from a small town called Marietta, she was fascinated. And when I told her how nervous I was to be a pledge, given that I'm so ugly and such a loser, she laughed, but not at me.

"Pretty is as pretty does," she said. "That's what Auntie Christiana always said. And she wasn't pretty at all. And she had lots of handsome boyfriends."

I almost pinched myself. Here I was having a nice coffee with a real girlfriend. When I told her I had to go, because I didn't know where I was going to find a fresh white carnation at two in the morning since the market doesn't open until six, Lindsay offered to pick me up at two thirty in her Porsche. There's another market she knows about that's open twenty-four hours. In fact, it looks like no more bus riding for me. Lindsay thinks we should go together every day during Pledge Week. How lucky am I?

# September 4

## Dear Diary:

Pledging is hard work. Take yesterday. Most of us were only half-awake when we arrived at the house for our three a.m. meeting, and we had to clean the entire house and scrub all the floors on our hands and knees with wet rags. No mops allowed.

"Handsies-kneesies," instructed Meri. "It's the only way to really clean a floor."

After that, we had to jog two miles carrying huge wooden bowls of pink Jell-O and hope against hope that it didn't jiggle too much.

"Your Jell-O bowls have been inspected," barked Gloria. "They're all smooth. If there's even the smallest crack in the Jell-O surface when you come back, you'll be doing it again. No walking, girls. Jog. We'll be watching."

Later, we were all summoned back to the house for more activities: Whoever could get the most credit reports for students on campus within sixty minutes would be able to skip house cleaning the next morning (I didn't win that one, since I don't really know how to break into computer sites, much less create them, like Lisa); more jogging with Jell-O bowls; and later, we all had to stand in the backyard of the house with apples on our heads while Meri and Gloria took aim with bows and rubber-tipped arrows. I was so nervous. We were each given seven apples. I didn't know what to do, so I just tried to send my mind somewhere else and closed my eyes. Each time—*ka-pow*—the apple went sailing off my head, punctured by the arrow. Meri and Gloria were obviously good archers. Poor Pledge Tina (a horsey girl who seems like a trophy wife in the making) started crying and sniffling, and I don't think it was a mistake when Gloria took aim and nailed her right in the mouth. She fell to the ground, writhing in pain.

"Tsk. Poor li'l pledge," whispered Meri.

"I have to go to the ER!" wailed Tina, who was nearly gagging as she pulled the arrow from her mouth.

"No hospital," barked Gloria, who examined her and saw that the inside of her mouth was only slightly bruised and bleeding. Then she froze, gaping open-mouthed at Tina, and screamed, "I see pink!"

She tore off the offending carnation, hurled it to the ground, stomped on it, and then gazed at Tina's blouse.

"There's blood. You'll have to get a new blouse. I'll give you ten minutes."

She ripped open Tina's blouse, yanked it off her body, and tore it in half.

"There's blood on your bra, too. Take it off. Walk topless to your room, pick up a clean bra and blouse, walk topless back to the house, and put everything on here. No driving. Wait. We'll give you a Jell-O bowl. You'll jog. Which means you have five minutes."

I think Tina had some sort of mental breakdown at that point. She burst into tears and wailed.

"This is bullshit! I'm not doing it."

Within minutes she was gone. She had to turn over her pledge book too, and Meri made her sign a fourteen-page legal document indemnifying the house and making Tina liable should she ever breathe a word about what happened. She was happy to do it.

"You're all a bunch of sicko bitches," she wailed, and she was off.

None of us dared say a word. Meri calmly stepped forward, flipped back her thick raven hair, and after a moment whispered,

"All my nostalgia is for tomorrow. Never for yesterday."

We stood there, letting her powerful words sink in. A moment passed, then Meri stepped up to Lindsay and quietly asked, "It's cloudy, Pledge Lindsay. Why are you holding an open umbrella above your head?"

Lindsay quivered.

"Auntie Christiana died of melanoma."

Meri gazed at her quizzically, and almost seemed to smile. Almost, but not quite. "That's good. I like it."

Before we left the house, we were all instructed by Gloria to purchase large pink umbrellas and hold them open above our heads day and night, indoors and outdoors, throughout the rest of Pledge Week—in solidarity with Lindsay and her sadly departed Auntie Christiana. Okay, that's a little strange, but it was nothing compared to what Meri instructed us to do this morning.

"You'll have several nights to complete this next assignment. Pose as prostitutes on the Grand Concourse, meet three tricks, get their mothers' maiden names and the home phone numbers of each trick and his mother. We'll be verifying the numbers. That's all. No one's asking you to do anything illegal. Come back to the house dressed appropriately tonight at eight o'clock. You'll be judged on your outfits. Then you'll begin."

Lindsay and I went shopping together after classes (Professor Scott was so perturbed when I refused to close my pink umbrella). Luckily, I knew just the type of clothes to get. I pretended I was Lisa. Would Lisa buy flirty plastic short-shorts with zipper sides? Of course she would. Would Lisa buy an apple-red blouse with a plunging V-neck? She wouldn't think twice. Lindsay's outfit wasn't as hookerlike as I thought it should be, but I didn't want to criticize her. Maybe she's never seen *NYPD Blue*. Personally, I've never known a hooker to wear such a lovely tunic dress. And in beige.

That night back at the house, Lindsay, Bethany, the rest of the pledges, and I were carefully scrutinized by Meri and Gloria. Bethany's outfit was beyond hookerish. I mean, she may as well have been naked. There was a shivery breeze out too, which meant that her legs were bound to get cold, since she was wearing only a garter belt, a bikini, and hose. But Meri gave her extra points, since she brought along an oversize lollipop. Nice touch, I guess. Meri seemed to like what I was wearing, but Bethany didn't.

"Very *Pretty Woman*," she sneered. "S-o-o-o 1980s."

Twenty minutes later we were all standing along the Grand Concourse, having been driven there together in a large van by Shanna-Francine, who promised to be back in three hours. We must have looked a bit freaky, since all of us were holding up pink umbrellas. A lot of cars slowed down to gape, but no one was stopping. Finally, one car pulled up and Bethany practically body-checked me and lunged forward, leaning into the man's open passenger window.

"Hey, guy, lookin' for fun?" she cooed.

Within seconds she was gone. I started to get nervous. Really nervous. I told Lindsay I didn't know if I could actually get in a car like that with a strange man—especially since we weren't really hookers and we weren't actually going to do anything. Wouldn't they be angry? Then she came up with a brilliant idea. We'd work as a team and keep going until we had six maiden names and six sets of numbers that we could divvy up between us. Unfortunately, cars didn't stop for us. Maybe it was because of Lindsay's beige tunic dress, or maybe because it looked like I was shivering (and I wasn't cold). A couple of other pledges got into cars, and three hours later, Shanna-Francine picked us up.

"Got one," smirked Bethany as we rode back to the campus. "This is easy."

Only one other pledge was successful. Another was crying. Her name's Alma, and she was practically inconsolable and wouldn't tell any of us what happened. When we got back to the campus, she handed her pledge book to Shanna-Francine. She was out. I guess that started a domino effect, or at least a domino-of-one effect. Another girl handed over her pledge book too. This is going to be a difficult assignment—and we only have three more nights. When Lindsay drove me home, I decided to risk hurting her feelings and mentioned that maybe, just maybe, her outfit was a little too "proper." Well, it turns out she was afraid of exposing too much skin, given the fate of her beloved Auntie Christiana, so I promised to coat her in the absolute highest SPF cream tomorrow night if she wears something just a little racier. She thanked me for my understanding and my strength, which she said was inspiring. I was shocked. Do I have strength? True, I haven't dropped out like other pledges, and I guess I did make a spectacle of myself the other day when I had all those Stoli shots, but honest, I don't think there's anything that Meri and Gloria could dream up for me that would make me feel any more humiliated about myself than I normally do. Maybe that means I'm some sort of doormat, or maybe it means I have a very high threshold for embarrassment. I should probably thank Bud for that. I consoled myself (and Lindsay) with the fact that Gloria had to pledge once, and so did Shanna-Francine, and Meri, too. Yes, even Meri. She was a pledge once. And look at her now.

When I returned to my dorm room, I was disappointed, but not surprised, to see that it was nearly as filled with garbage, half-empty food containers, and newspapers as before. Patty was asleep. It was three in the morning. I had to be back at the house at five. I'm so tired, and yet I'm wide awake. I'm also taking stock. True, I'm not done pledging, I'm not a sister at Alpha Beta Delta, but I already have two nice girlfriends—Shanna-Francine and Lindsay. And even though I probably won't make the final cut and they'll ignore me after that, at least I know that I have the capacity to make friends and be social. That's something, isn't it?

# September 5

## Dear Diary:

Bethany's gone! Vanished! She got in a car tonight and she never came back. Everyone's concerned, especially since all day there were rumors that, in her determination to win, she had already given three hand jobs, one dance party, and a really good spanking. I'm a bit creeped out, to tell you the truth. When we gathered at the house this morning, Bethany did seem a bit on edge, especially when Gloria criticized her "handsie-kneesie" scrubbing skills.

"Oh please, it's clean enough," snapped Bethany.

"Excuse me?" barked Gloria. "Did you say something? I think you need to redo the bathrooms."

After cleaning and scrubbing the house, we gathered in the living room, where Meri informed us of our greatest and most important challenge yet.

"Contribute to Alpha Beta Delta's Hoover File," she announced.

Now I know why Alpha Beta Delta has always been so powerful. Information. The Hoover File was started in 1919 at the height of Prohibition by Miss Anita Woolrich, Alpha Beta Delta's first president. It was Anita who learned that RU's Home Ec instructor, Miss Enid Louise, was a secret bootlegger for the school's trustees. The Hoover File has since grown to include any and all indiscretions over the years. Dean Pointer, the current dean, has long been in the pocket of Alpha Beta Delta, and so have all the board trustees and many professors. Lucky for all of us pledges, though, there are always new professors coming in each year, along with several who haven't yet been investigated. The Hoover File has been an Alpha Beta Delta secret for more than eighty years.

"Say a word about it to anyone and you're out," warned Gloria. "Two years ago a pledge tried to talk about it to her therapist. She's going to community college now."

All of us gasped in shock.

"That's right. Commuting from home. I think I've made my point."

Given that it's such an important assignment, we only have to get the dirt on one teacher, or one board member, but it has to be good. In other words, I'll probably have to learn things about several teachers over the next day or so, and pick the one that I think is most worthy of the file. But how on earth am I supposed to do that? With the exception of Professor Scott, none of my professors even know I exist. Lindsay was worried too. She admires her professors, and so she doesn't necessarily like the idea of digging up dirt on them. Still, we were both heartened by the fact that neither of us has had that many points deducted yet, so if we're not able to contribute anything worthwhile to the Hoover File, hopefully it won't hurt us too much. Meri's right. This is going to be a big challenge. And yet, before the meeting even broke up, Bethany smugly proclaimed, "Oh please, I've nailed this assignment already. Professor Hollingsworth is a cokehead. And he deals. And I should know."

There was stunned silence. Meri leaned in.

"Explain, Pledge Bethany."

"What's to explain? I do lines with him every now and then. Big whoop. Get this. He blew a hole in his nose cartilage three years ago. What a jerk. Still won't give it up. Says it reminds him of his Studio days, whatever the fuck that means. I've brought him a lot of customers, too. Anyone want to be hooked up? He's got Grade-A shit."

"You're not quite done," said Meri, though she was obviously pleased.

Bethany will have to visit Professor Hollingsworth—with Shanna-Francine posing as a new customer, only she'll be wired. Once they have the goods on tape, Meri will inform Professor Hollingsworth that evidence against him is now the sole property of Alpha Beta Delta, to be used or not used depending on his level of continued cooperation with the needs and requirements of the house. Still, Bethany was basically done with her Hoover File assignment. Lucky her, I suppose—or not, depending on how you look at it, especially given what happened tonight on the Grand Concourse.

Lindsay and I didn't have any luck tonight, even though she was wearing a more revealing outfit. And within seconds after our arrival, Bethany hopped into a car and she was gone. Really gone. When Shanna-Francine drove up in her van to pick us up, Bethany still hadn't returned. Shanna-Francine didn't seem too worried. She dropped all the pledges off, but Lindsay and I begged her to drive back to the Grand Concourse once more before dropping us off, just in case Bethany had returned and was still waiting. We waited and waited. Nothing. Lindsay started crying. Shanna-Francine shrugged.

"Them's the breaks," she cheerfully blurted. "We need to go. I gotta make Jell-O bowls for tomorrow."

"More jogging with Jell-O bowls?" asked Lindsay.

"Uh-huh. There's an obstacle course this time."

We were all silent on the drive back to campus. Was Bethany in any real danger? Maybe we should have called the police. True, I don't like Bethany very much, but I don't wish her harm.

# Apostolina

When I got back to my dorm room, I called her dormitory number off the Pledge List Call Sheet and talked to her roommate. Bethany had not come home. She hadn't even called. I asked for her cell phone number and called that. There was no answer, but I left a message, telling her that everyone was really concerned about her welfare, which was a total lie, but maybe it would get her to call Meri or Gloria and let them know that she was okay. I'm still worried. Whatever happened to Bethany could have happened to any of us.

# September 6

## Dear Diary:

Bethany's okay! Meri and Gloria got a package this morning with Bethany's pledge book and a Hello Kitty postcard. By now, Bethany's off on a plane to some obscure, strange-sounding Arab country. Her "P.S." read:

"Hey, anyone need a great summer job? Contact me!"

# September 1

## Dear Diary:

Tonight was the last day of pledging. I'm so nervous. I'll find out tomorrow morning if I make the cut. And get this. Thanks to Lisa, of all people, I was able to contribute to the Hoover File. Lindsay made a contribution too. She's so resourceful. With her disposable Kodak Insta, she caught Belinda Faith, RU's married drama coach, in a touchy-feely embrace with Sissy Carrington, a senior RU drama major and the girl everyone thinks is destined to become the next Meryl Streep. But unlike Meryl, she's now part of the Hoover File, along with Professor Faith. As for me, I called Mom yesterday to ask if she had any helpful hints regarding the Hoover File, but I ended up talking with Lisa instead, who's thrilled with the way her demo has turned out. She hired a junior high school garage band to write and perform the music but told them she couldn't give them credit since it would ruin her "mystique." But she did pay them twenty dollars and gave them free access for life to her Web site. I don't know how I managed to get a word in edgewise, but I told her about a "class assignment" I had, and how I needed to learn everything I could about my teachers, like if there was anything unusual about their past or present activities. She giggled.

"Gimme their names."

I didn't think anything of it, and besides, I was still zero-for-zero in terms of fulfilling my assignment on the Grand Concourse. Lindsay and I were a team again last night. And since we decided to wear even less clothing than the night before in hopes of convincing cars to stop, we were cold. To our surprise, a red Honda Civic screeched to a halt next to us.

"You girls work as a team?" asked the man inside.

We told him yes, and we climbed into the backseat together. Off we went. There was silence at first, and Lindsay nervously took hold of my hand.

"How much do you girls charge?" growled the man.

"Oh, there's no charge, sir," babbled Lindsay nervously.

That seemed to pique the man's interest. He pulled down a dark alley, stopped the car, and turned around to face us. He looked old, maybe thirty or so, and he was sort of handsome. He sure didn't seem like the type of guy who needed to "procure," as they say on *NYPD Blue.*

"I'll ask you girls again. How much do you charge?"

"She's telling the truth, sir," I anxiously responded. "We don't charge."

"Uh-huh." He was obviously thinking it over. "So what do you girls do? For free?"

"Nothing!" gasped Lindsay.

For some reason, that really seemed to make the man angry.

"I can still bring you girls in. You won't make entrapment just 'cause you're saying you don't charge."

Then he flipped out his badge. Oh my God, he was a cop. Officer Kyle Hanson, RRPD. *That's it,* I thought, *we're going to jail, I'll have to call Dad to bail me out.* How on earth was I going to explain this? Fortunately for me, Lindsay explained everything. Even though we're sworn to secrecy, she broke like a dam. She told Officer Hanson all about our secret Alpha Beta Delta assignment and promised that we would both stay away from the Grand

Concourse forever if he would just drive us back to the campus. Then she turned to me. Her eyes were misty.

"That's it. We're finished. But I won't go to Women's Prison, and I won't let you. It's not worth it."

I knew she was right, and I pleaded with Officer Hanson too. Please just drive us back. Lindsay and I would have to turn over our pledge books. It would all be over. Officer Hanson's brow furrowed.

"Maybe I can help you girls out."

Oh, I love Officer Hanson! He didn't drive us back to campus, and he didn't drive us back to the Grand Concourse, either. Instead, he took us to an even seedier area just near the farmer's market and asked if we would "play-act" for a little while longer. It was perfect. Boy, this area was just crawling with johns, and in the next hour, we helped Officer Hanson bust six in a row. His partner, Officer Roberta Wood, who was following us close behind the whole time, was the one who slapped on the cuffs while Officer Hanson read them their rights and sternly asked:

"Mother's maiden name?"

"You—what?" sputtered one of the johns.

"Mother's maiden name. And phone number. Part of RU's Community Clean-up Initiative. Give it up now or give it to a judge with your mother present. It's up to you."

One of the johns was Professor Alan Heim from RU. I figured, heck, that's pretty good—he can be my contribution to the Hoover File. Once we were finished, Officer Hanson gave each of us a big bear hug, along with a strict warning to stay out of trouble or else. Officer Wood said she'd drive us back to the campus, but before that, she treated Lindsay and me to coffee and doughnuts at a genuine diner where real officers hang out. She was so nice. She's close to retirement—she's been on the force for nearly thirty years. One of her daughters graduated from RU eight years ago, and now she's an assistant district attorney in Miami. That's where Officer Wood's planning to go once she retires from the force. She said we'd certainly given her something new and different to tell her daughter when she calls tomorrow (they speak every morning), though she swore she wouldn't say a word about Alpha Beta Delta. Phew. Then she addressed us both very firmly.

"As a mother, I should call your mothers. I know Officer Hanson was trying to be nice, but I'm not happy we helped you girls out. Now that I think about it, it makes me sick. So here's the deal. Every quarter, you bring your report cards to me. You dip below a 3.0, I call your mothers and tell 'em everything. Okay? We got a deal?"

"Deal," we said.

Officer Wood's the best. She drove us back to RU, but instead of having her drop us back at our dorm rooms, we asked her to drop us at Alpha Beta Delta, since Lindsay noticed the lights were on. She wanted to hand over her maiden names and phone numbers right away, and thought I should too.

"They'll be impressed by our initiative," she said.

Also, that's where her Porsche was parked, and she didn't want to get a ticket. Officer Wood chuckled at that one and gave us each a hug good night. We dashed up to the house and knocked. Gloria answered. No, we could not come in, and no, Meri was not available. That's when Lindsay proudly handed over our maiden names and phone numbers—all six of them. Now, Gloria may be what some people call a "hard nut," and I'm sure she has to be, given that she's second in command at Alpha Beta Delta and has to work so hard to shield Meri from unnecessary distractions, but she seemed genuinely surprised that both Lindsay and I had completed our Grand Concourse assignment. I was giddy with pride.

"And guess what?" I added. "One of the johns was Professor

Heim. From RU. That should take care of my Hoover File assign-ment, too, right?"

"Huh. Don't see why not," concurred Gloria. "Hold on."

She instructed us to wait and closed the door. Lindsay and I bobbed up and down giggling. We did it. A minute later Gloria swung open the door.

"Meri is devastated," she snapped.

"I don't understand," I said. I was completely thrown.

"Professor Heim doesn't count. In fact, Meri is deeply saddened by your attempt to cut corners and combine two assignments."

"I'm—I didn't mean to—"

"Excuse me, Pledge. Did I ask you to talk? Unfortunately for you, Meri's now seriously considering whether or not to ask for your pledge book back. At the very least, she'll be docking you points. This is bad. This is real bad."

She slammed the door and flipped off the porch light, plung-ing us into darkness. I was silent as Lindsay drove me back to my dorm, even though she did her best to cheer me up. It would all blow over by morning, she promised, but I wasn't so sure. And deep inside, I knew Meri was right. Using Professor Heim *was* cutting corners. Why didn't I see that? That's it—one stu-pid, lazy mistake and it's all over. I climbed into bed and pushed aside my diary. I couldn't even face writing about it. When I woke up this morning, I listlessly made my fresh facial masks and prepared my uniform, knowing full well that it was all use-less. To make matters worse, today was the last day of pledging. How pathetic to be asked to return my pledge book on the last day. I decided to write an e-mail to Mom and tell her every-thing. It'll be better for her to hear about this from me instead of learning about it though the Alpha Beta Delta alumni grapevine. Given that she was president, I'm sure she'll find it especially shameful. I logged on to my account. There were two

new e-mails in my in-box, both of them from Lisa. I clicked
open the first one.

From: <lisa@lisabixby.com>
Date: 7 September
To: <cindybixby@yahoo.com>
Subject: Get a Load of This!

Hey Sis:

Don't say I've never done anything nice for you. Ha! Double-
click this:

www.twinc.org

Your better,
Lisa

    Curious, I double-clicked the link. My browser popped open—
and suddenly on my screen was a large red animated title: "Toilet
Whores!" Then it whipped aside and revealed several small boxes,
each with a hidden-camera picture of girls in public ladies' room
stalls. I thought, *Has Lisa finally gone off the deep end? Is she managing a porn
site now? And is she starring in it?* That would be so incredibly wrong. I
clicked open one of the pictures. It took me a moment. Hold on. I
know that bathroom. I know that stall. It's an RU stall. Who the
heck is running this site? I scrolled to the bottom, which read: "All
Contents © Denisovich and Associates." That didn't mean anything
to me, so I clicked off and opened Lisa's second e-mail.

From: <lisa@lisabixby.com>
Date: 7 September

To: <cindybixby@yahoo.com>
Subject: They Can Hide, But Not from Me!

Hey Sis:

Just in case you don't, like, "get it," double-click below.

www.twinc-cert.com

Envy me,
Lisa

I double-clicked it. It was a confidential copyright certification and Visa CheckCard access routing site for "Toilet Whores" and Denisovich & Associates, along with its many domestic and foreign subsidiaries, all of them owned and operated by Mr. Charles Scott. I reread that last part twice. Mr. Charles Scott. Mr. Charles Scott. Ergo, Professor Scott. Professor Charles Scott. "Toilet Whores." Quickly, but zombielike—since I was beyond shock—I printed the site document, along with pages from the original "Toilet Whores" site. Twenty-two pages in all. I stuffed them in my bottom-fold portfolio briefcase. Later, I didn't breathe a word about it when Lindsay drove us to the market for our fresh carnations. She held my hand part of the way. She probably thought I was still smarting from the night before, along with the prospect of being dropped as a pledge on the last day. But that wasn't it. I was numbed by the fact that I had done it. Somehow—and with Lisa's help, of course—I was now on my way to becoming an Alpha Beta Delta sister. I mean, unless there was some sort of huge, impossible hurdle today, I was in. It's strange. I always thought there would be a big fanfare when I turned this particular corner in my life, when I crossed the threshold from loneliness and Loserville to freedom and happiness and

90

friends and fun. But instead it was unnerving. Sure, I was turning the corner, but was I ready? Here was real opportunity, a chance to become a part of everything I'd ever hoped for, but was I worthy? Was I a fake? Was I a phony? Would I be found out?

At the house, it was the same as any other pledge day—lots of handsies-kneesies and, just as Shanna-Francine had promised, an excruciating obstacle course with our wooden Jell-O bowls (miraculously, nobody cracked their molds). I was still functioning on autopilot when we were told to gather in the kitchen for a morning coffee break. Without saying a word, I handed my printout pages to Meri. While everyone drank coffee, chatted, and supplied Xanax to a few demanding sisters ("Like, morning is the perfect time to speedball," chuckled a sister, who downed six pills and three cups of coffee), Meri very calmly flipped through my printout pages, one by one, never once looking up at me, never once altering her stony expression. Then she cleared her throat, pushed back her hair, and softly announced, "Last year at Christmas, I traveled to Zululand in Africa, where I was presented with a small stuffed dik-dik—a fully grown deerlike animal that is specially bred for its miniature size."

Complete silence. We all absorbed her words, a few of the pledges nodding their heads knowingly—though for the life of me, I couldn't figure out what the heck she was getting at. Then Gloria barked orders.

"Everyone downstairs. To the basement. Now."

We silently filed out of the kitchen to the stairs. My heart was racing. What on earth was down in the basement? I looked up, hoping to catch a reassuring glance from Shanna-Francine. She looked away fast. A hand abruptly gripped my arm. Gloria leaned in.

"Meri is considering your contribution to the Hoover File. But she's still stung by last night's fiasco. You're not out of the doghouse yet, Pledge. Go on. Get downstairs."

The next eight hours were hands down among the worst of my

life. Lindsay and I, along with the two other remaining pledges, were instructed to sit upright on cold metal chairs. Gloria and Shanna-Francine bound our hands, then our feet, and then we were blindfolded. I was so scared. What would happen next? Then out of nowhere, music was playing. It was Mariah Carey's "Butterfly." At first, I was soothed. True, it was being played loud, but it is a very nice ballad.

*Spread your wings and prepare to fly!*
*If you should return to me, we truly were meant to be!*
*So spread your wings and fly, butterfly!*

The song played again. Then again. And again! It was louder each time.

*Spread your wings and prepare to fly!*

How much longer could I take this? Then it played again. And again. Louder. Louder.

*Spread your wings and fly, butterfly!*

After the fourteenth or fifteenth time, I had trouble breathing. Would I lose consciousness? The song started again. I heard a sudden, high-pitched wail. Was it Lindsay? Another pledge was softly crying.

*Spread your wings and fly, butterfly!*

Sudden silence. No more Mariah. Would she start singing again? More silence. Did I want Mariah to sing again? Was I going crazy? What if I needed to go to the bathroom? I was thirsty. My throat was parched. Suddenly blasting:

*Spread your wings and prepare to fly!*

I gasped for air. I could feel sweat dripping from my body. Then the song cut off midway—and another song blared. It was bouncy and upbeat.

It sounded familiar. But was it?

Oh my God, this was crossing a line. It was Hanson's "Mmmbop." I honestly don't remember how old I was when I first heard "Mmmbop," but even as a little girl, I was sophisticated enough to realize that this was definitely one annoying pop song, and it took me forever to get it out of my head.

Even Lisa loathed Hanson. I remember we were riding in the car with Mom one afternoon—she was taking Lisa to get a French manicure—when "Mmmbop" suddenly come on the radio. Lisa just snickered, then she studiously informed me:

"Hanson was way before N' Sync and 98 Degrees. Back then, boy bands were allowed to be ugly."

I honestly don't remember if the Hanson boys were ugly or not, but I definitely felt ugly when "Mmmbop" played again. I'm not sure when I started crying, but I could feel tears stinging my eyes and cheeks and my blindfold was damp. It couldn't possibly get any worse.

*Spread your wings and fly, butterfly!*

Oh no. Mariah. Again. Apparently, this was one time too many for one of the pledges. I heard a metal chair crash violently to the floor, along with a shrieking, excruciating scream.

"I want out, I want out! I'll give you my pledge book. Please!"

Then a quick rustling, a cruel slap. Another wail. Then the *clump-clump-clump* of someone racing in horror up the basement stairs to freedom. Freedom. Freedom from Mariah. Oh, please, no more.

*Spread your wings and prepare to fly!*

I'm not sure how many times this second round of Mariah lasted—I decided after the twenty-fourth spin that it was making things worse to keep count. It seemed unstoppable and ominous, as if I'd been dropped into a bottomless pit, only to land in a suffocating heap of pure Mariah-ness. There was no escape. Mariah was consuming me. Butterflies were everywhere.

Silence again. Complete silence. I braced myself. Something would be playing next, I was sure, and whether it was Mariah or Hanson, I was ready. Then my hands were unbound, then my feet. My blindfold was gently pulled from my face. Shanna-Francine's cheerful, bubbly face came into focus.

"That's it!" she blurted.

Lindsay, the other pledge (a nice girl named Maureen, whom I haven't gotten to know well yet), and I sat there completely overwhelmed. Were we really free to go? No more Mariah?

"You guys are done pledging," chirped Shanna-Francine. "That wasn't so bad, was it? Tomorrow morning, if you don't get a call from us by eight o'clock, you didn't make it. Sorry. But if you do get a call, we'll be welcoming you to Alpha Beta Delta. Isn't that cool?"

"Can you give us a hint?" pleaded an exhausted Lindsay.

Shanna-Francine erupted into giggles. Apparently, the very idea of giving us even the slightest advance clue was hilarious. Lindsay and I stepped out of the house together. We were both shaking. I almost told her she didn't have to keep her pink umbrella open since we were all done pledging, but then I remembered her Aunt Christiana. She offered to give me a ride back to my dorm room.

"Can you wait a sec?" I asked.

I raced back into the house looking for Shanna-Francine, finally finding her in the kitchen making screwdrivers for herself and Gloria, who was upstairs.

"Did you forget something?" she asked cheerfully. "I'd offer you a screwdriver, but I don't think you're supposed to be here."

I cleared my throat. Okay, this would have to be fast. I knew what the answer to my question would be, but I still wanted to ask. I still believe in the goodness of virtually everyone around me, and that includes Shanna-Francine. Especially Shanna-Francine.

"I was just wondering. I mean, it was so nice of you to invite me to the Smoker, and I'm really glad I got to pledge. I know you took a big risk choosing me."

"Oh please," she said.

"No, let me finish," I insisted. "I know I probably won't get a phone call tomorrow morning, but I was wondering, even if I'm not an Alpha Beta Delta sister, can we still be friends?"

She stared at me open-jawed for a moment. Then she stepped forward and took my hand.

"That's a really stupid question. Of course we can."

I'll admit it. I got a little teary-eyed.

"Someone took a risk on me, too, you know," she continued. "A girl named Tonya Hickerson. She graduated last year. She changed everything for me. I mean, I know everyone thinks I'm, like, kinda goonie and I talk funny—blah-blah-blah. But you should have seen me before. Total spazz-case. That's why I played 'Butterfly' for the Pledge Song Blast."

"You chose 'Butterfly'?!" I asked, trying my best to tamp the outrage in my voice.

"Think about it," she explained. "It's, like, a very deep song. It describes exactly what happened to me once I joined the house."

After Lindsay dropped me off, I stepped into my dorm room and started filling garbage bags, and not just with Patty's garbage, but with mine, too. Time to throw away my facial mask supplies, the cigarettes, all the pledge items I wouldn't need anymore. It was over. Tying off the bags, I carried them downstairs to the

Dumpster and heaved each one inside. Then I just stood there for a moment—amidst all the garbage and the flies and the horrible smells. I could hear it playing softly in my head.

*Spread your wings and prepare to fly!*

I smiled, trembling. Tomorrow morning I'll know for sure. And if I'm lucky, I'll be free—I'll be breaking out of my cocoon too.

*Spread your wings and fly, butterfly!*

Shanna-Francine is right. It is a meaningful song. I wish I had a copy of the CD now. I'd listen to it.

# September 8

## Dear Diary:

The phone rang at six a.m.!

"Meri prefers the least amount of disturbance possible, so you need to move your stuff in before eight o'clock."

I was thunderstruck. Who was this? Was this a gag?

"Hello? You there?" the voice barked.

"Is this Alpha Beta Delta?" I yelped. "Am I in? Is this Meri Sugarman?"

The voice on the other end snorted.

"No. This is Mary. Queen of Scots. It's me, you little bow-wow. It's Gloria. You're in, kiddo. By the hair of your chinny-chin-chin. Pack it up. And don't be late."

Then a click and a dial tone. The room was dark, but sunbursts were exploding; a supernova soared inside me; butterflies were everywhere. I screamed. Patty bolted up, her hair on end.

"Huh? Wha?"

"I'm in!" I screamed, leaping from the bed. "I'm moving to Alpha Beta Delta!"

I don't remember clearly what happened next, but I think I grabbed the phone, dialed Lindsay, and got a busy signal. When I replaced the receiver, it rang. It was Lindsay. She was screaming with joy. I screamed with her, jumping up and down. We were

97

chanting, "Oh my God, oh my God, oh my God, oh my God, oh my God, oh my God!"

How did I pack so fast? Who knows. I was a tornado. I vaguely heard the protesting voice of Patty, but I tried to ignore it.

"Cindy, stop!" she shrieked. "This is insanity. Look at yourself. De-realization, excessive hysteria, a worsening of your Separation Axis."

Maybe she was right—maybe I was a being bit too giddy, but I didn't care. Lindsay would be here any minute with her Porsche, so I had to be ready. I didn't even realize that I was singing:

*Spread your wings and fly, butterfly!*

Wow. I was done in a flash. I snapped my trunk closed. Patty was standing before me, her arms folded, brow furrowed. It kind of made me angry.

"Oh, be happy for me. This is a big day for me."

"She's insane. You know that, don't you?"

"What are you talking about?"

"Meri Sugarman. Insane and dangerous."

"Oh, stop it," I cried. "You're not a psychotherapist yet."

Then it dawned on me. She was jealous. Absolutely green with envy. And I was leaving. She would be all alone.

"We'll still be friends, Patty," I insisted. "This doesn't change anything."

"Insane and dangerous. I want you to hear that. I want you to take that in."

I was losing my patience.

"What? You think I should join a fraternity instead?"

I heard a honk outside from Lindsay's Porsche. It was time to go. I asked Patty if she would help me carry my trunk and suitcase downstairs, but she refused. I couldn't believe it.

"I cannot in good conscience . . ."

"Okay, fine, so don't help me," I bellowed.

I couldn't believe how weird she was being, but I thought, *I carried my trunk and suitcase by myself when I first moved in here, I can sure as heck carry them out.* I grasped the trunk handle and the suitcase and put one foot in front of the other. I would never know dorm life again. I would never again be cleaning up Patty's garbage. I could even start using white soap again.

"A real friend would be happy for me," I said softly. "A real friend would help me."

But she didn't respond at first. Her eyes were fixed on me.

"Insane and dangerous."

I angrily slammed the door. And I practically flew out of the dorm building and into Lindsay's waiting Porsche. We laughed and cried as we drove to Alpha Beta Delta. The sun was rising. I could see the house at the end of the block. We pulled up, popped the trunk, and gathered our belongings. Gloria suddenly appeared behind us and barked, "What the hell do you think you're doing?"

Then she snapped her fingers and two meek little sophomore girls squirmed past us and began hefting our luggage and trunks inside. It seems the house grants them "favors" for services rendered.

"What kind of favors?" I asked.

"They get to keep their scholarships," chuckled Gloria.

Then we were whisked inside for a wonderful buffet-style breakfast with Gloria, Shanna-Francine, and the rest of the sisters. All except for Meri. Shanna-Francine was preparing a tray to be taken up to her room. She was so delighted that Lindsay and I had made it. In fact, we were the only two chosen to join the house this year—a record low, and a sad commentary, too, according to Gloria, on the pool of Smoker applicants.

"So why was I chosen?" I asked.

"Shanna-Francine's graduating this year," said Gloria. "Alpha

Beta Delta can always use another Shanna-Francine."

I'm not quite sure what that meant, but then Shanna-Francine turned to me and merrily blurted, "Would you like to take Meri's breakfast up this morning?"

Would I? What an honor! Meri's room was on the third floor, and as I carried the tray up the stairs, I was careful not to spill her orange juice or jiggle her scrambled eggs, which were very nicely displayed on the plate by Shanna-Francine, who used a light dusting of freshly ground pepper and salt to make a smiley face on them. I finally reached the third-floor landing. There was only one room. The door was closed. What was I supposed to do? Should I just leave the tray at the door? I wasn't sure. I set it down and knocked—and it swung right open from the force of my knock. I gasped. The room was immense. Obviously, there used to be two rooms, or maybe three, but the walls had been knocked down, creating a gargantuan space. I didn't see Meri anywhere, so I figured I might as well bring the tray in and set it on a table. I stepped gingerly inside.

The room was fantastic. The snow-white carpets made a beautiful background for the lovely piecrust tables and the antique armoire and a large corner cabinet, hand-carved and painted pink, which housed a collection of Wedgwood and Chinese things. The walls were painted soft blue. The bookcase was overflowing, and when I looked closer, I was intrigued to see that they were all on the same subject: *Jackie: The Clothes of Camelot; Jackie: Mother, Maiden, Myth; A Woman Called Jackie; Jackie Under My Skin: Interpreting an Icon; Jackie's Halcyon Days*. I set the tray down on one of the tables and gazed at the frilly four-poster canopied bed. On the bedside table sat an ashtray with a few butts and a book: *My Way of Life: A Script for a Complete Woman*, by Jacqueline Onassis. Then I heard a whispery voice.

"Is that you, Shanna-Francine? I hope you remembered to butter my scones."

I gulped. "No, it's me. Cindy Bixby."

Then doors swung wide from the balcony. I didn't even know there was a balcony, but I could see that it was very big, with a large Jacuzzi that was gently bubbling. In swept Meri, an absolute vision in a white fluffy robe and turban towel, her face red and flushed. Just like a movie star.

"Oh, it's you," she whispered. "What's your name again?"

"Cindy Bixby," I gulped.

"That's right. Cindy Bixby. Gloria calls you our 'little bow-wow.' I don't think that's very nice, do you?"

Was this a trick question? I wasn't sure. I decided to be honest.

"I don't know. I've been called worse things," I limply offered.

"I don't think it's very nice at all," said Meri softly. "I think it's mean. I'll tell her to stop. As president-elect, I can do that. But let's take a moment to look at why she says it. And correct it. Would you like to do that?"

I didn't know what she meant. I was completely out of my league here. Correct what? The next thing I knew, we were in my room on the second floor. My suitcase and trunk were empty. The scholarship girls must have put everything away. Meri swung open my closet, revealing all of my clothes neatly hanging. Then, lightning fast, she took each item out, quickly assessed it, and hurled it over her shoulder until there was nothing left in my closet except for a few plain T-shirts and my Alpha Beta Delta pledging outfit. She sniffled. Was she crying? Did she have allergies?

"It's been a long road for you, hasn't it?"

Before I could answer, she charged out of the room. I stood there rattled. A few seconds later Shanna-Francine gleefully popped her head in.

"Meri wants you out front."

Twenty minutes later Meri and I were whisked off in a town car, both of us in the backseat. I couldn't see who the driver was. The partition was black and firmly closed. Where the heck were we going? Meri whispered, staring straight ahead, "A smart girl makes a genuine effort to find out what goes on at second base or on the ten-yard line, and she should know better than to draw to an inside straight."

Huh? I'm going to have to make a real effort to start understanding Meri. She's so sophisticated, and she says so many interesting things, and yet I always feel at a loss. Still, I was a bit concerned. I was already missing my first class, and I had no idea where we were going, or when we would be back. I cautiously reminded her that I did, in fact, have several classes to go to today. She giggled lightly.

"You're funny."

Wow. Meri is amazing. She didn't just take me shopping, she took me shopping! Remember that scene in *Pretty Woman*? Oh my God, forget it, this was better. We went everywhere. Lord & Taylor, Neiman's, Banana Republic, and lots and lots of superchic little boutiques. Meri did everything. After my complete measurements were taken at the first place, we blew into one store after another and Meri picked everything out: Yves Saint Laurent, Chanel, St. John Sport, Calvin Klein, Guess, Dior. And shoes. Way more than ten pair. I couldn't even keep track. At first I was bowled over. I told her there was no way in a million trillion years I could ever pay her back for any of these clothes, no matter how hard I worked or how many part-time jobs I took on. She softly chuckled.

"Pay? You're a funny bunny."

And on we went. This boutique, that store, even the fancy Rumson River Shopping Mall, where Meri greeted a group of young children, led them into Toys "R" Us, and sweetly announced:

"Go on. Take anything you want. Pretend I'm Michael Jackson. Only you don't have to put out."

Then we were off to the Lili Mar Lili salon. I was plopped into a chair. Meri pulled aside my hairstylist, whispered in his ear. A clip here, a clip there, then a dye job, a few more clips. I couldn't believe it. My mousy brown hair—gone. My stringy haircut—a thing of the past. I stared at myself in the mirror and ran my hands through my thick raven hair. Meri leaned in next to me.

"What do you think?" she whispered.

What did I think? I looked fantastic. I looked just like Meri. It was late afternoon by the time we returned to Alpha Beta Delta. Meri retreated to her room. Shanna-Francine and Lindsay gaped at me, flabbergasted.

"You're beautiful!" exclaimed Lindsay.

"You think?" I squealed, whirling in a circle, showing off my new canary yellow Chanel outfit. "Am I a hottie?"

Shanna-Francine suddenly clamped her hand over my mouth. "Shh. Don't ever say that again."

Uh-oh. I still have so much to learn. "Hottie" is on the Alpha Beta Delta list of undesirable words and phrases. Meri believes that "language is like a virus," and Shanna-Francine helpfully showed both Lindsay and me the long list of forbidden words that Meri has compiled as part of her duties as president, which include "Hottie," "Hella," "Wack," "Awesome," "Dude," "All that," "Tight," "'Sup," along with phrases like, "It's all good" or "All about"—which means that these words cannot be used in the form of "It's all about Donatella" or "I'm all about chillin' today"—as well as "I'm down," as in, "I'm so down for getting a dragon tattoo this afternoon."

After dinner—it was catered!—Lindsay and I joined Shanna-Francine, Gloria, Meri, and the rest of the sisters for movie night in the living room. It was foreign: *The Piano Teacher*, starring Isabelle Huppert, and it was kind of scary and creepy, but I wasn't too sure what was going on because we weren't allowed to turn on the DVD subtitling display.

"Learn French," whispered Meri.

Still, it was getting late, and when the movie ended, I politely told everyone that I had to go upstairs to study for my classes tomorrow. Everyone exploded with laughter. I swear, you'd have thought I'd just said the funniest thing ever. I looked over to Lindsay, who shrugged helplessly.

"Oh, let her," said Gloria, waving me away.

Tomorrow I'll be having my first class with Professor Scott since discovering you know what. I don't know how I'll face him. An hour later Lindsay hopped onto my bed. We had such a nice just-girls chat, and we playfully pinched each other. Were we really here? And was it really true, as Lindsay had heard downstairs, that we no longer had to go to classes? How is that possible? My door swung open. It was Gloria.

"You're really going to class tomorrow?" she barked.

"Of course I am," I said. "I can't fail. And besides, I want to go."

"You want to go," she said, like she was testing the words out. "Okay, look, do whatever you want, but that's not going to give you much time. The house is throwing a benefit tomorrow night. Meri's appointed you and Lindsay to organize it. Guests will be arriving by nine. Frankly, I don't see how you're going to pull it off and go to class too, but whatever. Just don't screw it up."

Then she was gone. Lindsay and I gulped. Plan a benefit? What did that entail? Deciding we'd figure it out in the morning, Lindsay said good night and retreated to her room. I guess it's time for me to turn out my lights now, but I can't sleep—just like last night. This time, though, it's not because I'm afraid or nervous or anything like that. I'm happy. I caught my reflection in the mirror. Who is that happy-go-lucky girl? This has all happened so fast. But it has happened. I'm really here.

# September 8

## Dear Diary:

Classes, shmasses. Ha! I sure have learned a lot about the house today. Whatever the girls of Alpha Beta Delta want, we get. Woo hoo! Trouble with your GPA? No prob. With the goods on Dean Pointer and most of the professors in the Hoover File, adjustments can be made. Want a better parking spot? Dibs on dessert in the cafeteria? Maybe even a spa weekend at the Cape? Not to worry. Just talk to Meri. She'll take care of everything. And planning the charity benefit? A snap.

"You don't really have to, like, do anything," babbled Shanna-Francine cheerfully, handing us a phone sheet. "Just make a few calls. Oh, and pick a theme."

Between us, Lindsay and I called the caterer, the party planner, and the DJ, and I picked a theme: "Camelot." It was perfect. I even ordered cute little matching pillbox hats for all the girls to wear. It was expensive, but Shanna-Francine said not to worry about that.

Later, when Lindsay and I strolled past the Great Lawn after lunch, we knew everyone was staring at us. And whispering. So this is what it's like to be envied. Oh, I love it! Suddenly bounding up to us was Bud.

"Cyn, whoa. Total hottie. Like, who knew?"

"Is a bee buzzing by?" asked Lindsay.

"Mmm. I think so," I answered, catching on.

"Someone should tell that poor little bee to move it—if he values his GPA."

Oh my God, it was so nasty. And easy. And fun. And Bud deserved it. He shirked away. "Hottie." Please. I think Lindsay and I are going to make a wonderful little twosome. I barely even notice that she's practically always shielding herself with an open umbrella anymore. It's just so Lindsay. Bud Finger. Ugh. The likes of him seem very far away now. Thank goodness for that. When we crossed the street, I saw Patty. I was so excited to see her, and I wanted to tell her all about Alpha Beta Delta, but Lindsay held my arm back.

"I think that's someone you used to know. Get it? NOKD."

"NOKD?"

"'Not Our Kind, Dear.'"

She was right. I'm different now. I'm better. I need to be careful. I looked down at the ground as we strolled past, totally ignoring Patty when she called out my name. That was hard. But it was absolutely the right thing to do. I've got to be strong.

The charity benefit was a blast. There was yummy food (and the catering guys were cute), and wine, and drinks, and we all looked so fabulous in our matching little pillbox hats. It was packed, too. Practically every RU professor, along with Dean Pointer, a very severe, tall man in his mid-fifties, was there, and they each had to pay close to three hundred dollars just to get in.

"All the proceeds are going to the National Scarpiella Foundation," Meri informed me.

I was confused.

"Wait a minute. Scarpiella's an Italian chicken dish with sausage."

"Your point being?"

Then she tittered and sashayed off with Gloria. There were lots of guys there too. Wow. I'm talking handsome guys from the RU football team, and the swim team and the soccer team too, though I didn't see Keith Ryder. Maybe he and Meri are still on the outs. I started getting a little drunk as the night wore on, and I think Shanna-Francine was too. She couldn't stop giggling. I mean, I know Shanna-Francine's the type to giggle loudly at any given moment, but she was really giggling up a storm now.

"Great 'shrooms," she blurted out. Then she handed me some mushrooms. "Here. Try some and pass 'em on."

She must have been really drunk to pick out a bunch of mushrooms from the buffet salad bowl. I nibbled on one. I was hungry, I realized, so I ate the rest of them and then figured, hey, maybe I should have a little salad with my mushrooms. Ha!

I should probably mention that it's four in the morning now and I don't think I'll be falling asleep anytime soon. I drank too much. That has to be it. I can't stop smiling. And giggling. Really. In fact, an hour or so after I had my salad, I was the life of the party, or so it seemed. Every word I heard struck me as hysterically funny. But probably the funniest word I heard all night was "umbrella." Ha! It still makes me laugh. Umbrella. Oh my God, that's so funny. Umbrella-umbrella-umbrella. Why is that word so funny? Why can't I stop smiling? Umbrella-umbrella-umbrella. That. Is. So. Fucking. Funny. Umbrella-umbrella-umbrella. I love me. My room is happy. It told me. Keith Ryder is superdreamy. Why wasn't he at the party tonight? Paisley. Ha! Paisley-paisley-paisley. He-he. Oh. My. God. I. Have. To. Stop. Now. I. Am. Just. Too. Damn. Much.

# September 9

## Dear Diary:

My life rocks! And guess what? The room I'm in is the exact same room that Mom was in when she was at Alpha Beta Delta, even when she was president (it was Meri who decided that presidents needed more appropriate quarters, so she knocked the walls down upstairs, and I totally agree with her on that). I e-mailed Mom this morning. I'll bet she's so proud of me. I'm really and truly following in her footsteps. Well, except for one thing. I'm not a cheerleader and I never have been (even though I did watch an old video of Mom cheering at an RU game once and tried out the cheers myself; I can do them!). And everyone knows cheerleaders meet the nicest boys. Oh, well. I guess I can't have everything.

Breakfast was late this morning, since everyone was still recovering from last night's Scarpiella Charity Ball. Meri and Gloria weren't there, which was nice, in a way, because Lindsay and I got to know the other girls a little better. Everyone was impressed to learn that Mom was president of Alpha Beta Delta when she was here, and one girl even suggested that I put my name in the running for president this year. According to the house by-laws, there have to be at least two candidates. I thought about it for a moment. It would be a nice tribute to Meri, being that I'm sort of her protégée (as Shanna-Francine said), and everyone's going to vote for her anyway. During the past two years, Shanna-Francine has been the one who's run against her, but she doesn't want to do it again this year.

"I mean, it's not like I had to do anything as a candidate," she said. "But you know, I've already lost twice."

Losing to Meri Sugarman would be an honor for me, and who knows, maybe it'll even put me in good stead if I decide to run for president next year after Meri graduates—though the thought of actually being president and assuming all of Meri's awesome responsibilities seems ridiculous.

"All those in favor of nominating Cindy, raise your hand," announced Lindsay.

Every single girl raised her hand. I almost cried. Most of these girls barely even know me, but they really seem to like me. One of them said I was a "good peeps." Can my life possibly get any better? Oh, yes, it can. To the amusement of everyone, I decided to go to my classes today. Heck, I know I don't have to, but I like learning, so there's no reason to stop now. I had three classes, and when I stepped into each room, it felt like I was royalty. My professors even knew my name. They were so thrilled to see me—and a little nervous, too—and in my last class, when Professor Macinhouser gave a pop quiz, he told me that I was exempt.

"But I want to take it," I insisted. "I studied."

He looked at me a little strangely, then bent down and whispered, "As long as it's clearly understood that I'm not forcing you to take it. I want that on the record. And I won't count the grade toward your GPA without your approval. Is that okay? Will that be all right?"

I assured him it was. I strolled lazily through the campus afterward. The sun was casting warm rays when I passed the football field. I almost gasped. The football team dashed out onto the field for practice. There was Keith Ryder, looking as superhandsome and cute as ever. I watched for a moment, but I kept my distance, especially when I saw a bunch of pretty girls in adorable cheer-leader outfits jog onto the sidelines and practice their routines. A couple of the football players offered a few horse whistles. It would be so incredible to be a college cheerleader like Mom and meet a cute football player like Dad, but I have other good qualities now. And I am in Alpha Beta Delta. I continued on from the field, mak-ing my way to the house. A town car pulled up alongside me.

"Woof, woof."

I whipped around. It was Gloria. The town car stopped and she swung open the passenger-side door, waving me inside. I climbed in back, sitting right between Gloria and Meri, who were sipping lemon-drop martinis.

"You can't woof at her anymore," whispered Meri to Gloria. "She's my little bow-wow now. Right, Cindy?"

It's funny. Having Meri call me her "little bow-wow" didn't feel nasty at all. In fact, it felt like an endearment. They were very amused when I told them I went to my classes today and took a pop quiz.

"You what?! What's the professor's name?" demanded Gloria.

I calmed her down. I told her Professor Macinhouser didn't force me at all, and it wouldn't count toward my GPA if I don't want it to, though I'm pretty sure I scored well.

"I think it's cute that you took a pop quiz," said Meri softly. "What else did you do today?"

There was nothing else to tell them, except for strolling past the football field, seeing the cheerleaders, and wishing that I could be one, but other than that, there was nothing special about my day.

"You want to be a cheerleader?" asked Meri.

"Sure, in my dreams," I chuckled.

Meri turned to Gloria, delicately asking, "Doreen Buchnar, right?"

"Mmm-hmm. She's still the one."

"Do we have enough?"

"Pff. We could write a book."

"Let's go. It'll be fun."

Gloria knocked firmly on the partition. "Driver. Football field. Now."

And off we went to the stadium. I had no idea what was going on. The car stopped adjacent to the field, and Meri swung open her door.

"Do you want me to hold your martini for you?" I asked solicitously.

She looked at me askance. "Why?"

Off she went, holding her martini, gently sidestepping down the steep slope in four-inch heels to the cheerleaders. She pulled one girl aside, and it looked like they were having some sort of conference. Then they laughed and air-kissed, and Meri returned to the town car and shut the door. We were on our way back to the house. She put her arm around me.

"Okay. The girl I was talking to is Doreen Buchnar. She's RU's Cheer Squad coordinator."

"Is she a friend of yours?" I asked.

"Don't be ridiculous!" barked Gloria.

"I'm—I'm sorry."

"Don't be sorry," said Meri amiably. "Your first practice is tomorrow at three. There's a home game this Friday. Gloria and I will try to come, but I doubt we'll be able to stay the whole time."

I was astounded. Did this mean what I thought it meant? I'm a cheerleader now? They want me? Doreen Buchnar wants me to be an RU cheerleader?

"It's not a matter of want," said Meri lightly. "It's a matter of survival. For Doreen, at least."

Boy, that Hoover File sure comes in handy. After dinner Lindsay and I painted each other's nails in my room. I admitted to being a little concerned. Just a little. I mean, yes, thanks to Alpha Beta Delta and the Hoover File, I'm getting everything I've ever wanted: I don't have to go to class if I don't want to, I have an amazing new wardrobe, I'm popular, I have friends, I'm envied, and now I'm going to be a college cheerleader, which means a nice boyfriend can't be too far behind. But is this ethical?

"No one's being hurt," offered Lindsay. "And we are being helped. It's like *Fantasy Island*. What's wrong with that?"

She had a point. A good one. Why shouldn't I be helped? After everything I've had to endure in my stupid, pathetic life, why shouldn't I be a college cheerleader? I ran my hands through my thick raven hair. A reassuring thought popped into my head. I deserve this. I deserve everything coming my way.

# September 12

## Dear Diary:

Fuckin' A, man, I'm a cheerleader. Actually, it's Doreen Buchnar who's always saying, "Fuckin' A, man." She's such a boisterous girl—a real city girl from New York City—and she was so completely welcoming when I showed up for my first RU cheerleader practice. The past few days have been so exciting: a whirlwind of cheer routines, cocktail parties at the house, dancing, and boys, boys, boys. Guess what? Lindsay has a boyfriend. Well, not a boyfriend-boyfriend, since they just met two nights ago at an Alpha Beta Delta fraternity reception, but a guy who really seems to like her and wants to go out with her. His name is Earl Fitzsimmons, and he's a supersweet guy from Little Rock, Arkansas (his family knows the Clintons!). During the reception, I saw them walk off together for a stroll. Earl even held her umbrella for her, and I think he gave her a kiss on the cheek too. I didn't see her for the rest of the night, and when I woke up in the morning, her Porsche was gone. An hour or so later she drove up to the house and I dashed out. I had to know everything.

"Let's go somewhere for a coffee," she squealed.

I climbed into the Porsche and we took off. Oh my God, she had a big hickey on her neck. I also noticed several footprints on the inside of the car's roof, which didn't make a lot of sense to me until she told me, "He has to share a room at his fraternity, so we slept in my car."

"Why didn't you bring him back to the house?"

She shot me a look. Didn't I know? Shanna-Francine had told her all about all the mics and the surveillance, even though it's supposed to be a secret. I'm so stupid. I had completely forgotten.

"It's creepy," said Lindsay, her mood darkening. "And totally unnecessary."

"But it's just until the election's over next week," I insisted.

"Uh-huh. So they say."

Over lattes, Lindsay was brutally honest with me. She thinks Meri goes too far. Way too far. She doesn't even like her anymore. In fact, she wouldn't mind in the least if Meri lost the upcoming election. I had to laugh at that. Everyone loves Meri (including me). Who wouldn't vote for her? They're certainly not going to vote for me.

"Don't be too sure of that," she said evenly.

Uh-oh. It seems Lindsay's been leading some sort of super-secret grassroots campaign to convince the girls to cast their vote for me, which is such a dumb idea. What the heck do I know about running a sorority?

"Well, for one, I bet you'd let us watch movies in English," bellowed Lindsay. "And you wouldn't have some stupid list of forbidden words, and I doubt someone as nice as you would blackmail people either, or try to ruin them if they didn't do what you told them to do."

Now I was really confused. Wasn't it Lindsay who said living at Alpha Beta Delta was like living on *Fantasy Island*? I was the one who had ethical problems, not her (though I don't anymore).

"I should have told you about this," she whispered anxiously. "But I was afraid."

She leaned in close. When I was away at practice yesterday,

none other than Patty Camp had come to the house looking for me. Lindsay was the one who answered the door, and right away she told her that I was, like, so not available, and wouldn't be available ever, period (Patty's NOKD). But then Patty started crying. I was her only friend, she insisted, and she was very concerned about my mental well-being, and she promised to go away and leave me alone forever if she could just have one conversation with me—just to make sure I was holding up okay. Lindsay took pity on her and invited her in, and they went to my room to wait until I came home. A few seconds later Gloria charged in.

"You. Get out," she barked at Patty.

Lindsay thought this was pretty rude, and she attempted to intervene—no one on the street had seen Patty come inside, and she would only be waiting for a few minutes—but it was too late. Patty was off like a gazelle. She practically ran out of the house. Lindsay was outraged.

"What was that about?" she screamed. "There's no party going on. No one knew she was here. What? Is it against the rules? More dumb-ass rules?" Then she bitch-snapped her fingers in Gloria's face. "That's totally wack. I am so not down for that."

In a huff, she stomped down the stairs, drove straight to the video store, came back, slumped on the couch, and popped a DVD in the player: *Far from Heaven.*

"I know, I know, it's a stupid movie, but I was trying to make a point," insisted Lindsay. "A sorority is not a fascist state."

Meri made her point too. A few moments later she stepped into the living room and sat right next to Lindsay, calmly sipping an apple martini, watching the movie with her.

"They do get the look of Sirk right, don't they?" she whispered delicately. "Not the emotions, but the look."

"I like all of it," responded Lindsay harshly. "I think it's deep. And original."

That's when Meri told Lindsay a little story. A true story. Meri's dad is the chairman and chief operating officer of Versalink, this superhuge conglomerate that Lindsay says is bigger than even Viacom or AOL Time-Warner. I guess that's pretty big. As it turns out, Lindsay's dad works for Tallyride, the biomedical and pharmaceutical research division of Versalink. Uh-oh. Meri also told her how "saddened" she was to learn that Lindsay's been attempting to "coerce" girls to vote against her in the upcoming house election. That really knocked the wind out of Lindsay, since all along she'd thought her grassroots campaign was secret, and she hadn't yet learned about the surveillance from Shanna-Francine, so she naturally thought that the other girls must have turned against her. But more than anything, she was completely freaked out for her dad.

"Brother, can you spare a dime?" asked Meri gently.

Then she stepped up to the TV, pressed the DVD eject button, and handed her the disc. Completely rattled, Lindsay tossed it into the fireplace and turned on the gas. *Poof. Far from Heaven.* Up in flames. Again.

"My hot tub needs to be drained and cleaned," said Meri sweetly. Then she was off, leaving Lindsay trembling and terrified.

"She must have been having a bad day," I asserted firmly. "Meri would never do anything to hurt your dad. That's just silly."

Lindsay looked up at me from her latte and smiled. I was so nice, she said, and so willing to see the good in everyone, which is why it's been so easy for her to convince the other girls to vote for me.

"Stop doing that!"

I was adamant. I do feel bad for Lindsay, but at the same time, I think she's way overdramatizing. She's even decided not to see Earl anymore, since she's afraid that Meri will blackmail him, too (which makes no sense at all). True, bugging and surveillance isn't exactly normal—but I doubt shielding yourself with an umbrella

24/7 is high on anyone's hit parade of "normal" behavior either. We all have our idiosyncrasies. Look at me. I was a total and complete loser, but thanks to Meri, I have everything now.

I didn't go to class later. I just didn't feel like it. At cheer practice, I did a little better than the day before, even though I made a total fool out of myself when I slipped and fell off the pyramid. I hit the ground hard, face forward. Then I heard a sudden, piercing whistle, and suddenly I was levitated. I was being carried in the air and back to the locker room by three totally handsome football players. I was dazed at first. Did I smell a cigar? *Whoosh.* I was carried right past Keith Ryder. Oh my God. He winked. At me! The players set me down gently in the locker room and I assured them that I was okay, nothing was broken, I wasn't even bruised. But one of the players insisted on massaging my calf, and I have to say, it did make me feel a little better, though all I could think about was Keith. He winked!

There was a big surprise in store for me when I returned to the house. Two small helicopters were landing, one on our front lawn and the other on the lawn of the adjacent house, and Meri and Gloria were escorting the girls inside them, along with many of the girls' boyfriends.

"You've got two seconds to change," snapped Gloria.

Then off we went, soaring into the sky. We were on our way to Le Loup, a superfancy restaurant on the top floor of a skyscraper three towns over.

"I hear the room rotates!" squealed Shanna-Francine.

I'd never been in a helicopter before. I was a little nervous, and I tried not to look out the window, but then I figured, that's silly, this is fun, I should look. I gazed out tentatively. Whoa. We were high in the air already. I could see the top of our house, the front lawn, and a small figure hunched on the patio in the back of the house. I gasped.

"Lindsay?"

Shanna-Francine shrugged. "Handsies-kneesies."

Boy, these girls know how to party. We had the entire restaurant to ourselves (it really rotates!). I was a little sad, though. It seemed like practically everyone there had a boyfriend except for me. After dessert (it was flaming!), we had cordials, and Meri sat down next to me and lit a cigarette.

"How's my little bow-wow?" she inquired softly. "How's practice going?"

I told her everything was fantastic, more than fantastic, more than I ever could have hoped for, and it was all thanks to her. The only thing missing from my life was a nice boyfriend, but since I've never really had one before, it wasn't like it was actually "missing" from my life, just absent, as usual.

"Hmm, I can't help you there," she mused. "I mean, I suppose I could, but I'm not worried. I have faith in you. You'll find a boyfriend."

Meri has faith in me. Wow. As Doreen Buchnar would say, "Fuckin' A, man." It turns out she was right, too. This morning I woke up completely optimistic and decided to go to my classes. Why not? It was game day, the day when RU cheerleaders are required to wear their outfits from dawn till dusk. As if they could stop me. I felt like a movie star. People stopped to chat with me— it seemed like everyone was planning on going to the game tonight—and Professor Scott said I had "nice gams," which is complimentary, I guess, though coming from him it was kind of skeevy. I hadn't bothered to read Jonathan Kozol's *Savage Inequalities* for his class today (I've been way too busy), but he didn't seem to mind at all. In fact, I had to leave class early, since it was time to go to the football stadium and prep for tonight's game.

I'm not really much for sports, and I never really knew what was going on when I watched football on TV with Dad, but the game tonight was unbelievably exciting. In between cheers, I couldn't take my eyes off Keith. He made one touchdown after another with the help of Jesse "Pigboy" Washington, this really huge black guy who ran ahead of Keith to protect him whenever he was running for the goal line. Unfortunately, Meri and Gloria didn't come, but I did see Shanna-Francine and a couple of the other girls in the stands, and farther up in the bleachers, I thought I saw Lindsay sitting with Patty, but I must have been imagining things. Lindsay may be in the doghouse with Meri right now, but I seriously doubt she'd risk making things worse by going to a football game with Patty. Poor Patty. Maybe I'll sneak her a note or an e-mail sometime and let her know everything's okay. It's sweet of her to be concerned—and kind of annoying, too. She's seen me around campus, she knows I have new friends, and if that really was her in the bleachers, she knows I'm an RU cheerleader, too. What does she think? I'm depressed?

RU won the game, and right after, Doreen and the cheerleaders invited me to go to a kegger at the Kappa Kappa Kappa frat house, but I was exhausted. I've partied so much this week, and truthfully, I wanted to find Meri and tell her all about the game and thank her, too, for making so many of my dreams come true. I also wanted to look for Lindsay and see if there was anything I could do to help her out of the fix she was in with Meri. Maybe I can negotiate some sort of truce. Boy, am I glad I didn't go to that kegger. After I changed out of my outfit, I walked out of the stadium and strolled through the parking lot. It was pretty empty and beer cans were everywhere. One by one, the parking lot streetlights started to go out. *Great*, I thought, *I'll be walking in complete darkness.* Car lights suddenly swept past—aiming right in my face. Blinded, I held my hand up, and I heard a bark, then I was knocked backward to the ground. It was Rags.

"Need a ride to the kegger?" asked Keith.

My heart did a billion somersaults. Before I knew it, he was picking me up off the ground. I was standing right before him— he was holding my hand, he was staring into my eyes, he was smiling. I could barely talk. Somehow I managed to communicate that I was going straight home to Alpha Beta Delta. I gasped. His hand was running through my hair.

"What happened?"

"Huh?"

"You colored your hair."

I almost lost my footing. If he knew what my hair looked like before, that means he actually noticed me before—which makes absolutely no sense at all. I tried to respond in a supercasual way, but as usual, I ended up sounding so jerky.

"Just felt like a change. Why? Don't you like it? Is it ugly? Should I change it back?"

"Well, Rags thinks you look good no matter what your hair color is."

Ah. Compliments from a dog. I was in safe territory now. I could relax. He was still holding my hand. Then he said, "Want to go out?"

Okay, that threw me. Big time. *Don't be a ding-dong,* I thought. *Do not fall into a trap.*

"Sorry, no can do. Tell Rags I would, 'cause I think he's s-o-o-o handsome, but I promised my parents no more interspecies dating."

He laughed. That made me happy. *We can joke,* I thought. *We can have this kind of a fun, jokey friendship. Like brother and sister. Like homely sister and hot-hot brother. But it won't be mean, and I won't feel bad.* He kissed me on the cheek.

"C'mon. Let's get out of here."

A trillion thoughts boomeranged through my head as I rode with him in his Range Rover. Did "Let's get out of here" mean,

"Let's get out of here and I'll give you a lift home?" or did it mean, "Let's get out of here and go back to my place and, like, suck face 'cause I'm bored and then I'll kick you to the curb like the skank that you are and forget your name?" He flipped on the radio, KCCA, RU's alterna-dance station. He gazed at me, moving his head to the beat. Imitation is the sincerest form of flattery, right? I moved my head to the beat too, only I'm such a fuddy-duddy I must have looked like some sort of freaky bobbing-head RU dashboard thingie. In the backseat, Rags let out a slight moan. Great. Criticism from Rags on my head bobbing. Thanks, Rags.

"You like dancing?"

"Oh, I love dancing!" I exclaimed.

What I should have said was, I loved dancing with my oversize teddy bear when I was eight years old in front of my family on Christmas Day, and I loved slow-dancing ineptly with Mr. Sherman at my high school prom (but I did go to the prom, points for me). That was the extent of my public "dance" experience. But obviously he took it to mean something else. He whipped the wheel. We screeched into the parking lot at Swingles, Rumson River's hottest dance club. *Oh no*, I thought, *now you're in for it*. In a flash we were on the dance floor, and I totally panicked—but then I remembered, wait a sec, I have been able to learn my cheer routines, I'm not completely uncoordinated, and I also remembered watching *A Charlie Brown Christmas* with Lisa once, and imitating the way Shermy and Pigpen danced—with their arms held out straight, their heads hanging loose, kind of twitching this way and that way to the music—and I thought, maybe I could sort of combine some cheer moves with a modified *Charlie Brown Christmas* dance and I'd be okay. So that's what I did. My arms flew this way, my head jerked that way, and I guess I made a real spectacle of myself or something, because Keith started laughing, and then he imitated me, and a lightbulb must have gone off in his head or something because he cried out, "Charlie Brown!"

We laughed. He has such a nice laugh. Phew. I pulled that off. After we finished dancing, we went for a drink, and he told me all about himself, and how he came to RU on a football scholarship and never really studied or anything in high school. But now he likes classes and he likes reading, and he sort of feels like he wasted his high school years because he was so busy being "the cool guy."

"I don't give a shit about being cool anymore," he said.

*Hey,* I thought, *hang with me. You'll be desperate to be cool again in no time.* But then I figured, this is probably a typical thing—like when movie stars complain about being famous and wealthy and having everything come to them too easily in *People* or *In Style.* I guess being cool can be a burden, especially when you're cool and superhot like Keith is and maybe wonder what it would be like to actually be uncool, since it's something you've never been before.

"Everyone assumes I'm stupid, you know? Like Meri. 'Cause I play football."

Ah-ha. So that's what this was about. Keith wants help getting back together with Meri. Would homely sister help hot-hot brother get back together with his ex-girlfriend? Of course. I'd be honored.

"Meri's so nice," I enthused, trying to smooth the way for him to ask me to pass a message on to her or tell him what she's been up to lately. I wanted him to trust me. He gazed into my eyes.

"I don't want to talk about Meri."

Then he leaned in and kissed me. On the lips. Just like that. His lips were warm. Mine were chapped (they still are). He didn't seem to mind. When he kissed me again and he held me in his arms and I closed my eyes, I could still see the strobe lights flashing and feel the thump-thump-thump of the bass, and I suddenly realized (duh!) that Keith didn't want my help reuniting with Meri at all. Why? Because Keith Ryder likes me! It was true. I could feel it. It was the lightest, purest, loveliest feeling I've ever experienced in my entire life. Then the bass kicked in louder—much louder. A new song was blasting, and just as Keith's lips moved to the nape of my neck, I heard a high-pitched voice singing clear as a bell.

*Tune my motor up!*
*Oh, baby, tune it, tune it, tune it, make me purr!*
*Tune my motor up!*
*Oh, baby, yeah!*

I shrieked, jerking back.

"Sorry," Keith said. "I wasn't going to give you a hickey, I swear."

*Oh, baby, tune it, tune it, tune it, make me purr!*

"What the hell is this song?!" I screeched.

"'Tune My Motor Up.' Haven't you heard it? It's on KCCA all the time now. Her name's Lissa, with two s's. Something like that."

"There's a whole CD of songs like this? That's impossible!" I must have sounded like a complete idiot.

"No, it's just a single. Some indie dance label. What? You don't like it?"

I decided it was best not to offer an opinion. And I really didn't want to reveal that my little sister, Lisa, with one s, is also *Lissa*, with two s's—the singer who everyone was shaking their booty to on the dance floor. I suddenly felt so violated. I was silent as we rode away from the club. Did Keith really embrace me? What was happening? And was Rags really happy hanging out in back all this time? Does Rags go everywhere with Keith?

"I had a nice time tonight," he said gently.

I turned to look at him. Oh my God, the nicest smile ever in the entire world. I apologized profusely for freaking out at

Swingles—I was so tired, I said, I just needed to get some sleep.

"You want to hang out sometime?"

Do I want to hang out sometime? As Doreen Buchnar would say, "Fuckin' A, man, you bet I do!" But I played it cool.

"Maybe."

"Oh. You have a boyfriend?"

"Are you kidding?"

"No."

Then he pulled over, cut the engine. We were a block away from the house.

"I'd pull up, but, you know . . ."

I knew. Meri. Oh boy. What was I doing? I had just gone dancing and made out big-time with Meri's ex-boyfriend, and now he wants to go out with me. Nice move, Cindy. I sighed heavily.

"Maybe this isn't such a good idea."

"Or maybe we shouldn't tell Meri. To hell with Meri."

He grinned. Oh God, how was I supposed to say no to a grin like that? Then he touched my cheek.

"Or, you know, maybe I should just forget about going out with a girl who's smart and pretty—'stead of just pretty. Guess I'm outta my league, huh?"

Then he leaned over and kissed me. Really kissed me. After I floated out of his Range Rover, down the block, into the house, and upstairs to my room, I was ready to open the window and float outside, up to the moon, and into the stars. Keith Ryder thinks I'm smart. And pretty. And he likes the way I dance. And he wants me to come "hang out" at his place tomorrow night and maybe "grab some dinner," then maybe rent a movie or go for a walk or "whatever we feel like doing." I almost feel like crying. Everything in my life is perfect now.

# September 13

## Dear Diary:

Today was the 13th. I woke up past noon. It almost felt like I was still asleep. I stepped clumsily into the shower, pulled the curtain shut, turned on the water—and stopped cold. I could hear it faintly in the background.

*Spread your wings and prepare to fly!*

Something was wrong. I suddenly felt very tiny and very vulnerable. Then the curtain whipped open and Meri yanked me by the hair, mashed a chemical-soaked handkerchief to my face, and that was it. I was out. Everything was black.

I didn't learn everything until I came back later this afternoon and crawled beneath the covers. By dinnertime I was still in bed, shivering in horror, my teeth rattling. I've never been so frightened in my life. Shanna-Francine brought me tea. That's when I found out how it all started.

"Oh, God, I really shouldn't be telling you this," she blurted. "But everyone else knows, so what does it matter?"

It began last night. Lindsay, Shanna-Francine, and a few other girls were watching a late-night DVD—Meri-approved *I Am Curious (Yellow)*; foreign, of course. They suddenly heard an abrupt screech of a tape rewinding, then a voice, then a screech, then a voice. Shanna-Francine gestured to Lindsay to turn down the movie. Now they could hear it: a male voice on tape.

"Or maybe we shouldn't tell Meri. To hell with Meri."

The tape screeched back.

"To hell with Meri."

It screeched back again and again.

"To hell with Meri. To hell with Meri. To hell with Meri. To hell with Meri."

Then it screeched again, farther back this time.

"Want to go out?"

*Screech.*

"Want to go out?"

*Screech.*

"Want to go out?"

A sudden violent crash. Then several more. It sounded like Meri was hurling all her Wedgwood and Chinese things against the wall. Gloria bellowed.

"Jesus, calm down, we'll take care of it!"

Silence, then stomping from above. Gloria called out from the stairs on the third floor, "Shanna-Francine. Now."

Shanna-Francine ran like the dickens up to Meri's room. When she stepped in, she saw that every single breakable object was shattered, dotting the snow-white carpeting with spiky shards; the armoire doors were ripped loose, exposing the DAT surveillance equipment; a long, tapered bedpost was gouged into the wall. At the far end, Meri was silently standing, her back to the room. Gloria was retrieving a pink Alpha Beta Delta insignia pad, pen at the ready. She barked, "Get in here."

Shanna-Francine cautiously stepped in—*crunch-crunch-crunch* across the shards. Meri whispered, still facing the wall, "Two problems, two solutions."

Silence, and then, "Shanna-Francine? Break into Building

Sixty-six. Tonight. I'll need Keith Ryder's folder. Gloria? I need a roofie, a small bottle of chloroform, and a digital camera. We'll reconvene in an hour and make our plans. We'll commence with our duties at seven a.m. tomorrow."

"Anything else?" asked Gloria.

Meri turned around. Shanna-Francine nearly yelped. Meri's hair was disheveled—a sight she had never seen before. But even more unsettling were her eyes: blacker than black and intensely focused. She calmly turned on her espresso frother, allowing its concentrated hiss to mask her voice.

"No, that's it for now. And remember, girls, as president-elect of Alpha Beta Delta, I never asked you to do anything illegal."

The front door slammed downstairs. Meri stiffened. Then she gestured to Gloria, who turned up the volume on the DAT. They could hear me walking in and being greeted by Lindsay. Pleasantries were exchanged, along with my dreamy little pronouncement.

"Tonight was the most romantic night I've ever had."

I do remember saying that, and I also remember assuring Lindsay I would tell her more tomorrow. I was tired, I told her. I was going to bed.

"Stupid little bow-wow," chuckled Gloria.

Meri smiled—just slightly—and added, "Woof, woof."

Shanna-Francine was off. She had a mission. It was the dead of night when she tried to jiggle open the door to Building 66 at the far end of the campus. No go. It was locked. A few moments later there was a loud *kerplunk*. She had just pushed herself through a window and hit the floor. Hard. Staggering a bit as she stood, she took stock of her surroundings—and all the file cabinets. It took her nearly an hour, since she'd forgotten Keith's last name and spent almost all of her time simply looking for a senior with the name "Keith" before she suddenly remembered "Ryder." Then she pulled it out. Keith Ryder's complete medical file.

Back at Meri's room, Shanna-Francine listened nervously as Meri dictated her plan.

"You're sure she's out of town?" asked Gloria.

"Positive," said Meri. "I reviewed his room surveillance. She's gone for a week."

"Who were they talking about?" I asked.

Shanna-Francine scrunched up her face.

"Oh, God, I really shouldn't be telling you this."

But of course she continued. I almost wish she hadn't. The next morning, Shanna-Francine was given a key to the house of Dean Pointer. With Gloria standing imperiously behind her, she quietly turned the lock and stepped inside. They made their way to the liquor cabinet. After completing their duties, they retreated to a large walk-in closet and closed the door. Gloria checked and rechecked her digital camera. Everything was ready. It was eleven a.m. Right on schedule. A few moments later the front door opened. They could hear Dean Pointer's phlegmatic laugh and Meri's soft chuckle, as if they'd just shared a really good joke. Shanna-Francine peeked through the closet door slats.

"Like, I've never seen Meri dressed that way before," she told me. "Her skirt was slit up to here, you know? Blouse slit w-a-a-a-y down to there. She was practically falling out."

And Dean Pointer was all eyes. Meri made herself comfortable on the couch.

"Wife out of town?"

"The whole week," he said, his eyes locked on Meri's décolletage.

"Mmm, goody." She stretched, languidly repositioning herself, then sighed heavily. "I don't know what's with me. All day I've been feeling it. A tiny little tingle. Right down there. Know what I mean?"

It looked to Shanna-Francine like the dean was about to have heart failure right then and there. But he was quick to respond.

He loosened his tie, took off his jacket. He was shaking. He couldn't believe his luck. He may have even growled. Meri petulantly protested.

"Let's have a drink first. A Harvey Wallbanger. Think you can do that for me, Dean?"

Shanna-Francine had never seen someone mix drinks so fast. One-two-three—the Galliano, the orange juice, and, of course, the vodka, which had just been enriched with a dissolving tab of Rohypnol by Gloria and Shanna-Francine.

"He has the cutest Tom Collins glasses," she blurted to me cheerfully. "I think they're, like, antique."

"Keep going," I insisted, my horror rising.

Dean Pointer handed Meri her drink. They clinked. She cooed, "Bet you can't down it all in one gulp. I can. I can do that, you know. I open wide. And take one big gulp."

The Dean grinned rakishly, gripped his glass, and knocked it back—chug-a-lugging till it was empty. Meri smiled seductively, then she stood up and gently rubbed against him, leading him backward, whispering, "You know why it's called a Harvey Wallbanger? True story. There was this guy named Harvey who lived in Newport Beach. He just loved to spike his screwdrivers with Galliano. But one night, after a really hard day at work, he had one drink too many. One after another after another. Then he fell right back against the . . ."

*Bang.* She didn't even have to push him. He tumbled with a thud to the wall and slowly sank to the floor, his eyes rolling back. Meri looked at her watch. She sighed impatiently.

"We're running two minutes and forty-two seconds behind schedule."

Shanna-Francine and Gloria stepped out of the closet.

"Oh my God, is he dead?" blurted Shanna-Francine.

"Mmm. He may wish he was," said Meri.

But she decided on a change of plan. Shanna-Francine would have to take care of Dean Pointer on her own.

"She wanted to take care of you personally," Shanna-Francine told me.

I didn't need Shanna-Francine to tell me the rest. I lived it. After Meri attacked me in the shower, I woke up. I was dazed, my head was throbbing. I was completely naked. What was I doing in this strange bed? I could feel dry, prickly skin. Naked skin. An older man was slumped on top of me. He was nude. I screamed.

*Click-whirr. Click-whirr.*

Before me, Gloria was taking pictures with her digital camera. Behind her, Shanna-Francine was covering her mouth with her hands, her eyes wide with disbelief. And standing in the doorframe, Meri, half-smiling, running her hands through her thick raven hair. I tried to scream again—but my head was pounding, the room was spinning, I couldn't move. Then Meri plucked a large needle from a knitting basket and gave a firm stick to the dean's ass. He yelped awake, jerking his body from on top of me, his mouth in a perfect O.

*Click-whirr. Click-whirr.*

The dean bellowed, "What the hell is going on here?"

Meri leaned in and smiled. "I've got a picture. I've got a dirty picture."

Minutes later the dean and I were dressed, and Meri was leading me out of the house. She ordered Shanna-Francine and Gloria to walk. Meri and I would be taking the town car together. We rode in silence. I looked out the window. The world was speeding past—faster, faster still. I didn't know what to think. I didn't know what to say. But finally I couldn't hold back.

"You can't do this to him," I said. "It's going too far. You can't do this to me."

Meri looked at me. She spoke very softly, but her words thundered through me.

"Why not? It's just more for the Hoover File. And the beauty of it is, what screws Dean Pointer can also screw you. Get it? Oh, and Keith Ryder is off-limits. Period. End of sentence. And your little ambition to be house president? Please. You'll always be my little bow-wow. Woof, woof."

Then she pressed a button, the passenger door flew open, and her legs violently kicked. I was suddenly flying through the air—or so it seemed—and then I hit the pavement hard, tumbling violently. I screamed. A car horn blasted. I was in the middle of oncoming traffic. I flung myself forward, finally squashed against a grassy knoll, my limbs sprawled out. I heard voices.

*What screws Dean Pointer can also screw you. Get it? Get it? Get it?*

I heard more voices. Louder. More insistent.

*She's insane. You know that, don't you? Insane and dangerous. Dangerous. Dangerous. Dangerous.*

I stood up. I felt so stupid. Would she even talk to me? After I so cruelly rejected her? I wouldn't have blamed her if she didn't. I walked four miles back to campus, stumbling to the hard cement several times, and by the time I reached the Great Lawn, I was sweating profusely, my hair was in wild disarray, my clothes were scuffed and torn, my arms and face were bruised. I could hear whispers. Everyone was shocked. Who was this walking train wreck? But I ignored them. I kept going—one foot in front of the other. I finally reached the door and tried to push it open. It wouldn't budge. With all my might I slammed against it, forcing it to open against all the piled garbage and the empty food containers and the crumpled newspapers.

"Cindy?"

I whipped around. Patty was racing down the hall. The next thing I knew, I was engulfed in her arms. I sobbed—great big messy sobs. I told her everything. And I wailed.

"Why don't you hate me?"

"Because I understand," she said plaintively.

I don't deserve Patty. Still, I felt weakened, and I screamed, or more accurately, croaked, "Please don't diagnose me! I don't think I can take that right now. What am I going to do?"

Patty's eyes narrowed. She was thinking.

"For you? Nada. Nothing we can do. Not right now, at least. But we better give this Keith Ryder guy a big heads-up."

We ran. I knew exactly where Keith would be. Today was the annual Red Cross Blood Drive at RU, and all of the sports teams and cheerleaders were required to participate to set a good example. We barreled into the cafeteria. There was a long line of students, cheerleaders, and football players, and taking a seat right next to Nurse Gertie, an aging member of RU's nursing staff, was Keith, happily rolling his sleeve up, completely unaware. Poor Keith. With Shanna-Francine's unwitting help, Meri had doctored his medical records, which now revealed that Keith has several STDs, including gonorrhea, chlamydia, genital herpes, and anal warts.

"Anal warts?!"

That's what Nurse Gertie yelped. Loudly. Within seconds, everyone in the cafeteria knew that Keith Ryder, RU's star quarterback, has gonorrhea, chlamydia, genital herpes, and anal warts. He bolted up out of his chair and swiped his folder—only to have it plucked by a teammate. After that, sheer bedlam.

"Whoa! He's a walking transmission!" shrieked a student.

Everyone was laughing, jeering. He angrily knocked his way past, trying to grab the folder as it was gleefully hurled from one student to the next—then he saw me standing with my mouth agape. He charged toward me, then very suddenly stepped backward. Patty gasped.

"Uh-oh."

I whirled. Standing right behind me was Meri. She reached out and gently ran the back of her hand against my cheek.

"Aw. See? Keith has learned. Don't fuck with Alpha Beta Delta. 'Cause we don't just fuck with the past, we fuck with the future."

Then she was gone, and when I turned back around, I saw that Keith had already left. Patty grabbed my arm.

"C'mon, let's go."

We went back to her dorm room. For obvious reasons, the university had not required her to have a new roommate after I left. I pushed aside a clump of garbage and sat on the filthy bed. It flashed in my head, *Yes, Patty may have problems, but they're solvable problems—and they won't be helped by my criticisms.* My problems, on the other hand, looked like they were just beginning. I sniffled. "What now?"

"Don't stir the hornet's nest," she advised. "Until we can figure out what to do, go back to the house, act as if everything is normal, and pray that she's satisfied. Remember, she's HPD."

"Huh?"

"Histrionic Personality Disorder, along with Rapid Cycling, maybe Perceptual Disturbances. Allow her to think she's in complete control. The sun rises and sets at Meri's command."

"I'm beginning to think it does."

"Good. Then you won't have to fake it. Tomorrow's Sunday. Go through the motions. Stay far away from Keith. And now that she's seen us together, don't come near me. By Monday I'll have figured out some way for us to get in touch."

"Monday?" I wailed. "That's so far away."

"Exactly. Meri's won. Let her believe that."

Everything did seem normal when I stepped back into the house. But there was something in the air. When I entered the kitchen, a few girls quickly looked away from me, then darted out like frightened little mice. No need to be seen with me, I guess.

"Handsies-kneesies," barked Gloria.

I leaped out of my skin. Gloria thrust a scrub brush into my hands.

"The kitchen floor. It's disgusting. Meri wants all of us to eat off it tonight."

For the next few hours I scrubbed and scrubbed and scrubbed—extra hard, just in case Gloria's remark about "eating off the floor" was not a figure of speech. Finally, I was finished. I put the brush in the mop bucket—and a foot kicked it over, sending dirty water splattering everywhere. Gloria stood before me. She winked.

"Life sucks, doesn't it?"

I wanted to rip her limb from limb (and I swear that I am not a violent person), (again), but I contained myself, barely, remembering Patty's words: Do not stir the hornet's nest. For the next hour or so, I handsied-kneesied until the floor was positively sparkling. Then I grabbed the bucket and dumped it into the sink. Phew. I stood for a moment. I didn't know what to do next. Should I stay here and wait for more orders? Did I dare go back to my room? I took a gulp and walked out, passing the living room on my way to the stairs. Meri, Gloria, and a few of the girls were sipping martinis and watching a movie (Eisenstein's *Alexander Nevsky*; very old, black and white, silent, obviously torturous to watch). I didn't miss a beat. I walked up the stairs, and it suddenly occurred to me that Lindsay was not among the girls gathered with Meri. *Lindsay*, I thought. *I have to see her.* The house might be bugged, but at least I could give her a hug and somehow let her know that I finally understood, even if it was too late. On the second floor I strode gingerly to the end of the hall and swung Lindsay's door open. I shielded my eyes. It was so bright. I didn't know what I was seeing at first. Lindsay was in bra and panties, tied to her bed, her skin abnormally red. Shining above her were five immense megawatt heating lamps. I nearly screamed, and I swept in to help, but the intensity of her whispers halted me.

"Go away," she pleaded. "Please. Go away."

I backed up in horror—right into Shanna-Francine.

"Uh-oh. I don't think you should be in here," she blurted.

Then she merrily led me to my room (if it's possible to seem like you're always happily skipping along even when you're not, then she does it). She told me everything about the night before. After she finished, I asked her a question—but I was really directing the question at Meri, hoping that she'd be reviewing my room surveillance either tonight or tomorrow morning.

"Do you think Meri will forgive me?"

Shanna-Francine tittered, then threw her arms up.

"How the heck should I know? C'mon down for dinner!"

She smiled toothsomely, as if nothing was out of the ordinary. Was she really this stupid? I told her I wasn't hungry. I haven't moved an inch since. It's past midnight now. No one has come into my room, but around nine thirty, I did hear Gloria in the hallway. She laughed.

"You have enough color. For now. I'd stick a meat thermometer in you, but what's the point?"

Then a series of clicks. I was relieved. The heating lamps were being turned off. Afterward, I could hear intermittent moans from Lindsay's room. I don't think I'll be able to sleep tonight. Or ever.

# September 14

## Dear Diary:

I haven't left my bed all day. Around three o'clock, Shanna-Francine popped in.

"Sleepyhead. Isn't it fun to sleep in on Sunday?"

I couldn't help it. I had to know, even if it was a risk; I had to know about Lindsay.

"Is she okay?" I asked.

"Aw, she's doing great." Then, like an excited cook, she gave me the rundown. "First, Gloria used lavender oil to soothe the burn, then she used apple cider vinegar to keep the blisters from popping, then she slathered her whole body in aloe vera. Isn't that cool? It was, like, an all-natural treatment. Except for the Tylenol 4, but that's codeine, so that's okay. Want some? There's extra. I just took three."

I politely declined. She walked off, and I shivered involuntarily. I had to do something to distract myself. I was going nuts. I decided to write an e-mail—but I was careful. Who knew if my hard drive was being scanned?

From: <cindybixby@yahoo.com>
Date: 14 September
To: <lisa@lisabixby.com>
Subject: Hi

Hi, Lisa.

Guess what? I was at a nightclub near RU and I heard your song!! I couldn't believe it. My little sister! I hope the single's doing well. How good does it have to do before a record company decides to hire you to do a whole CD?

Everything's going great for me at school—and at Alpha Beta Delta. I love it so much here! All the girls are so nice, especially the house president, Meri Sugarman. Next week we cast votes for the new president, and everyone's voting for Meri. And they should!

Please write me back as soon as you can (please please please). I'm dying to know how things are at home—and, of course, I want to hear all about how the single has changed your life.

I love you so much and I'm so proud of you and I hope you write me back immediately.

xxxooo
Cindy

A minute later I almost cried with joy. She had already sent something back.

From: <lisa@lisabixby.com>
Date: 14 September
To: <cindybixby@yahoo.com>
Subject: Re: Hi

* * * THIS IS AN AUTOMATED RESPONSE * * *

Dear Fan:

There is s-o-o-o-o no way I can read all my e-mails. And no way I can answer them (forget that). But I totally appreciate that you took the time to tell me how much you love my first CD single, "Tune My Motor Up"! I love it too. And I love you. (But of course, if you ripped it off the Net for free, I hate you, and will prosecute you to the fullest extent allowed by law. Sowwy! My lawyer told me to say that.)

Oh, and if you're wondering, yes, this is Lissa. I haven't had time to change my site name, but you know it's me.

By the way, I'm told my single is really collectible and will be worth lots of money in the very near future, so buy tons of copies, and tell your friends to do that too.

Worship me,
Lissa

My blood sugar must be low. I feel woozy. I can't write any more. I think I'm going to crawl back under the covers. It's safe there . . . I think.

# September 15

## Dear Diary:

The day began innocently enough. I showered, had breakfast with the girls downstairs (no one would look at me), and Shanna-Francine happily brought eggs, scones, orange juice, and coffee up to Meri's room. I didn't dare go to Lindsay's room, but I overheard one girl mention that she was "rapidly improving." Maybe it was all over. Meri had made her point—and that was that. I had certainly learned my lesson; *From now on,* I thought, *keep your head low, do whatever Meri says, and do not go near Keith.* That last part stung. True, Keith and I had spent only a few hours together, and it's not like I came to know him real well, but he was so sweet, and in a lot of ways it felt like we were similar in a "mirror-opposite" kind of way. He was tired of being cool and hanging with cool people who thought he was stupid; I was tired of being uncool and hanging with people who thought I was ugly. And yet, it didn't feel like either of us was "trying" to be anything when we were together. We were both relaxed. We were ourselves.

I gathered my books. I figured I might as well stay out of everyone's hair (even though a bunch of girls had booked a town car for a "spa day") and go to my classes. As I made my way to the door, I heard a whispery voice behind me.

"Go placidly amid the noise and the haste, and remember what peace there may be in silence."

I froze. It was Meri. She was standing at the top of the first-floor landing, half-smiling, looking down at me with what seemed like pity. She continued.

"If you compare yourself with others, you may become vain or bitter, for always there will be greater or lesser persons than yourself."

She was quoting "Desiderata," by Max Ehrmann, a prose-poem writer who, along with John Swinton and John Spargo, was considered the embodiment of forward-thinking socialism in the early 1900s, but who's since been taken up by navel-gazing New Agers and people who like to cut out "happy thoughts" and paste them on their notebooks or pin them on corkboards or refrigerators. Yet in Meri's case, it seemed like she was (maybe) communicating something different. Was she trying to tell me that she understood my lifelong struggle to change myself (but how could she really understand, since she has no reference point in her own life?)? Or was she, like Ehrmann, advising me to stop comparing myself with others (which is a nice thought in theory, but how can you not compare yourself with at least some people some of the time?)? Or was she not-so-subtly mocking me (this seemed the most likely, but with Meri, who knows?)?

"Thank you," I said, slightly trembling.

What else was I going to say? I stood there like a ding-dong. Should I go? Was I waiting for orders? More poetry? Meri wasn't moving either. She stood at the top of the stairs, her eyes meeting mine. Then she slowly crooked her hand into the shape of a gun and took aim at me.

"Bang," she said softly. "Bang-bang." She burst into melodious giggles. Then *poof*. She was gone. Back upstairs.

Move quickly, I told myself. I was out the door and walking through campus, holding my head down. Do not stir the hornet's nest. Everything will be okay. Besides, didn't Patty say she'd figure

140

out some way for us to be in touch? How was she going to pull that off? If the poplar trees were bugged, and obviously all the streetlamps in the football stadium parking lot and all the streets within the university were bugged too, where would it be safe?

In my literature class, Professor Scott handed out a test. I really wasn't up for it, especially since I've been way too scared to look at any book lately, much less study, so I politely declined. My request was denied. In fact, Professor Scott took pleasure in informing me that this test would count as two-thirds of my final grade this semester since I had "declined" to take other recent tests. If I failed, then I would fail his class. I sighed anxiously. Professor Scott, as well as my other professors, had obviously been informed by Alpha Beta Delta that Cindy Bixby's test-denial privileges were over. My eyes glazed over the questions. I perked up. I was in luck. All the questions were about *Wuthering Heights*. At this point in my life, I practically have that book memorized. I answered each question correctly, but I wasn't happy. Was I Catherine? Was Keith my Heathcliff? Were we doomed? Was our love for each other all-consuming and destructive?

"Time's up," snapped Professor Scott. He snatched the test papers from my desk, his smile tight and mincing.

*Toilet Whores*, I thought. That made me feel better. It even made me smile. I was also relieved—in a larger sense. If things were now back to normal, was that so bad? I did come to Rumson U. to study and to learn. After my next class, I stepped onto the Great Lawn. Nothing was different. Couples were making out, the Abercrombie & Fitch boys were strolling past and chuckling (those guys are beginning to creep me out), people were on their way to their classes. I even saw Randy and Nester hacking (*Where is Bud?* I wondered, but then I realized I wasn't that interested). Life would be calm now, it would be normal. Not great, nothing special, but normal. Meri had spoken, and she was finished.

The sudden whirring of a police siren jolted through me. A crowd of gawkers quickly gathered. Were the police coming for me? Was I under arrest? Would I be going to jail? Then every fiber in my body cried out "No!" There was Keith, in handcuffs, being led to a police car. What was happening? The crowd was excitedly chattering.

"They found everything in his football locker. Crystal meth, steroids, gay porno mags."

"Oh my God, that explains the anal warts!"

"He's, like, so off the team. Permanently."

I had to save him! I pushed violently through the crowd. None of it was true—I had to tell the police everything. *Officer Wood can help me,* I thought. I was sure of it. When I got closer, Keith saw me. His eyes widened in terror, and he shook his head. The siren blasted. He was off. He was gone. This was my fault. Oh, all my stupid-stupid hopes and dreams; this was the price. Everyone around me was still chattering, delighted by the scandal. I wanted to kill them all (and I know I'm repeating myself, but I am not a violent person, even though I've been having lots and lots of violent thoughts lately, and I'm not pushing them away). I started crying. Boo-hoo. Poor me. Poor, stupid, jerky me. I wiped my stupid eyes. The crowd was dispersing. "Show's over!" I felt like screaming. Then I saw Patty across the street. She was standing with Bud Finger. Huh? What were they doing together? Still, today was Monday. Patty and I could talk. Being with Patty would make me feel better. I was even up for being diagnosed. I made to cross the street, and Patty's eyes widened and she shook her head—just like Keith had. Then she whispered in Bud's ear and they darted away. Was the world caving in? I guess I can't be seen with anyone now. Do not stir the hornet's nest. Pretend everything is normal. I made my way to cheer practice and apologized to Doreen for being a few minutes late.

"Late for what?" she snorted.

"Um, practice?" Oh, I should have seen it coming. Fuckin' A, man. Talk about slow on the uptake.

"Sorry," Doreen chirped. "I really don't know who the fuck you are. Or why the fuck you're here. Are you some kind of fuckin' stalker? Some kind of fuckin' cheerleader stalker? You better get the fuck out of here. 'Cause, like, if you don't go, I'm fuckin' calling the police."

That night at the house, the girls and I were forced to watch Andy Warhol's *Sleep*, a six-hour experimental film in which a single mounted camera watches a man sleep. Throughout, there were spurts of giggles and laughter from Meri, Gloria, Shanna-Francine, and the other girls, but that probably had less to do with the film and more to do with the Ecstasy tabs they had popped sometime after dinner. Lindsay and I were the only ones who dared to say, "No, thanks." Thank God. We exchanged sympathetic glances whenever we were certain Meri and Gloria were distracted (I have to say, even though she recently endured her worst possible nightmare, Lindsay now looks beautifully tan).

My anxieties have anxieties. Keith is facing serious jail time. It's all my fault. And I keep seeing Patty's face—her look of terror, shaking her head.

I am Alpha Beta Delta's Typhoid Mary. Hang with me and your life is ruined.

# September 16

## Dear Diary:

At five this morning, I was abruptly pulled from bed by Gloria and forcefully pushed into the bathroom—right toward Meri, who was ominously snapping plastic gloves onto her hands. I was barely awake. What was happening? Fifteen minutes later, after goo was squirted into my hair and my head pushed beneath the bathtub spigot to rinse, Meri turned me around to face the mirror. My beautiful thick raven hair—gone. I was mousy brown once more, only it actually seemed a little worse (if that's possible). Meri and Gloria exchanged a look and suppressed chuckles. Then Gloria blindfolded Meri and handed her a large pair of scissors. An errant clip here, a clip there. Voilà. It was done. My lovely Lili Mar Lili coiffure was reduced to a dreadful frizzy clump. I was beyond dowdy.

"Woof, woof," whispered Meri. She ran her fingers through my locks. "Now you really are my little bow-wow."

"Well?!" snapped Gloria. "What are you standing there for? Don't you have classes today?"

I meekly padded back to my room. Uh-oh. Several girls were trooping out carrying all of my clothes—all the Chanel, the St. John Sport, the Calvin Klein, the Dior, everything. I stepped inside. All of my frumpy old clothes were back. They were on the floor, and Lindsay and another girl were wearing oversize, mud-clumped boots and stomping on them. Lindsay shot me a look. "Sorry," she mouthed, and I knew she was.

I did my best to keep a low profile throughout the day. I didn't see Patty, though I kept a furtive lookout. I also heard whispery comments about Keith. He's out on bail. He's also facing felony drug possession charges. He may drop out. I don't care that I'm ugly again, I don't care that everyone is staying away from me. Hello, loneliness. Hello, rejection. Welcome home. I embrace you. But not Keith! I'd give anything to save him—and even though he'd probably never love me or talk to me again after I did, I wouldn't care, because I'd always know that there was one time in my life when a wonderful and handsome and super-dreamy (and smart!) guy gently pressed his lips to mine. It happened. I wasn't dreaming.

# September 17

## Dear Diary:

When is the other shoe going to drop? Nothing happened today—and by that I mean, nothing terrible. I don't like it. I know it's not over. I can feel it in my bones.

# September 18

## Dear Diary:

I had a terrible panic attack in class today. I knew what it was. I read about them while flipping through Patty's DSM-IV when I lived with her. Seemingly out of nowhere, my heart started racing, I couldn't breathe, I couldn't swallow, it felt like I was choking. I wanted to scream, "I'm dying!" I had to walk, or run. I muttered excuses, bolted out of the classroom, and walked and walked and walked and walked. By the time I came back to the house, my feet were throbbing. I scurried to my room, closed the door, and took off my shoes. My feet were bleeding, the skin was torn loose. I curled up into a ball on the bed. I was safe.

"Woof, woof!" snarled a voice outside my door.

Oh God, someone help me. When will this end?

# September 19

## Dear Diary:

Today was election day at Alpha Beta Delta. Meri won by a land-slide. Big surprise. "California Dreamin'" and other songs by the Mamas and the Papas blared throughout the day and well into the night during the Alpha Beta Delta Presidential After-Party, since today is also "Mama" Cass Elliot's birthday. Everyone came: Dean Pointer, most of the school's professors, all the coolest students. If you didn't know any better, you would have thought, "Wow, this is a real kick-ass party."

# September 22

## Dear Diary:

*Save Keith!* That's all I've been able to think. Most of the girls were gone throughout the weekend, except for Lindsay and me. We've been like the walking dead, exchanging banalities—we don't dare talk about what we're really feeling. Sunday was nice. We went to Long John Silver's. Was Long John Silver's bugged too? I doubt it, but Lindsay didn't want to risk it. She opened her notebook and wrote: "I will not be a victim. And I won't let you be one either."

I wrote: "Which means what?"

"Destroy Meri Sugarman."

I nearly screamed. I grabbed the pen.

"Are you crazy?!"

"Maybe."

Okay, I had to help her think straight. Her tan was starting to fade, and I didn't want either of us to inadvertently cause Meri to order another torturous session under those heating lamps. I thought, *What is the safest possible solution?* I wrote: "We should start applying to other schools. Transfer midyear, or in the fall."

"Destroy Meri."

"We can't!"

"Haze the bitch."

"We won't win!"

"We'd better. Or Keith goes to jail. And God knows what else."

"How?"

"I don't know."

She trembled and closed the notebook. Then she anxiously flipped it back open, tore out the page we'd written on, ripped it into tiny little pieces, and ate them. Without saying or writing another word, we finished our Chicken Planks and Hush Puppies, and as we strolled back to the house, she sweetly put her arm around me and shielded us both from the sun beneath her umbrella.

# September 23

## Dear Diary:

*Save Keith!* The thought was blaring through my head when I woke up this morning. Why should he have to pay for my sins? Wasn't there some sort of middle ground that could be negotiated? Okay, he's off the team, he's "unpopular," but does he have to go to jail? Lindsay's been punished for her transgressions, and so have I, but neither of us is facing a future as bleak as Keith's. It's just not fair. I'll gladly take more punishment to keep Keith out of jail. *Maybe that's the solution,* I thought. At breakfast I asked Shanna-Francine if I could take Meri's tray up. She looked to Gloria for approval.

"Fine," she said, clearly not interested. "Don't drop the tray."

My hands were shaking as I walked up the three flights of stairs to Meri's room. The air seemed thinner as I reached the top. Was I having another panic attack? I couldn't swallow. Her door was open. The room looked empty. I took a gulp, walked in, and set the tray down on a piecrust table. All evidence of Meri's temperamental rampage on the thirteenth was gone. The room looked exactly the same as it had before. She even had the same book open on her bedside table, *My Way of Life: A Script for a Complete Woman,* by Jacqueline Onassis. I took a quick glance and read: "In Zululand, I was presented with a small stuffed dik-dik—a fully grown deerlike animal that is specially bred for its miniature size."

Hold on. Jackie O. had a dik-dik? Did Meri also have a dik-dik, or was she just quoting? And if she wasn't quoting, did she want all of us to believe that she did, in fact, have a dik-dik? A sudden gunshot blast nearly made me scream. Then another, and another. I glanced out the window. Several large birds tumbled from the sky. Meri breezed in from the balcony holding a shotgun.

"Blackbirds are boring," she airily intoned. Then she stopped. "Oh, it's you. My little bow-wow."

I smiled tentatively (doing my best to look away from the shotgun), and given Meri's adoration of Jackie O., I decided to keep the moment light by mentioning Grace Coolidge, the lovely First Lady and wife of President Calvin Coolidge, who was Jackie O.'s fashion predecessor in the mid-1920s.

"She was America's first ambassador of women's sportswear," I said with forced good cheer. "She even wore flapper outfits. In fact, she was so admired that she was given a special gold locket by the French garment industry. Isn't that fascinating?"

And then nothing. Silence fell. It fell hard. Like a huge white mountain collapse: *ba-boom!* Meri took two steps closer to me—deliberately, slowly—her eyes never leaving mine. Was this it? Would she shoot me? Would she bite me? A sick foamy nausea rose up inside my stomach. I couldn't take it anymore. I was ready to burst.

Then the words just tumbled from my mouth: I was the one who was deserving of more punishment—much more—I was the one who had betrayed not just her, but the whole house. Keith's future at RU was already ruined, so what could be gained by sending him to jail? Send me to jail. Punish me more. And finally, I appealed to her vanity. She was too wise to punish Keith with jail time; after careful consideration, she would realize that it was me, Cindy Bixby, who deserved more.

The next few seconds felt like an eternity. Meri ran her hands through her thick raven hair. If thoughts were racing through her mind, her face didn't betray them. Finally, she spoke.

"You're right. You do need to be punished more."

"Yes," I gushed. "Yes, I do."

She outlined a course of action. I shrieked.

"I won't do it!"

"Of course you will," she said softly. "Because what hurts Dean Pointer can also hurt you. Remember? Oh, and I'm not just talking about headlines, though they'll be so much fun. 'Dean Pointer Drills Coed.' I like it. But what I really like are the little details, and how many people they'll affect. Cindy Bixby's diabolical blackmail scheme. Everyone will be shocked. She fucks the dean, takes a few pictures, and suddenly she never has to go to class, and her GPA just keeps going up and up, and so do Lindsay's and Keith's. Did you know Versalink owns six daily newspapers nationwide? Daddy loves a scoop—a scoop with pictures. Dirty pictures. Your family will be so embarrassed. Everyone will be."

I stood firm (how, I don't know). I sputtered, "I don't care, I won't do it."

"So you want Keith to go to jail?"

"You're saying—"

"I'm not saying anything. You told me you wanted more punishment. And I'm agreeing with you."

I had to do it. If there was a chance that this would ultimately save Keith and keep him out of jail, I didn't have a choice. At lunchtime I stormed into RU's cafeteria, walked right up to Keith, brutally slapped him across the face, and loudly accused him of date rape. Well, one look at me and no one believed it. Except, of course, for the Lesbian Feminist Clique. Within hours, they were following him from class to class, holding up signs that read: "Use Your Hand!" and "Enemy to Womyn!" and "Lesbians Don't Rape!"

"Did you give her anal warts, too?" they screamed.

"Look! He's got a cold sore!" shrieked another.

Students ran screaming. Shanna-Francine skipped up to me.

"Poor li'l Keith," she blurted. "Guess he won't have a date for the Oktoberfest Dance this year. Are you going? Guess what? It's going to be seventies retro. Isn't that a scream?"

That afternoon I was also required to lodge a formal complaint with campus police and local authorities (to Officer Wood, no less, who was so kind and sympathetic; if I'm ever really date raped, I'll know where to go). Keith now faces not only felony drug possession charges, but aggravated assault and rape. Meri was right. By forcing me to ruin Keith's life more, she was punishing me more.

When I returned to my room tonight, I was calm. I'm not sure why, only I can't help but think that even Meri must have a limit. Keith has now been completely destroyed. Yes, there's probably more punishment in store for me, but it won't necessarily affect him. And maybe after it's all over, Meri will quietly intervene and keep Keith from serving time. Am I being naive?

Tears are rolling down my cheeks now. I'm crying for Keith. Happy tears, actually. It's all over, my love. You're safe now.

# September 24

## Dear Diary:

Someone did a hit on Rags! All anyone knows is that the car was pink. He's at Rumson River's TLC Animal Hospital now. I'm not much for praying (Mom goes to church, but Dad doesn't, and Lisa and I have never had to go), but I got on my knees tonight and prayed for Rags.

# September 25

## Dear Diary:

They say that wartime criminals sometimes bond with their captors. That's what happened to Patty Hearst, this really nice (and superrich) girl who was kidnapped by a group of schizoids. She bonded with them, and then they turned her into a scary bank robber. Will that happen to me? What's next? Am I about to knock off Rumson River Savings & Loan? I only ask because I had a delightful morning with Meri. Honest. After most of the girls had left for the day, Gloria ordered me to handsie-kneesie the kitchen floors. *Big deal*, I thought. I've actually come to enjoy handsies-kneesies. It's relaxing. Then I heard the *clickity-clack* of high heels. Meri was in the kitchen.

"I just love honey cake," she whispered breathily. "Don't you?"

We were off in her town car. We visited several specialty food stores to buy just the right ingredients: the freshest cinnamon, the finest almonds, the plumpest raisins. She was so relaxed, even chatty. We talked about boys.

"It's a good idea to take fifteen minutes or so before a guy picks you up to think of ten things to talk about," she advised. "Especially if it's your first date, because if conversation stops, then you'll always have a handy topic."

Definitely a good idea, I said (and it is) (not that I would know, but still).

"And don't let the first date get too hot. You're just getting to know each other. It's boring to end up in some sort of late-night dilemma. Guys can get embarrassed so easily, and you don't want to have to scold him and tell him you're not that kind of quick-neck girl."

"Quick-neck girl?" What an antique-sounding choice of words. Was I listening to Meri? Or Jackie O.?

Back at the house I made honey cake for Meri, and as we waited for it to bake, we did a *Cosmo* quiz called "Do You Have What It Takes to Be Popular?"

There were lots of questions, like: "Can you get into a terrif mood with last year's dress for this year's big date?"

We both answered yes to that.

"When you meet a new guy, do you look for price first or personality?"

Meri answered, "Price. What a dumb question."

Finally, I tallied up the scores. Oh no. Meri didn't do well at all. Her Scoring Key read: "Ouch. Not too good, dear, but nothing you can't fix. Work on your ability to get along with others, and try cooling that nasty temperament."

But of course I read her a different Scoring Key: "You go, girl. Not only are you popular, you're even-tempered and take an active interest in other people's lives. No wonder everyone wants to be with you."

She gleefully clapped upon hearing this. That was actually my Scoring Key I was reading (which astounded me, because I have never, ever been popular, but if *Cosmo* says I have it in me, then I guess it's in me somewhere, though it's probably long dead and buried by now). I read the Scoring Key meant for her as mine.

"Oh, I'm so sorry," she said. She really did seem sympathetic. "It's a big world out there, Cindy. You'll be a lot happier if you try and like the people in it."

We had coffee with our honey cake. It was delicious (if I do say so myself). Then Gloria charged in and they "smoked a bowl," which is drug talk for smoking marijuana from a small pipe. They smoked several bowls, in fact. The kitchen was soon filled with smoke, and it felt like I was getting high too. My head was getting lighter, I started feeling paranoid (just a bit), and I didn't know what to do when Gloria thrust the "bowl" in my face.

"Go on. It's primo shit."

I didn't have a choice. I took a big puff, then coughed—awful, painful, hacking coughs. They laughed at me. Then they were gone. *Poof.* I was alone in the kitchen. My mind was racing faster and faster: I just had a very nice morning with Meri, which could mean that it's all over, which could mean that Keith is saved, which could mean that he won't go to jail, which could mean that Meri will stop, which could mean that I am seriously kidding myself, which could mean that this is just the calm before the storm, which could mean that things are going to get even more terrible, which could mean that there's nothing I can do about it, which could mean that I'm doomed forever. I gasped.

"Patty."

I ran out of the house. I couldn't wait any longer. Patty had to help. She promised she would. I wasn't stupid, though. I darted behind the dorm building alleyways. I didn't want to be spotted by anyone. Finally, I turned the corner to my old dorm building. I couldn't believe my timing. There was Patty, turning the opposite corner and carrying two large garbage bags to the Dumpster. My heart sang. Patty may still find all her problems and ailments "fascinating," but at least she was making some sort of effort to deal with them. She was actually cleaning her dorm room. I was about to run down the alley—but I stopped in my tracks when I saw Bud turning the corner carrying a garbage bag too, and then Nester, and then Randy, and then Keith! What the heck was going on? Was everyone enabling Patty? And did they know that her room would probably be back to its old state within days? One by one they hurled their bags into the Dumpster. *Get a hold of yourself,* I thought. Whatever was going on in Patty's world wasn't important right now—well, it was, of course, since I want nothing but good things and happiness for Patty, but my focus was elsewhere. Patty's garbage and her "fascinating" ailments could wait; right now, she and I had to figure out some way to keep Keith from going to jail. They saw me as I walked toward them. Practically simultaneously, they fiercely shook their heads. I held back a sob. They slammed the Dumpster shut and made a quick beeline around the corner, completely abandoning me.

I am now truly alone. It's three o'clock in the morning as I write this. I tried calling Mom, but our phone number's been disconnected (no doubt due to Lisa's rising celebrity). Why hasn't anyone given me the new number? And even if I were able to reach Mom or Dad or Lisa, would they be able to help me? Can anyone?

# September 21

## Dear Diary:

The morning looked harmless enough outside my bedroom window. Fluffy white clouds were pinned against a shiny blue sky, but I was wary—and heck, why shouldn't I be? Fluffy white clouds mean nothing to me now. When I looked at my alarm clock, I nearly yelped. I'd overslept by a good three hours. Dressing quickly, I walked downstairs and I was surprised to see that no one was there. The house was empty. And yet, far off in the distance, I could hear laughter, I could hear music. What was going on? Had the house suddenly been transported during the night? If I stepped outside, would happy little Munchkins herald my arrival? And more important, if the house had been transported and whipped into the sky (by a helpful tornado, of course), had it thoughtfully landed on top of Meri?

I swung open the door and strode onto the campus, and it really did seem as if I'd just walked into some sort of Technicolor dreamland. On the Great Lawn, kids were happily mingling with adults next to various food and crafts booths. A large banner proclaimed: RUMSON UNIVERSITY'S ANNUAL PARENTS' DAY! Oh my God, I'd completely forgotten.

"Yo, Cindy! Meet the old man!"

I whirled. There was Bud standing next to his father (whom I'd never had the pleasure of meeting back in Marietta), extending his clammy hand toward mine, eyeing me up and down, his mouth crooked into a dirty smile. Eeeow. Double-eeeow. Like father, like son—like get-me-the-heck-out-of-here-now. His hand felt moist against mine as he shook it.

"Damn, you're right," he said to Bud in an overly excited raspy voice. "She's a real freak mommy."

They laughed and laughed, like two hiccuping hyenas. Did I really need this? Did I even deserve it? And would I have to knee Mr. Finger in the balls to get him to let go of my hand? I forcefully yanked it back.

"So nice to meet you, Mr. Finger, but I've really got to go. It's my car. The bivalve on my distributor is furbulating."

I dashed away, zigzagging past the cluster of kids and parents. From a distance, I saw Patty. She was standing mortified with her mother and father, both of whom were tall, very athletic-looking, and well dressed. Her father was staring off in another direction, with a look that said he'd rather be anywhere else but here. Her mother seemed to be tersely scolding, and her fingers were picking and plucking imaginary dirt and lint from Patty's blouse and hair. Then she cruelly jabbed at Patty's midsection. Twice. Patty looked up. She caught my eye. I almost burst into tears. The look she gave me said it all: This is where I come from, this is why I am the way I am, this is what I must overcome. Then she shamefully looked away and defensively batted her hands against her mother's heartless assault. I stepped away, but I didn't run. I didn't want Patty to think I was repelled by what I saw, but I also wanted to give her the dignity of privacy. A gentle breeze wafted my way. My spirits lifted almost instantly. My heart sang! I'd know that Grand Torpedo Magnum Wrap cigar smell anywhere. I pushed through the crowd, I joyously gasped, "Keith!"

And then I stopped short, nearly sputtering.

"Dad?!"

Warm arms enveloped me. I felt so safe. I couldn't believe it. Dad came for Parents' Day.

"You look beautiful," he gushed.

Wow. If ever I have doubts that Dad loves me unconditionally, then I'll just have to think back on this moment. There I was, with my horrible frizzy haircut, my old frumpy clothes, and all he could see was the daughter he loved. Oh my God, that's so incredibly corny and stupid, but it's true. He just went on and on about how proud he was of his "little girl, all grown up, standing on her own two feet." If only I could have told him that I was terror-stricken and under siege, but I was mindful of Meri, the bugged poplars, and her terrifying ability to ruin the lives of anyone I confided in or cared about. So I just smiled.

"College is s-o-o-o-o great," I squealed, sounding like a major ding-dong.

"Your mother's here too," he enthused.

I gasped. Mom? Here? Dad stepped away, promised to get the three of us some cherry punch, and pointed me toward the east side of the Great Lawn, where Mom was waiting. I had a tumble of feelings. What would I say to her? Why didn't she warn me about Alpha Beta Delta? And what, if anything, had she contributed to the Hoover File (and was it juicy)? Then I saw them. I nearly jumped out of my skin. I wanted to scream. There they were, standing together; Meri, Alpha Beta Delta's reigning president, and Mom, Alpha Beta Delta's former president, girlishly chatting and chuckling like two old friends, the early morning sun bathing them in beatific rays. I blinked several times. Could I even tell them apart? They suddenly shared a very broad laugh—were they talking about me?—and simultaneously flipped back their hair. The ground seemed to vibrate beneath me. A voice pierced through the haze.

"There she is! There's our girl!"

I could barely focus. All I could see was the very tip of Meri's

French-manicured finger, looming forth like a dagger in a 3-D movie. I was abruptly engulfed. Mom hugged me tight. Looking up, I saw Meri's face. Her smile was so docile, so gentle, with that aw-shucks-this-is-just-too-touching-for-words look, but it was swiftly dropped, for the briefest of moments, when she brought her forefinger to her lips in a venomous "shh" motion. Mom released me from her arms. Meri beamed with good cheer.

"She was a worthy little adversary," she cooed, no doubt referring to the election.

"Well, now, we can't all be president," chimed Mom, giving my hand a friendly squeeze.

Then Meri bid us good-bye and whirled off. Were her parents here? And did they, by chance, have horns?

"Tsk. Where's your father? I always lose him at these types of things, " clucked Mom. We sat on a bench. The silence between us was aching. I gazed at her for a moment, strangely seeing her in two different ways. On one hand, she looked impatient and aloof, like it was a chore to sit with me; on the other hand, she seemed awkward and uncomfortable, even vulnerable. I was so confused, and I was also angry, and I guess it's the anger that won out, because I suddenly blurted out, "I'm not dumb, you know. I finally figured it out. 'Elaine Bixby at MSN' blocks my e-mail."

The words were barely out of my mouth when I realized that tears were streaming down my face. Did I really just say that? Was I that bold? Mom looked genuinely confused. Oh, but how could she be! My fury was rising. Why doesn't she just say it? I'm a disappointment, I'm the black sheep, I am not the daughter she wants. But instead she said, "MSN? I haven't had that e-mail address in over a year. Remember? When we got DSL? We're all Yahoo now. You, me, your sister, your father."

Oh my God, oh my God. I. Am. Such. A. Bunhead. But the floodgates were open; it was too late now.

"I'm sorry I'm not like you," I stammered. "I guess if I were, maybe then you'd like me."

Mom eyes welled up with tears. Stop! Rewind! I have never seen Mom cry before. Never ever ever ever ever. What had I done?

"Maybe when you have kids someday, you'll understand," she sniffled. What did that mean? What was she telling me? She struggled to explain. She was never very smart as a girl, her grades were average at best, but she did have her charms, her popularity. Then she met Dad. And then she had me.

"You were such a bright young baby," she said. "Everyone thought so. And you're right. You and I are different. You were completely different from how I was when I was growing up. You were so smart. And you read so much. Every day. Book after book after book. I was so proud of you. I still am. But sometimes I felt . . ."

"Felt what?" I asked tentatively.

Mom thought for a moment, then she took my hand and leaned in, whispering conspiratorially, "Let's put it this way. I know exactly how to prepare your sister for life."

We chuckled. I was starting to get it. The mom sitting next to me was, in fact, uncomfortable and vulnerable, even though I had thought she was acting impatient and aloof. She was feeling one thing, and I was seeing and feeling something else entirely. How messed up is that?

"But you," she continued, choking back a sob, looking down at her hands. "What could I possibly help you with? I guess I just felt so inadequate at times. Like I wasn't good enough for the job, or smart enough when it came to you. Oh, I love you so much, Cindy, I know you know that—I know you do. You've always been the special one. I know you know that."

That was it. Major waterworks. Practically Niagara! We hugged and we cried. My mom is intimidated by me? I make her feel inadequate? What a joke. A feeling of relief washed over us both. She attempted to collect herself. She dove into her purse and frantically scribbled "elainebixby@yahoo.com" on a piece of paper, wrote down our new home phone number (which was changed, as I thought, due to Lisa's rising fame, and which Lisa was supposed to give to me, though she forgot, no doubt since I'm not her manager, agent, lawyer, or fan club president), and even wrote down her own superprivate emergency cell phone number, which no one has (expect for Dad and Becky Randel, Mom's Personal Shopper at Neiman Marcus). Dad took us to dinner that night. It felt like I was on vacation. I was freed from all my worries and fears about Meri and the house. After dinner they walked me back to Alpha Beta Delta, and on the way, Dad pointed out where he first saw Mom.

"Right over there," he said, pointing to the far end of a parking lot. "She was just walking to her car, and I thought, 'Hey, now there's a looker.' I saw her two days later at my first football game. She was cheering. Well, let me tell you, I was barely able to play the game after that."

They chuckled and held hands. They looked young again, like two college students in love—but in a far more innocent time. I gave them a wave as they drove off from Alpha Beta Delta, then turned around and stifled a gasp. From above, I saw the silhouetted figure of Meri observing from her bedroom window. I gulped and walked into the house. My parents may have lived in more innocent times, but I was bracing myself for the far more dangerous present.

# September 29

## Dear Diary:

"Bud Finger, at your cervix."

Oh, I hate Bud so much. The past few days have been relatively peaceful. (I wake up, go to classes, come home, and shut my door. That's it.) But this morning, as I was walking down the hall to class, I heard Bud's stupid little pronouncement behind my back. I turned right around to face him. I think I like violence now. Besides, I have been known to kick Bud in the balls, so would anyone really be surprised if I ripped his head off? But I had barely turned when he hurled a small pack of Hostess Ho Hos right at me and then ran down the hall. They tumbled off my chest to the floor. *That's disgusting*, I thought—the package was already open, one of the Ho Hos was gone, and the remaining Ho Ho had a large bite out of it. I swiped it from the floor and looked for a trash can. The loose Ho Ho fell out. The mushy cardboard backing had writing on it with black Sharpie: ".qɘƧ nɘV γttɒЯ ooM"

Very nice, Bud. For old times' sake, he's telling me to "Moo?" And the rest? Bud-style gibberish? Thanks, but no thanks. I picked up the loose Ho Ho, tossed it in the trash, and I almost threw away the cardboard backing when it suddenly occurred to me. This was no gibberish—this was a message! I stood for a moment. Was anyone watching? Did anyone see him throw the Ho Ho at me? I suddenly felt like Spy Girl Barbie. Lisa and I used to love playing Spy

Girl Barbie in the backyard when we were little. We had so much fun dreaming up secret missions for her. But then Lisa wanted to change her name to Mata Hari Barbie, which meant that Spy Girl Barbie was suddenly very slutty and never wore panties anymore. *Think,* I thought. *What would Spy Girl Barbie do?* She'd pretend everything was normal, that's what she'd do, then she'd find a "secure location" where she could calmly examine the message. As nonchalantly as I knew how, I stuck the cardboard backing inside my copy of Céline's *Journey to the End of the Night* (Professor Scott's syllabus was becoming very predictable, and yet it seemed an apropos book for Spy Girl Barbie and me since, like Bardamu, we were also in the midst of a scandalous battlefield), strolled into the ladies' room, held my head low, walked into the last stall, locked the door, and sat on the toilet. I stared at the message:

"Moo Ratty Ven Sep."

It made no sense. Should I be holding it up to a mirror? Luckily, I still had my Chanel pressed powder compact and mirror from my Pledge Week supplies. I retrieved it from my purse and placed the mirror opposite the cardboard backing message. It now read: ".qɘƧ nɘV γɈɈɒЯ ooM"

That made even less sense. I was beginning to get frustrated. Was this really a secret message?

"Anagram!" I suddenly gasped.

Oh no. Did anyone hear me? I didn't see anyone when I walked in. But more important, I hate anagrams, and crossword puzzles, too. Brain teasers are for people with too much time on their hands (people like Bud). *Okay, focus,* I thought. *How difficult can an anagram be? Especially an anagram by Bud.* I pulled my official pink insignia Alpha Beta Delta notebook from my knapsack and got to work. As I arranged each letter and each word, my heart started beating faster and faster and a huge smile was spreading across my face. I would be saved. Keith would be saved. And even though, somehow, Bud was involved, I would no longer be alone. I cracked the code. The message read: "Patty's Room Seven."

Oh, God. Tonight at seven, I could go to Patty's room and everything would be all better. I was exhilarated. The rest of the day was a complete breeze, and I kept hearing Lindsay's words, or seeing them, actually, since she had written them down: "Haze the bitch."

That sounded pretty damn good to me. Hazing Meri Sugarman. Bring her down hard. Make her cry. Why not? After everything she's done? Watch out, Meri. Little bow-wow bites back. Still, as the sun started to set, I got anxious. I was at the Great Lawn sitting on a bench beneath an oak tree (bugged, I'm sure, like the poplars), wondering how I would make it to Patty's room without anyone seeing me. Sure, I could go through the dorm building back alleys, but once I was in the building, wouldn't people see me going down the hall to her room? Did I need a disguise? Where would I get one? Or did I have to somehow find a way to reach her second-story dorm room window and climb inside that way? Would I need rope? Or a ladder? Wouldn't that look suspicious? What would Spy Girl Barbie do? I smiled knowingly. She'd create a diversion, that's what. It was almost too easy. At about quarter to seven, I scurried down the back alley to Patty's dorm building, looked both ways, darted inside the front entrance, breathed a huge sigh of relief upon seeing it was empty, then took off my mule and gave a firm whack to the fire alarm. It blared deafeningly. I scampered back out, slammed myself against the wall just around the corner, and waited for the inevitable— hoping against hope that Patty would know it was me and stay in her room. Sure enough, students started pouring out of the building, and they didn't seem too happy about it either (I think I broke up a beer bust), but the crowd was large enough so that I was easily able to mingle, hanging my head low; no one seemed to notice that I was walking in the opposite direction. My heart was going topsy-turvy. Eureka. I did it. I flew down the hall to Patty's room and knocked on the door. It swung open. I nearly screamed. It was Keith.

"Hey, sexy," he said, grinning.

He pulled me into his arms and planted a scorcher—right on the lips—led me in, and kicked the door closed. *Oh, never let me go,* I thought. I was in Keith's strong arms. He may be facing jail time, but in this moment, in this small and tender moment, he was mine. I heard a door click. Stepping out of the bathroom was a huge figure. It was Keith's teammate, Jesse "Pigboy" Washington. His face was dotted with lipstick kisses. And stepping out after him was Patty. Completely thrown, I disentangled from Keith, pulled Patty aside, and whispered urgently, "What's going on? You and Pigboy?"

"Jesse's fantastic," she cooed. "A little hypomanic, a few anxiety phobias, but otherwise . . . well, let's just say, no more Mallomars for me."

It was too much to process. *Keep the focus,* I thought. I whipped out my notebook and wrote: "How do we save Keith?"

"That's what we're here to figure out!" she exclaimed.

I gasped, covering her mouth. She pushed it away.

"We're safe. This room's safe."

So that's why everyone was helping Patty clean her room. With Randy and Nester's help, Patty had learned that practically every room in every dorm, sorority, and fraternity is bugged, including Jesse's, Keith's, Bud's, and Randy and Nester's. They found tiny mics implanted in couches, a few in phone receivers, still more in bathrooms. It was Bud who told them to leave everything in place. If Meri knew mics were being discovered or removed, she'd be on to them. Next, they decided to search Patty's room, but since it was so jam-packed with garbage and newspapers and half-empty food containers, they decided to completely clean it out first. To their delight, they realized that Patty's garbage had actually acted as an obstacle to the Alpha Beta Delta sisters who had bugged all the rooms—either that, or they had decided not to bother upon stepping knee-deep in it (who can blame them?). The room was "clean." I suddenly exploded with anger.

"Haze the bitch!" I bellowed. "Bring her down. Make her cry."

"Whoa. Slow down, gunsmoke," said Patty. "Let's not get ahead of ourselves. We need to help Keith."

She was right. What was wrong with me? Keith put his arm around me and kissed my cheek. He was so understanding. He even said he was worried about me. Me. With all the trouble that he's facing, he's been thinking of me. The school is now considering whether or not to expel him, given all the charges against him. A hearing is scheduled for next week. We ran through the options. I could step forward and recant my date-rape charges, but given the drug possession charges against him, would anyone believe me? And besides, we didn't have any way to prove that the drugs were planted. And even if I did go forward and put the kibosh on the date-rape charges, wouldn't that tip off Meri and prompt her to give the photos of Dean Pointer and me to her father's newspapers?

"Everything's in Meri's room," I said.

That's where the DAT tapes are, the digital camera with pictures of Dean Pointer and me, the Hoover File, which I've heard is quite literally a large accordion file bursting with incriminating papers, and God knows what else. But how on earth could we get everything out? And does Meri keep every single day's recording of the entire campus, or does she tape over them with the start of each new day? If she erases everything, which seems likely, then we'd having nothing to prove our side. There were so many questions, and even though I'm the one inside the house, no one could figure out how I could go about getting everything out of the house without Meri learning about it, even if I did have help from Lindsay, who was sure to be game for anything. We were at an impasse. The future looked bleak. Especially Keith's. Patty looked at her watch.

"We're running late, cutie," she said to Pigboy.

It seems Patty and Pigboy had made a date to go to RU's Cinema Revival tonight to see the late show of Fellini's *Amarcord*. I was shocked. We had problems—real problems—especially Keith, and they're skipping off to a movie? But Patty assured me she was on it. She was in the process of diagnosing Meri. She was certain that a thorough examination of Meri's psyche would reveal a solution, possibly several. Well, that sounded like a bunch of hooey to me, and besides, how we would we all meet up again? I can't smash the fire alarm every night.

"You won't have to," she said. "Starting tomorrow night, you'll have a reason to be here."

"What are you talking about?"

"Tomorrow night you'll be going out on your first college date with Bud."

The room shifted. Was I hearing right? She continued, oblivious to my rising horror.

"It's perfect. You'll go out on a date, make a good show, and then you can come to this dorm building whenever you want— you know, to make out with Bud. Don't sweat it. We've already worked out the details. Everyone's in on it."

"I don't like this at all!" I protested.

"Oh, Cindy. Relax. All work and no play? Allow yourself one night of peace."

She walked out with Pigboy and closed the door. Behind me a lighter flicked. There was Keith, smiling, looking superdreamy as always, sitting on the couch, lighting a cigar.

"Heard you went to the prom with Bud," he chuckled.

"Not funny," I said, and it wasn't.

Who was he to make fun of me? I laid into him. I suppose he would have taken me to the prom in high school, right? Puh-lease. Would he have even noticed me in high school? Fat chance.

Besides, what was our current relationship (if you could call it that) based on? We've been brought together by mutual tragedy, nothing more. And look at me now, I protested. I was ugly again, I was plain, just like before. The last thing I needed from him was pity. I told him I wanted to help him out of his fix and then move on with my life and hopefully transfer to a new school in the fall. That's it. Then I realized that while I was in the midst of my tirade, I hadn't even looked at him. I defiantly met his eye—and I melted.

His gaze was so warm and so sympathetic (and so handsome). He responded to everything I said, gently, truthfully. No, he would not have taken me to the prom if we had known each other in high school. Why? Because he was in a trap of his own making, though he didn't realize it at the time. He was the "über dude," he dated all the hot girls (and yes, he was prom king), and yet, in the back of his head, he knew something was wrong. In his junior year he met Tracy Parham, a new girl at his school. She was apparently quite brilliant. And a loner. They were assigned to be lab partners in Science III one semester, and to Keith's surprise, they had a ball together. Keith had never spent time with a girl like Tracy. She was witty and challenging and, no, she wasn't the hottest girl in school on the surface—that was Ginger Pantelope, whom Keith was dating at the time—but he was attracted to her, and not just physically, though that was part of it too. What did he and Ginger Pantelope have to talk about, anyway? Did they even talk? Yes, the sex with Ginger was great, no question about that, but what if he were with Tracy, and they had great sex, and they had fun, too? Wouldn't that be better? And ultimately, wouldn't that make her even hotter than Ginger? He never found out. After he casually mentioned Tracy to his friend Dennis Roemoser, Keith dropped Tracy like a cold potato. How could he go out with a girl whom all his friends considered a "scugly ho-bitch," if they even knew who she was. What was he thinking? Maybe he needed to beat off more.

"But Meri was the limit," he confessed.

Did he really come to college to repeat high school? Would he end up like his uncle Roger (a guy whose life peaked when he was a college linebacker, and who now had a huge potbelly, a bitter wife, and a nowhere job on a car lot)? If he really wanted to explore his options—which he had never even contemplated doing before—wouldn't it be a good idea to start now? He could start by dropping Meri, a girl who seemed like a repeat performance of Ginger and every other girl he had ever dated, or more accurately, "just fucked," because they certainly didn't want anything else from him, and the feeling was mutual. Maybe it was time to be a lone wolf. He started slowly. He began by paying more attention in class. He made an intriguing discovery. He is not a dumbass. No, he's not a brainiac, either, but he did come to see that if he really and truly studied, maybe harder than other people have to, his grades improved. But even more important, he enjoyed it. He liked learning cool, new things. And after he dumped Meri and bumped into me when I arrived for the Smoker, he had a flash. He could tell I was smart; I had that look about me, just like Tracy. He walked home slowly that afternoon and fantasized about what it would be like to have everything: his way-cool winning streak on the football field, a really high GPA, and a girlfriend who was smart and sexy and fun to be with and who wouldn't think he was just another dim-witted dick with a six-pack.

I'm so selfish. My thoughts are always about me—my pain, my troubles, my obstacles. Maybe it was time to step outside of myself and consider other people's feelings for a change.

"How's Rags?" I asked softly.

He tensed. Rags was still in recovery. Thank God his internal organs are fine, but both his hind legs are broken. He needs to stay at the animal hospital just a few more days, and then he'll be released to Keith, who's going to have to keep a round-the-clock vigil to make sure that Rags doesn't try to wriggle or move too much while his legs heal in their casts. I was sitting right next to him as he told me this. He was speaking in deep tones. I watched his lips move, forming each word. Should I kiss him? Would that be too forward? Should I wait for him to kiss me? Would that be the proper thing to do? But what if he didn't want to be kissed? He's not a dim-witted dick with a six-pack. Would he push me away? Would I ruin everything? *His lips are so cushiony.* That's what I was thinking: *That's what they feel like, that's what they feel like right now,* because in the midst of my thoughts, my body ignored my brain and my lips were upon his and his hands were holding my cheeks so gently and then we tumbled off the couch and we were on the floor and he was on top of me, engulfing me, his body pressed urgently to mine. I should take a moment here to say that, yes, this was fresh territory for me (of course), but P.S., I didn't need any instructions or helpful hints. Before I knew what was happening, my blouse was off, his shirt was flung aside (okay, not to be too superficial, but he does have a pretty amazing six-pack), and then he suddenly picked me up off the floor, set me gently on the couch, and sweetly smiled.

"So, uh, how about a little date rape?"

I burst out laughing. Then I playfully bit his ear.

"Well, you know, as long as you understand that 'yes' means 'yes.'"

I lost my virginity tonight. Keith and I made love. I've read and heard so many things about what "it" would be like—you know, "it hurts," "the earth moves," "church bells peal," "oh, sweet mystery of life," that sort of thing—and all of them are true. But what no one tells you is how beautifully still and motionless everything feels afterward. When I left Patty's room (Keith gave me the sweetest kiss good night), I walked through the campus on the way to the house. I took the long way.

Nothing was different except for the air. It seemed lighter, even clearer, as if the world's entire supply of oxygen had been freshly renewed. It wasn't me who had changed, it was everything around me. Suddenly everything was crystal clear. I stepped into the house, walked up the stairs to my room, and thought, *The clouds have finally lifted. Now I can see where the earth meets the sky. Now I know what's truly important.*

# September 30

## Dear Diary:

Gloria's voice was singsongy and dripping with sarcasm. "Your date is waiting for you downstairs."

I had almost forgotten (conveniently). In order to help Keith (my love, my sweet, my everything!), I was required to go on a public date with Bud Finger. He was waiting for me in the living room, yukking it up with Meri, who was sitting opposite like a pensive, gently inquiring parent.

"There's our girl," said Meri sweetly, spotting me as I stepped down the stairs. "You didn't tell me Bud was your high school sweetheart."

"Cindy rocks!" exclaimed Bud stupidly. "Did she tell you we went to the prom?"

"No, she didn't," gasped Meri. "It must have been quite a night."

"Can we go now?" I asked assertively. I mean, fine, this will somehow help Keith, but enough is enough. Then I saw it. Bud had a small booger dangling from his left nostril. Could things get any worse?

"Let's take a picture," enthused Meri. "A picture of the high school sweethearts on their first college date."

"Hey, I'm down for that," said Bud.

He had no idea that his choice of words made Meri flinch, like she'd just been stabbed in the abdomen. I responded firmly, twisting the knife in further.

"I am not down for that. I want to go. Bud? I am all about leaving. Right now."

Before we left, Meri pulled me aside, whispering gently but threateningly.

"You seem a little headstrong tonight. Something wrong?"

"I don't like being made fun of." I can't believe I was being so blunt.

"Is that what you think I was doing?"

"Forget it."

"Oh, but I can't. As president of Alpha Beta Delta, it's my duty to make note of everything. Academic achievements, social engagements, general disposition. Your disposition is unacceptable." She smiled, just slightly, running her hand through her thick raven hair. "Besides, you're my little bow-wow. I only want what's best for you. Understood?"

"Yes," I said, slowly deflating. Now was not the time to fight. No battle would be won here. Retreat.

I climbed petulantly into Bud's 1993 Plymouth Neon Expresso Coupe with confetti-patterned seat covers.

"Whoa, she's a hottie," he said, grinning lasciviously. "Nice rack, too."

"Wipe that damn booger off your nose!" I snapped.

He immediately became silent, like a cowed puppy dog, driving, furtively wiping and rewiping his nose with his sleeve. Then he gingerly asked, "Where are we going?"

"Where people go on dates. Think you can figure that one out, big guy?"

He gulped, silent once more. I suddenly felt so ashamed. What am I, some sort of dating expert? That's a laugh. I sighed.

"Do you like Long John Silver's?"

"Yeah. Hush Puppies rock."

At the restaurant I ordered Chicken Planks. Bud attempted to make conversation.

"So, uh, you know, you've never told me. What's your sign?"

"My sign? I've got one on my back. It says 'Moo.'"

He gulped, looked at his plate, toyed with his Hush Puppies.

"You look very pretty tonight."

"Oh, Bud, knock it off."

"Hey, I'm just trying to help, okay? A lot of people are trying to help you. Especially that Patty girl. You know, your friend? Hello? The one you blew off? Fine, blow me off, but what did she do to deserve it? Huh?"

I was being lectured on my lax ethics by Bud Finger. And he was right. But I wasn't going to completely cave.

"We're not talking about Patty right now. We're talking about you. And me. And how you've always treated me. At least I learn from my mistakes and try to change. But not you. You're still Bud. Same old, same old. And guess what? You don't offend me anymore. You just bore me."

"Hey, I'm here, aren't I?" he screeched, his voice catching.

I looked up. His jaw was set, defiant, but he was trembling, too, and his eyes were stung. Is Bud Finger capable of change? Is it conceivable that he might one day become a better, or more bearable, person? The answer is no, of course, but he might try, at least on occasion. He'll peddle his little tricycle up the hill, and even though he'll just reach the top and then plummet backward to the bottom (and be relieved that he did), he might try again.

"More Hush Puppies?" I quietly asked. "They're on me."

"Whoa, big spender," he chortled.

He ordered four more servings of Hush Puppies. I could take a moment here to explain why Bud is not a very polite eater. But some things are obvious.

I told him to take the long way home. I was in no rush to get back to the house. For a few minutes we rode silently, and then he flipped on the radio.

*Oh, baby, tune it, tune it, tune it, make me purr!*
*Tune my motor up!*
*Oh, baby, yeah!*

We had a good laugh. Apparently, Bud's been getting a lot of mileage on campus by telling everyone that he and "Lissa" are tight, though he's neglected to mention that she's my sister (no problem). He was full of questions. Is Lisa going to be recording a full CD (if she is, I'm leaving the country)? Why won't she answer his e-mails (why should she)? Did I think she was a one-hit wonder (please, God, yes)? Did I know she had a huge gay following (Lisa will take any following)? We finally pulled up to the house. Bud thought we should make it look good (including a good night kiss, but I warned him, no tongue), and he reminded me to casually mention to the girls that we've made plans to meet at his dorm room tomorrow night.

He pulled out all the stops. He gallantly opened the passenger-side door for me and even held my hand as we walked to the door. His hand was moist and clammy. He gazed into my eyes. It was like a parody. Still, I reminded myself, he was trying, and like he said, he was here. His meekness surprised me. He very sweetly touched my cheek, brought his lips to mine. I could smell the Hush Puppies. Then he jammed his tongue down my throat and I nearly screamed, but I knew I couldn't; he was darting it in and out, in and out, like a piston-plunging earthworm (was he digging for truffles?). But then I realized, he can't scream either. I grabbed his balls and squeezed them hard. Really hard. He gasped, leaping back. I brought my finger to my mouth. Shhh. He was slightly stooped over as he walked back to his car.

The house felt empty when I walked inside. I didn't trust it. Holding my head low, I scurried up the stairs and into my room, firmly closing the door. Just seconds later there was a forceful knock. Oh God. What now? I swung it open. It was Lindsay. She was smiling unnaturally.

"How was your date with Bud?" she chirped. Then she pushed her way in, closed the door, swiped a piece of notebook paper and frantically wrote: "Keep talking about Bud."

Nervously, I told her about my "wonderful" date with Bud—and I gaped in horror at the notebook paper as she furiously scribbled: "I overheard Shanna-Francine telling Gloria that you keep a diary. If you do, hide it or destroy it. No one's gone through your room yet, but they will."

I swiped the pen and wrote: "Can I sneak it to you in the morning? And then sneak it back at night to write in it?"

She responded: "Risky, but we can try."

"Thank you, thank you, thank you!" I wrote.

She grabbed the pen. "If anyone asks, I'm going to the movies by myself tomorrow night. I'll be in Bud's room playing you."

I almost cried. Everyone really is helping me. Even Lindsay. I took the pen to write more, but then we heard the front door slam downstairs. She grabbed the paper, quickly and silently folded it, then stuffed it in her mouth and swallowed.

"He even gave me the sweetest kiss good night," I said, continuing my Bud monologue.

*Eeeow. Really?* she silently mouthed. I nodded, my expression appropriately repulsed. Then we said our good nights. I changed into my nightgown, turned on my night-light, and was just about to settle in when I heard a fist pounding—*boom-boom-boom*—against my door.

"Yes?" I gulped.

"How was your 'date'?" asked Gloria in a sickeningly sweet voice. Then I heard giggles and Meri softly adding, "Woof woof." Then nothing. They were gone. It's two thirty a.m. now. Another sleepless night. Is this the last night I'll be able to write my thoughts down? I can't let Meri see my diary! If I have to burn it myself, I will. I'll hate it, but I'll do it.

# October 1

## Dear Diary:

I brought Meri her breakfast this morning. *Be obedient*, I thought. *Do not arouse suspicion.* Meri and Gloria were furiously snorting lines of cocaine when I stepped inside.

"I hear coke's making a comeback," I said cheerfully, if lamely. "Especially in New York."

"Oh, really?" asked Meri, looking unusually bright-eyed. "Never went out of style here."

"You fuck with me, you're fuckin' with the best!" bellowed Gloria. They exploded with giggles. I set the tray down.

"*Scarface*, right?" I asked subserviently, recognizing Gloria's movie quote.

The "coke" version of *Scarface* with Al Pacino is one of the few Meri-approved remakes or homages, since she admires its "mise-en-scène," and has further noted that it's become a powerful influence on New Black Cinema, from *New Jack City* to practically everything directed by Ice Cube. But they didn't hear me. They were quoting away, rapid-fire, faster and faster, back and forth.

"One more Quaalude and that bitch is mine!" shrieked Gloria.

"I kill for fun," fired back Meri.

"Hey, baby, what's your problem . . ."

". . . you got that look in your eye like you ain't been fucked in a year."

"Fuck the Diaz brothers."

"Fuck them all."

"I'm gonna bury dem cockroaches."

More giggles. Then Gloria lost her balance, fell backward, and knocked over Meri's breakfast tray. *Splat.* Eggs and juice dribbled all over the snow-white carpeting. I didn't even wait for the order. I was down on my knees. Meri turned to me and spoke very quickly. I tried not to stare at the tiny dab of cocaine clumped on the very edge of her nose.

"Listen up, little bow-wow. You won't be going to class today. Gloria and I are taking the girls shopping, but you'll be staying here with Lindsay. I'm assigning you both to Shanna-Francine."

It seems that Meri has taken an interest in the upcoming Oktoberfest Dance, or rather, she's decided that it needs the management expertise of Alpha Beta Delta. In other words, it's another event she wants to control. She swept out of the room with Gloria. I picked up the last clump of eggs with my hand. Uh-oh. The carpet was stained. I would need to get a brush and a mop bucket and maybe even some carpet cleaner from the kitchen. Then I froze. It dawned on me that I was only a few feet away from Meri's armoire and her precious DAT surveillance equipment. And to my right, Meri's walk-in closet, which is rumored to contain the Hoover File and the digital camera with pictures of Dean Pointer and me (and God knows what else). What was stopping me? All I had to do was walk in the closet, or swing open the armoire. I could bring an end to this now. I could smash everything to bits. I stood very slowly. My heart began racing. I felt dizzy. Was I going to faint? I tried my best to focus, and in that moment, I had a realization. I wasn't just doing this for Keith, or for myself. By destroying Meri and everything Alpha Beta Delta stood for, I would be saving an entire generation of kids at Rumson University—and not just the ones attending this year, but the ones who'll be here next year, and the next year, and the year after that. I suddenly felt very noble. Okay, so maybe what I was doing wasn't on a par with the heroics of, say, Susan B. Anthony, who fought so bravely for the rights of women in the nineteenth century, mostly because her Quaker faith told her that everyone was equal under God's eyes, with no distinction between male and female, which I guess says as much about the Quaker faith as it does about Susan when you think about it. (I've never met a Quaker, to my knowledge, and I doubt they're easy to spot, since I'm assuming modern Quakers don't dress like that guy on the Quaker Oats box, or at least I hope they don't, since he looks so wide-eyed and kind of lobotmized.) So no, maybe I won't be remembered in the history books, I thought, or by the kids at Rumson University, but then a real hero simply sees an injustice and takes decisive action, right? That's all I had to do. And the armoire was so close—so temptingly close. I put one foot in front of the other, and finally, there I was, standing right in front of it. *Open it*, I screamed to myself, *open it and smash everything inside, or find a lighter and torch it all. Anything. Just do it.*

"What the hell are you doing?" snapped Gloria behind me. I could feel her breath on the back of my neck.

"Um, looking for a towel," I gulped.

"I hear you keep a d-i-i-i-iary," she sneered. "Is it true? You keep a d-i-i-i-iary?"

"I used to. In high school. And when I lived in the dorms. But who has time for stuff like that now?"

I nervously turned, forcing a self-deprecating laugh, now face-to-face with her. I don't think cocaine agrees with Gloria. Her head seemed to be vibrating, and I could hear the *snap-grind* of her teeth rhythmically mashing against each other. *Keep the focus*, I thought. *Do not arouse suspicion.*

"I should finish cleaning up."

"Forget it. Mamacita's here today."

Mamacita, I learned, is a lovely Mexican woman in her late seventies who personally cleans Meri's room top to bottom once a month (Meri pays her a fortune). *Lucky me,* I thought. *No more handsies-kneesies on the snow-white carpet.* Gloria escorted me out of the room and closed the door, and I saw her carefully lock a deadbolt. I had no idea that Meri's room had locks. Obviously, this is going to make whatever plan Patty might be coming up with that much harder—or maybe impossible. Oh, why didn't I attack that stupid armoire when I had the chance? But now that I look back on it, I'm glad I didn't. If there's any evidence capable of clearing Keith's name in the armoire (or in the closet) and bringing down Meri once and for all, I would have ruined everything by going insane and destroying it.

I heard the *whirr* of a helicopter as we walked down the stairs. Though Mamacita lives only two towns over, Meri apparently prefers that she be flown in to Alpha Beta Delta. Downstairs in the living room, I was greeted by Shanna-Francine and Lindsay, both of whom were surrounded by stacks and stacks of 8-track tapes and several large picture books, like *Fashionable Clothing from the Sears Catalogs: Mid-1970s,* and several Time-Life yearbooks, all of them from the seventies, like 1974 and 1977. But my eye was on Meri. Through the living room window, I saw her sweep out onto the front lawn and greet Mamacita, who was very cautiously stepping out of the helicopter. She is, without doubt, the tiniest woman I've ever seen (and very frail). They exchanged air kisses, and then Meri led her inside and pointed directly at me.

"That's the little bow-wow who stained my carpet. I asked for cranberry juice this morning. I don't know how you'll get it up."

Mamacita just nodded. Her eyes were doll-like and vacant. Did she understand a word Meri was saying?

"Mamacita's been with the Sugarman family for two generations. Isn't that right, Mamacita?"

Again she nodded vacantly.

"Hi, Mamacita!" exclaimed Shanna-Francine, giving a wave.

This time her eyes seemed to brighten, though she wasn't look-ing directly at Shanna-Francine, but at a point seemingly beyond her. Is Mamacita blind? After leading her to the staircase, Meri, Gloria, and the rest of the sisters were off. They boarded the heli-copter and *poof*—they were gone, off to a local airstrip. There they would board a private jet bound for Dallas, where they would spend the morning shopping and enjoying a late lunch. Then they'd spend the afternoon and early evening at a nearby ranch riding Ardennais—an ancient breed of horse from the Ardennes region on the border between France and Belgium, known for their compact size and immense, muscular legs. Their evening plans were open, though Shanna-Francine mentioned that they might go clubbing in Austin.

"Don't you love the Captain & Tennille?" squealed Shanna-Francine.

She pushed a tape into an 8-track player (where the heck did she get that?) and forced Lindsay and me to listen to the complete Captain & Tennille songbook, including her favorite, "Muskrat Love." It seems Shanna-Francine has come to the conclusion that a seventies theme for the Oktoberfest Dance is a bit too generic and "like, done to death," but a Captain & Tennille–themed dance would be "so awesome." Well, I can think of worse seventies-era groups to plan a dance around, and much better ones, too, but I wasn't about to disagree, and neither was Lindsay, who exchanged weary glances with me whenever Shanna-Francine shrieked with delight over all the little touches and decorative ideas she was coming up with. Lindsay was more intent, thank God, on planting several seeds within earshot of Shanna-Francine, like when she asked me, "Do you and Bud have any special plans for tonight?"

"Not really. I think we're just hanging out at his dorm room," I answered stiffly. Oh, I'm just the worst actress. "We'll probably order a pizza or something."

As the morning wore on, Shanna-Francine's party plans grew more elaborate. (Could we actually fly in the real Captain & Tennille for the dance, she wondered? Were they "gettable"?) She turned to me, cheerfully commanding, "Like, you need to take notes, don't you think? You should get your notebook from your room. Don't you think?"

I didn't feel like arguing. Off I went. Still, when I reached the second-floor landing, I was shocked. Mamacita was still hobbling up the stairs, one at a time, in an effort to get to Meri's room. At the rate she was going, she probably wouldn't make it to Meri's room until the late afternoon. I touched her shoulder, just to let her know that I was there, and asked her (speaking slowly) if there was anything I could do.

"*Lléveme,*" she said.

I wasn't sure what that meant, but when she held her arms out, I got the general idea. The next thing I knew, I was literally carrying Mamacita in my arms like a small infant. I was terrified. True, she was light as a feather, but what if I dropped her?

"*Usted es una muchacha dulce,*" she said sweetly, and it must have been a compliment, because she smiled when she said it.

We finally reached Meri's door, and it occurred to me—how would Mamacita get inside? Then she pulled out a truly gargantuan key chain with color-coded keys and very slowly began to finger through each one, presumably looking for the right key. Honest, I just wanted to be helpful, but when I reached for the key chain, she viciously slapped my hand back and screamed at the top of her lungs.

"*Si usted toca las llaves, usted es una mujer muerta!*"

I stood traumatized. What was she saying? Luckily, Mamacita could be heard all the way downstairs, and Shanna-Francine helpfully screamed back up.

"If you touch her keys, you're a dead woman!"

"*Si. Comprende,*" I said, nervously backing away from her.

It was nearly seven o'clock when I told Shanna-Francine that I was off to see Bud. Mamacita was gone. (She kept calling me "*puta disimulada,*" or "sneaky whore," when I carried her down the stairs and into the arriving helicopter; if I were a vindictive person, I would have dropped her, but I didn't.) Lindsay was gone too. She said she was off to see *Amacord* at RU's Cinema Revival, and it took some doing to convince Shanna-Francine that she had to see it by herself.

"I need to be alone when I commune with Fellini," she explained. "It's like going to church."

Shanna-Francine understood. Apparently, she "communes" at least once a year with *The Sound of Music* and pretends to be little Liesl. She also told me that I was "like, so lucky" to find a special someone like Bud. My stomach did backflips. Even if I am able to help Keith and make everything turn out right, will I ever be able to live this down? Leaving the house, I almost darted behind the dorm building alleyways in order to make my way to Patty's, but then I remembered, I have nothing to hide. My affair with Bud is common knowledge. Still, old habits die hard, and as I got closer to her building, I detoured down an alley and saw Lindsay hiding. She was standing just behind the Dumpster—obviously waiting until I had entered the building before stepping inside and going to Bud's room. The setting sun was shining bright, and her umbrella was closed by her side. I almost cried with gratitude. In order not to be spotted, Lindsay was enduring the sun's punishing rays. As quick as a mouse, she fell into step behind me, holding her head low. We didn't say a word to each other as we made our way inside the building and walked down the hall. Behind me, I heard a knock and a door opening.

"Yo, Cindy," said Bud, a bit too stiffly. I guess I'm not the only lousy actor around.

I turned my head. Lindsay gave me a thumbs-up as she stepped into his room and closed the door. I don't care what anyone says, that's friendship. Going into Bud Finger's room, alone and unprotected, goes way beyond the call of duty. Okay, so I knew they weren't going to be doing anything—they'll just be making noises and stuff to sound convincing on the surveillance tapes—but groaning with sexual ecstasy in the presence of Bud Finger, oh my God, that's harsh. Poor Lindsay!

*Keep the focus,* I told myself. I strode down another hallway and stepped up to Patty's door. Did I need a secret knock? We hadn't planned on one. I gave a quick knock, hoping they would somehow recognize it was me. Pigboy swung the door open and all but yanked me inside. Music was blaring. Patty was giggling—and she was dancing, too, shaking it to the left, shaking it to the right. Pigboy joined her, and they both cheerfully sang along:

> *Has your girlfriend got the butt?*
> *Tell 'em to shake it, shake it, shake it, shake it!*
> *Shake that healthy butt!*
> *Baby got back!*

"Isn't this a great song?" exclaimed Patty.

I was about to say that Sir Mix-A-Lot's a bit passé, but then I realized what a complete killjoy I'd be if I did; Patty and Pigboy were having such fun shaking their respective big butts. And besides, when I heard a quick staccato knock, I knew in an instant who it was. I swung open the door and there he was. Keith (my love, my sweet, my everything!). But he moved so fast that I couldn't get a word out. He swept me into a sweet embrace, kicked the door closed, and grabbed my butt, shaking us both to Sir Mix-A-Lot.

> *Shake it, shake it, shake it, shake it!*
> *Shake that healthy butt!*

Okay, I admit it. I don't care if he's "over." I like Sir Mix-A-Lot. A lot. Then I heard another knock. Was there another couple waiting outside to shake their butts? As it turned out, it was a pizza delivery boy, and for the next hour or so, Patty, Pigboy, Keith, and I had such fun sharing pizza and laughing. It almost felt like this was a normal double date (not that I would know what a "normal" one was), but it wasn't. When Patty served coffee, the mood turned grim. We knew what we were here for. As it turned out, Patty, Pigboy, and Keith had already met for several strategy meetings about Meri, and a very complete plan was already worked out, but for reasons of security, they didn't want to tell me everything. I didn't like that. I'm so tired of secrets and clandestine maneuvers behind my back, but they assured me it was for my own safety. Besides, they insisted, I was about to be informed of the first maneuver—because it involved me.

"Our first step is to cause Meri 'Induced Anxiety Syndrome,'" announced Patty intently. "We'll cause her fantastic stress. Hit her where she lives. Then she'll be weak and vulnerable. Then we can really strike."

Pigboy handed me a small laboratory vial filled with creamy-looking black liquid, which had been given to him by Randy and Nester, who had gotten it from Bud, who had gotten it from Wolfgang Rimmer, one of his earth science lab buddies. It was Keith who advised me to make a practice run with it tomorrow, then strike the next morning, and everyone thought this was a good idea. I was foolish enough to ask what the creamy-looking black liquid would do. I'm still shuddering. I'm back at Alpha Beta Delta now, in my room, and I'm afraid to write anything more. What if my diary is discovered before I make my practice run? True, getting my diary from Lindsay at night and handing it off in the morning is working, but I can't be too careful. "Operation Hazing Meri Sugarman" has begun.

# October 2

## Dear Diary:

The practice run went well. Thank God. In fact, this plan is going to be a whole lot easier than I thought. After all, Shanna-Francine doesn't seem to mind anymore when I ask to take Meri her breakfast in the morning. Is this too easy? Am I tempting the gods?

"Who knew you were such a hooch?" chuckled Gloria when I returned from my afternoon class.

I froze. Think fast, Cindy. Gloria knows what she knows from listening to Bud's room surveillance, which means that Bud and Lindsay must have put on quite a show last night—at least verbally. I nearly burst into tears at the thought of poor Lindsay caught in such sordid circumstances, but I offered a weak smile instead.

"Well, we did go to the prom together," I said, and that seemed to suffice.

Tomorrow morning I strike. I'm so nervous. I know everything will work out perfectly, but what if it doesn't? What if I'm caught? What if everything turns to complete disaster? Okay, I've got to stop writing about this. I think it's scaring me more.

# October 3

## Dear Diary:

No one blinked when I asked to take Meri her breakfast this morning. Holding the tray, I simply put one foot in front of the other, and as I climbed the stairs, I couldn't help but ponder all my weaknesses, and how they've brought me to such a dangerous place. Yes, I've been rejected my entire life, I've been a loner, I've been an outsider—boo-hoo for me—but that's also allowed me to be an observer, hasn't it? Am I so blind? Why have I always wanted to be just like the girls who've always been so mean to me? Maybe I've only allowed myself to see the good things about them, or all the things I've wanted for myself. They were popular, they had friends (and they had cute boyfriends, too). I had all of that (for a brief moment); I was part of Meri's circle, I was "in." And the sick thing is, if I had run across a girl who was a loser like I was before, and I had been given only the slightest bit of encouragement, I bet I would have been really mean to her. Do I have to completely despise what I was in order to become something different? Before I left Patty's the other night, she told me, "We'll always be fighting the Meri Sugarmans of the world," but I don't think that's true, at least in my case. I think I'll be fighting myself. I really don't want to go back to being lonely and depressed all the time. Done that, been there. True, I guess I can console myself with the fact that I do have a small circle of friends now with Lindsay and Patty (and okay, maybe Bud, too), and you might even say that

I have a real boyfriend with Keith, but once we've succeeded in destroying our shared enemy, what then? Won't everything return to normal? Normal for me is misery.

*Oh, baby, tune it, tune it, tune it!*
*Make me purr!*
*Tune my motor up!*

I cringed as I climbed the second flight of stairs. One of the girls in the house bought Lisa's CD single. For a second or so, I thought of Madonna. What if Lisa becomes as big as Madonna? Madonna is, after all, a real person, and she does have several brothers and sisters. One of them is gay and designs her clothes (or something like that), and another is supposedly a bitter, raging alcoholic. These are my options? Barring any lesbian tendencies, which I don't think I have, I guess that means I can look forward to a future just as lonely and depressed as always—with the added bonus of alcoholism. Thanks, Lisa.

By the time I started climbing the third set of stairs to Meri's room, my hands were shaking. The salt and pepper smiley face that Shanna-Francine sprinkles on Meri's eggs every morning was now jolted into an angry and deranged expression. My heart was thumping out of my chest, my throat was parched. Would I faint? Would I collapse? Could I really go through with this? I honestly don't know how I did it.

Meri's room was stone-still when I walked inside. The porch door was slightly ajar. I could hear the Jacuzzi gurgling. I would have only a few minutes, if that. I set the breakfast tray down and silently crept into Meri's bathroom, gently pulled aside her shower curtain, and spotted her medium-size bottle of Aveda Black Malva shampoo. I was quick. I screwed the top off the bottle, retrieved the laboratory vial from my pocket, and dumped its gooey liquid inside. Then I screwed the cap back on, gave a good shake to mix it all up, stuffed the vial in my pocket, tiptoed back into the room, picked up the breakfast tray, and made to set it down on one of Meri's piecrust tables as if I'd just stepped in from the hallway—and that's just when Meri breezed in from the porch in her white fluffy robe and turban towel.

"You look sick," she observed cheerfully. "Is my little bow-wow sick?"

"Let's stick a thermometer up her ass and find out," snickered Gloria, who had just walked in.

"I'm okay," I offered meekly. "I didn't sleep well last night."

"Fine, whatever," said Meri, waving me away.

I returned to the kitchen. Shanna-Francine and Lindsay were already going over more plans for the Captain & Tennille–themed Oktoberfest Dance. I am now learning much more about the Captain & Tennille than I ever thought possible. Did I know that both the Captain and Toni Tennille originally toured with the Beach Boys (no, but I'm not surprised)? Did I know that Toni Tennille was a featured singer on Pink Floyd's "The Wall" (no, but that's more than weird)? To Shanna-Francine's delight, Lindsay has tracked down a mail-order house that sells official "Captain" hats, each with a different Captain & Tennille song title stitched on the back. We decided to order four hundred of them. The decorations and the music were beginning to firm up, but we were also at an impasse, at least as far as Shanna-Francine was concerned. Lindsay had learned that Toni Tennille is, in fact, available for public appearances (and she comes fairly cheap, too, which I guess is no big surprise), but even though she and the Captain are still married and live a quiet life in Nevada, they no longer make public appearances together as the Captain & Tennille.

I was suddenly stunned by a wailing, bloodcurdling scream— and I thought, *Oh, come now, Shanna-Francine, an appearance by the real*

*Captain & Tennille will not make or break the dance.* But then I realized that Shanna-Francine was not screaming, and neither was Lindsay. The screams were coming from upstairs. From the third floor.

We flew up the stairs and raced into Meri's room, along with a bunch of other girls. We were flat-out shocked by the sight before us. It was pure horror. I have never before witnessed anything like it, at least not in real life. Remember that scene in the original *Psycho* when Anthony Perkins is finally grabbed by the police and he drops the knife and his wig falls off and he seems to wail and disintegrate before your eyes? Here it was, playing out before us. Meri was standing just outside the bathroom in a towel, and her mouth was abnormally wide, and she was howling loudly, almost like a banshee, and she was pulling at large, ratty clumps of matted hair. All of her thick raven hair—it was gone! Then she sank to her knees and rocked violently back and forth, howling and howling. No one knew what to do. Even Gloria was completely astounded. Meri's howls grew louder and more high-pitched, and her back was arching and contorting. What would happen next? Would she melt? Can I keep her broom? I wanted to jump up and down and scream "Yes! Induced Anxiety Syndrome! She's weak, she's vulnerable, it worked!" But I wasn't about to give myself away.

Unfortunately, one of the girls did something awful. It couldn't have lasted more than a second, but that's all it took. She laughed—then immediately sucked it back, though futilely. Meri froze. Her screams died. She was still bent over on her knees, but she was absolutely motionless, like some sort of psycho alien fetus about to be reborn after being burned to a crisp by a blowtorch. She stood, slowly but regally, using both of her hands to wipe the few remaining tufts of hair from her bald head. Her eyes glistened like two opaque cough drops—just like a shark's. She stepped before her full-length mirror.

"Okay, we'll find out who did this," she whispered. "In the

meantime, we'll tell everyone I've had chemo. I'll get tons of sympathy. In fact, I feel the need for lots of sympathy. Right now. From everyone in this house."

The house of Alpha Beta Delta turned into a House of Horrors that night. One by one, Lindsay, Shanna-Francine, and the rest of the girls (including Gloria), were ordered into Meri's room for our new "chemo cut," a new bald do that we were ordered to inform all within earshot was done voluntarily out of love and unity for Meri, our president, who had only recently endured painful chemo and hair loss while fighting her cancerous affliction.

This is Induced Anxiety Syndrome? Patty underestimated Meri, to put it mildly. I didn't cause increased anxiety; I had thrown a rock at a hornet's nest—and now stood directly in the path of the swarm. After we were all shaved, we were ordered to sit in the living room and wait for Meri to descend from her room. Gloria had taken off in the town car. She returned forty minutes later, carrying what looked like a large hatbox, and charged up the stairs. None of us said a word. We were all terrified—and bald. Then Gloria raced down the stairs and stood ramrod straight at the living room entryway.

"She's coming," she barked.

Meri walked majestically down the stairs. Several girls gasped. Meri was wearing a large black bouffant wig, made by hand from actual human hair, we were told, by the good Sisters at the Abbey of Crewe, who create them exclusively for female parishioners who endure unsightly hair loss from chemo. The point was clear. The wig wasn't just big and black. It was blessed.

"One of you has betrayed me," said Meri softly, her eyes newly lambent. "But I won't accuse anyone. Yet. Not without proof."

I tried not to shake, or to cry. Oh my God, wasn't it obvious? I had brought Meri her breakfast this morning. True, lots of girls meet with Meri during the day in her room, and go into her bathroom, too, but I was the last one in her room before she took the shower that left her bald. The empty laboratory vial was practically burning a hole in my pocket. I still hadn't disposed of it. There hadn't been time. It took all my strength to remain absolutely still and not give myself away. And then, seemingly out of nowhere, Meri shrieked at the top of her lungs, "Handsies-kneesies!"

If you weren't aware of what was going on at Alpha Beta Delta, or who was in charge, or what we were all enduring, you'd prob- ably be taken aback by the sight of several bald girls on their hands and knees scrubbing every wall, floor, and surface within reach, while one girl, in a large black bouffant wig, serenely kept watch and airily offered helpful hints and maxims.

"Make sure your clothing choices are as versatile as an actress's wardrobe. Be ready for any role," and "Only wear hot pink if you have an absolutely flawless complexion," and "It's always best to sit on hard chairs. Soft ones spread your hips."

Still, all the scrubbing and the cleaning gave me a good oppor- tunity. And I took it. I was alone in the kitchen on my hands and knees when I realized it was now or never. I placed the laboratory vial on the floor, quickly covered it with my scrubbing cloth, and jammed my hand down repeatedly until I was sure the vial was reduced to tiny little pieces. Then I scooped it all up and dumped it into the trash. Even better, Lindsay and I were ordered to empty all the garbage bags in the house in the back Dumpster. Talk about a lucky break. Now there was nothing to link me to Meri's Aveda Black Malva shampoo, which Gloria and Meri had already identi- fied as the likely source of the poison (they sent it off to Professor Joseph Adelson, the chair of the Science Department, who prom- ised a full inventory of its contents by morning, and who wasn't about to cross Meri given the information regarding his past petty embezzlement from the university that has long been a part of the Hoover File).

I'm sitting in my bed now. It's already past three a.m. It's strange being bald, though it's not as upsetting to me as it is to the other girls, since my hair was already a motley wreck thanks to Meri's blindfolded haircut. I don't know when I'll get the chance to tell Patty what's happened. I was supposed to meet up with everyone tonight in her room—with the cover of seeing Bud in his room for another "date," of course. I should have tried to call Bud, but I didn't have a chance. Who knows what Meri's got prepared for us tomorrow? Or the next day. Or the day after that. I don't think I've ever been with a group of girls so completely demoralized. All of their individuality and free will seems to have been shorn off right along with their hair. Meri has us in her grip. Will she be serving us little Dixie cups with poisoned Kool-Aid next? No, she wouldn't do that. She won't kill us. That I'm fairly certain of.

# October 4

## Dear Diary:

Oh my God, oh my God, oh my God, oh my God! I'm in big trouble! The day began normally, which should have been my first tip-off that things were about to go wrong. More than wrong. Disastrous! Breakfast was the same as always (except that we're now all bald) (of course), and I even took Meri up her breakfast tray. She seemed in good spirits, and I wasn't nervous at all when she told me to bend my head toward her. It seems she needed to adjust her lipstick, and my shiny dome was a handy reflective surface (or so she said). Then she chuckled and waved me away. That was it. No one was giving us any special orders—the day would be unfolding like any other. I went to my classes, and I was careful to tell everyone who asked that I had shaved my head voluntarily out of sympathy for Meri, who had just undergone chemo. I could detect a hopeful glint in some of my professors' eyes, but I was quick to point out that she was making a speedy and very full recovery. Still, my focus was elsewhere. Where was Patty? Or Keith? Or Pigboy? They needed to be informed that their Induced Anxiety Syndrome plan was a complete bust.

Between my third and fourth classes, I darted into the cafeteria, bought a package of Hostess Ho Hos, stuffed them into my purse, and then walked calmly into the last stall in the ladies' room. I worked fast, and a few minutes later I darted inconspicuously to the Great Lawn. There was Bud, as always, hacking with Nester and Randy.

"Yo, Cyn, babe!" he called out.

I wanted so desperately to scream, "No!" but I had no choice. I endured it. Bud ran up to me, his "girlfriend," and gave me a big, sloppy, tongue-plunging kiss—in and out, in and out, it just didn't seem to stop—along with a firm slap on my ass. I heard a few snickers and derisive laughs.

"You can let go of my ass now," I said through gritted teeth.

"'Sup with your hair? It's kind of hot."

I smiled broadly, hoping that anyone who happened to be watching would assume that we were two ordinary college sweethearts. Eeeow.

"I just wanted to say hello between classes," I said feebly, then tossed the pack of Hostess Ho Hos at him and took off.

Would he get it? Would he just eat the Ho Hos and leave it at that? On the cardboard backing, I had desperately written "Grim Stres Roni Re!" which, if he was as good at deciphering anagrams as he was at creating them, would read "Meri is stronger!"

Unfortunately, I was too late. It was lunchtime when I turned the corner to the house, and I could see Gloria and several of the girls on the front lawn. They were ritualistically ripping clothes apart and hurling them haphazardly to the ground. As I stepped closer, I stopped breathing. They were my clothes, and on the ground with them were all of my personal belongings and papers. Everything was ripped apart or completely mangled. I thought about running in the opposite direction—and finding a handy bridge I could jump off of—but I kept going straight ahead, because I couldn't help but think that they had nothing on me. I had destroyed the vial, and the Dumpster was emptied this morning. This had to be about something else. It was Gloria who spotted me first.

"Dead girl walking!" she cried, pointing at me. "Rimmer ratted you out."

Gloria took pleasure in telling me the details. It seems Meri had a meeting this morning with Professor Adelson, the chair of the Science Department, who confirmed that her Aveda Black Malva shampoo had, in fact, been contaminated with several compound chemicals, including polypropylene glycol, disaccharides, and dithiothreitol—all of which had been requested for an unspecified experiment only two days previously by one Wolfgang Rimmer, a German-born science student who cracked under the pressure and revealed that he had created the concoction at the request of Alpha Beta Delta's Cindy Bixby, though he claimed to have no idea what she would do with it.

"I've never met anyone named Wolfgang," I yelped, and there was at least some truth to that.

Why Wolfgang had covered for Patty and Nester and Randy and Bud and not for me was beyond my comprehension at the moment. Still, it didn't do him much good. Meri had arranged for his student visa to be revoked. It's back to Deutschland for little Wolfgang. And straight to hell for me.

"We're done here," said Gloria with a snort, who ordered the girls inside and turned to me. "You never existed at Alpha Beta Delta. Get it? You're DOA."

"It—it's not true," I stuttered.

"Aw. Nice try."

*Ka-chink.* I leaped out of my skin when I heard a rifle cock. Meri stepped outside in her black bouffant wig, holding a shotgun, aiming it right at me, absolutely red with rage. She roared, "I wish upon you a thirty-year yeast infection. But since I can't do that, I'll kill you. But not with this gun. That would be too simple. This gun is symbolic. Your death will be slow. For starters, I'm lowering your GPA to 1.6. If it stays that low beyond the semester, you'll be asked to leave RU. Think of it, Cindy. Community college. Commuting from home. Classes with Inbred Pig People. Beyond that, let's just say I have a few other tricks up my sleeve."

"It's not true," I whimpered in vain.

Tears were running down my cheeks. What other "tricks" was she talking about?

"It's always the quiet ones," mused Gloria.

"Yes, it is," agreed Meri. "The quiet little bow-wows." Then she stepped up very close to me and patted my cheek. "One has watched life badly if one has not also seen the hand that considerately kills."

She was quoting Nietzsche. She couldn't have read him. She must have seen it on a refrigerator magnet. But I wasn't any less terrified. Then they walked back into the house and left me standing there. I must have a hearty constitution of some kind because I didn't crumple to the ground or run into traffic. Instead, I worked fast, gathering everything that was salvageable and stuffing it into my newly mangled suitcase. Then I heard the front door click open. I shuddered, bracing myself.

"Let me help you," said Lindsay, stepping out onto the lawn. Then she smiled very oddly. "I guess you'll be moving in with your boyfriend now, right?"

"What?"

"Your boyfriend. Bud. You're moving in with him, right?"

Oh, I love Lindsay. She's always thinking.

"Yes," I said a bit too theatrically, hoping that the mic in the poplar tree would pick me up. "At least Bud still loves me."

"Do not help her!" bellowed Gloria, who appeared suddenly at the door.

Lindsay quickly dropped the pile in her hands and scurried back into the house. Gloria slammed the door shut behind them. I picked up the clump Lindsay had left—and my diary slipped out.

Oh, Lindsay, Lindsay, Lindsay! What a quick thinker.

I made my way to Bud's dorm room. Boy, was he glad to see me—especially when I pushed myself in, clamped my hand over his mouth, and made like I was kissing him. Then I told him how "happy" I was that we were going to be living together, but at the same time, I was writing on a piece of notepaper: "Does Patty know what happened?"

He wrote back: "Everyone knows. No meeting tonight. Too risky. Patty says to stand by."

"If you touch me inappropriately tonight, I'll kill you."

"Chill out!"

"I'm serious. Did you give Patty my message?"

"What message?"

"Grim Stres Roni Re!"

"What?"

I sighed heavily. I couldn't even continue my phony monologue. Obviously, Bud had just eaten the Ho Hos.

It's nighttime now. Bud is sleeping on the floor (he insisted; I didn't argue). A thought keeps popping into my head: *I am not breakable.* I'm not exactly sure what that means, except that I'm not ready to give up yet, and obviously Lindsay isn't either. And neither are Patty and Keith and Pigboy. Hazing Meri Sugarman. It still has a nice ring to it. It might not be possible, but it's a worthy goal.

# October 5

## Dear Diary:

I've been feeling very angry today. There's been no meeting, it's still too "risky." In Western Lit, Professor Scott handed out a test, but mine was pregraded. On the top sheet, he had already written a large F in red Sharpie. You want to play that way, Professor Scott? Fine. I'm not afraid of anyone anymore. I'm way too far gone for that. I'm filled with hate. It's probably not very healthy (I read somewhere that maintaining a constant ill temperament can lead to heart failure, high blood pressure, and constipation), but it is making me feel newly refreshed and very focused. I kind of like it.

# October 6

## Dear Diary:

Ahhh! Still no meeting yet. At lunch today in the cafeteria, my prepaid semester lunch card was mysteriously invalidated. I didn't care. I paid for my lunch and sat by myself at a table, cheered by the thought that, unlike the sisters at Alpha Beta Delta, I did not have to keep shaving my head. My hair is actually starting to grow back. True, there's only a light fuzz now, but it's a start. I toyed with my peach cobbler (at least that's what they call it) and was considering throwing it away and leaving the cafeteria when I glanced up and saw Keith. There he was (my love, my sweet, my everything!), gazing at me from afar, sitting alone at a table at the other end of the cafeteria. My heart swelled, I smiled back, and I thought of that scene in *West Side Story* when Natalie Wood saw this handsome guy, Tony, across a crowded dance floor—and then suddenly there was lots of weird smoke and strange red strobe lights and they were dancing together. I've always loved that movie (even though Lisa made fun of it because she thought the dancing gang members were, "like, so flaming"), but there was no weird smoke or strange red strobe lights to bring Keith and me together. It didn't matter. Well, that's not exactly true. I would have appreciated a bit of swirling smoke, at the very least to obscure my peach-fuzz head, but we were still able to gaze silently at each other, and he even took a big risk by quickly blowing me a kiss. No one was watching us, but I figured I'd better get the heck out of there in case he blew me another. The last thing either of us needs is for Meri to learn that our love is still strong.

As I walked outside to my next class, I thought of poor Natalie Wood, who lost her boyfriend in a fight because she was Puerto Rican (even though she wasn't in real life). I also thought about Meri. I can't get her out of my head. There she is, completely unstoppable and serene. I remember her once telling me that her favorite fruits are quinces, which I had never heard of, so I looked them up on the Internet and learned that quinces are pear-shaped and very hard and have a strong acid taste. Frankly, I'd like to grab a few quinces and mash them right in her face, and thinking about that sort of makes me smile, but it also makes me sad. Meri was my idol, she was everything that I've always wanted to be, and now all I can think about is doing terrible things to her, which probably doesn't say much for my state of mind. I also thought about Bud, who told me this morning that we should go out on a date tonight to keep things "looking real." But I think it's real enough that we're living together in the same dorm room. Too real.

It's two in the morning right now, and Bud is, of course, snoring on the floor (in fits and starts, like a carburetor), and I can't sleep. Everything is way too strangely calm. My entire life has been Ziplocked and put into the back of the freezer and forgotten about. I want my life back. And I don't care if it's lonely and miserable like before, because at least I'd be alive. What if Patty and Pigboy and Keith can't come up with a plan? What if everything stays the same and Keith goes to jail and I'm stuck living with Bud? Every time I try to go to sleep, thoughts like that keep waking me up.

# October 1

## Dear Diary:

I didn't fall asleep until four this morning, but when I woke up at seven, I panicked. Something was wrong. Bud was gone—he wasn't snoring on the floor, which is really strange and slightly ominous when you consider that Bud never wakes up more than ten minutes before his first class of the day (he doesn't bother with a shower or shave until well after lunchtime; the fact that I know things like this pains me). I was barely awake when I saw a piece of paper on the door, and large letters that said: "Destroy This After You Read It!" Oh my God. I flung the covers aside and raced up to the door, reading the note:

"Meeting tonight in P's room at eight. Important: Do not come earlier or later. Check hallway carefully before going to door. Confirmation will come by phone. At seven thirty, phone in B's room will ring three times to indicate that everything is a go. If no rings at seven thirty, meeting cancelled. Destroy note now!"

I grabbed the note to pull it off the door and it wouldn't budge. Bud didn't tape it or tack it. In his infinite wisdom, he had used four pieces of gum to stick it into place, which meant that it took several minutes for me to rip it off in sections, and even then, I had to use Bud's tiny Swiss Army knife to scrape off the rest. I had destroyed the note, but I had also left a series of deep scratches and gouges in the door. But who cares about Bud's door? I didn't.

I was levitating with happiness. There would be a meeting. There was hope.

The rest of the day was uneventful, though I did see a bald-headed Shanna-Francine leading a group of bald-headed Alpha Beta Delta girls to the school's auditorium. Her plans for the Oktoberfest Dance are obviously well under way. Posters are up all over campus announcing it ("Love Will Keep Us Together!" they blare), along with the scheduled appearance of "special guest star" Toni Tennille (I guess even Alpha Beta Delta can't rouse the Captain from retirement). They're also charging a heart-stopping sixty-five dollars a person, with proceeds slated to go to the Alpha Beta Delta Charitable Trust, which means that Meri must need a new bauble or two. I looked closely at the small crowd of bald-headed girls, but I didn't see Lindsay, and no one was obscured by an open umbrella. That made me nervous. Still, I was heartened in one way. I was still standing. Maybe now that I'm out of the house and out of Meri's sight, she's forgotten about me (I know, I know, but I can dream). Beyond canceling my lunch card and telling all of my professors to fail me, nothing else has happened.

I practically flew back to Bud's room at six. Time quickened as I waited for the three rings. My mind was fritzing out, leap-frogging from one negligible thought to the next: Will Clay Aiken ever come out of the closet? Has Patty ordered a pizza (I hope so, because I'm hungry)? How will I explain this semester's grades to Dad? In years to come, will Lisa be as "gettable" as Toni Tennille? I was barely breathing at 7:29. My eyes were glued to my Timex. I counted the seconds. Finally, at seven thirty on the dot, three astounding rings! I wanted to jump up and down and scream for joy, but I knew I couldn't risk alerting anyone (namely Gloria or Meri) who might be monitoring Bud's room surveillance. The next half hour was painful, but I calmed myself by organizing Bud's CD collection. All of his music is stolen off the Internet except for his

Kylie Minogue CD, which he actually paid for because he thinks Kylie's "doable." Honestly, she's pretty and everything, but it is kind of weird watching a thirty-seven-year-old woman prance around half-naked in videos like she's a teenager or something, and "Can't Get You Out of My Head" is definitely up there with "Mmmbop" in terms of highly annoying pop songs, but then what do I know? "Tune My Motor Up" has climbed to number thirty-seven on KCCA's all-request playlist.

I was unusually calm right before eight p.m. I was Spy Girl Barbie. I was once more on a mission. I opened the door just a crack and peeked out into the hallway. The coast was clear. Quick as a rabbit, I darted down the hall, slammed myself against the wall as I neared the corner, took a peek, then turned the corner and stepped right up to Patty's door. I knocked quickly but firmly. The door swung open and I nearly screamed with delight at the sight of a bald-headed Lindsay, who pulled me inside and shut the door. We jumped up and down, holding each other, giggling and laughing.

"Shh. There's mics in the hallway," exclaimed Patty.

I calmed myself. I couldn't believe it. The room was jammed. There were Patty and Pigboy (holding hands, so sweet), and Randy was writing furiously in his notebook, and Nester was taking pictures, and Bud was just sitting there (looking stupid), and Lindsay was opening up several to-go bags, revealing a Long John Silver's dinner for everyone. I almost started to cry, but then I realized that someone was missing. Then there was a knock and I swung open the door and there was Keith and I couldn't help it, I was all over him (and he didn't seem to mind). I could only vaguely hear Randy and Nester chiming in behind me.

"Those two are doing it."

"Doin' it and doin' it and doin' it, yeah!"

"Have you missed me as much as I've missed you?" whispered Keith in my ear.

"Impossible," I squealed, sounding superdumb and way too girly, but I couldn't help it.

"Hush Puppies are getting cold," said Patty cheerfully.

Keith and I extricated ourselves from each other long enough to eat dinner. And to listen intently to "The Plan," though frustratingly, most of it's being kept from me for reasons of security. Everyone in the room is involved. The target date for bringing down Meri is the twelfth, this coming Sunday, at Alpha Beta Delta's Captain & Tennille Oktoberfest Dance, though a number of maneuvers will be going into play well before then. Everyone was talking at once, but I couldn't understand a thing. Why did Nester need to round up more than thirty-seven cameras? And what did that have to do with *The Matrix*? And why was it so important for Pigboy to become "friendly" with Walter McCall, a Trinidad student who's also known as "DJ Mo Ghee" (he thinks "Lissa" is "wack," so I'm inclined to like him no matter what he'll be doing). My involvement is apparently crucial on Friday the tenth, and for that I'll need to shave my head on a regular basis so no one will suspect anything (not that there's all that much to shave).

"The entire house is going to Vegas the night before," said Lindsay urgently. "We're scheduled to fly back on the tenth at around noon, so you'll have to make sure you're done before then."

Then she handed me a copy of Alpha Beta Delta's front door key. But the plan made no sense. I'm supposed to scurry into the house on the tenth before noon, preferably before eight a.m. so no one's around, and then steal the Hoover File, the digital camera with pictures of Dean Pointer and me, and a mound of DAT surveillance tapes, which Lindsay has confirmed from a loose-lipped sister are all neatly arranged and catalogued in Meri's walk-in closet.

"That's impossible," I said, explaining the obvious obstacle.

For a moment everyone was stumped—but it was Keith who came

up with the solution. I shudder to write it down. I don't think I can.

The meeting was too short. After we were done with dinner, Patty told us we all had to leave since she was concerned that Meri or Gloria or their spies might become suspicious that they're not picking up me or Keith or anybody else on any room surveillance.

"We can't compromise our safe house," she explained, and she was right.

Still, I had to ask, "Why am I still standing?"

And by that I meant, why hasn't Meri reduced me to roadkill? After all, as I pointed out, Induced Anxiety Syndrome had hardly been a success, so what was stopping her from completely destroying me?

"You're the mouse and she's the cat," shrugged Lindsay, and Patty agreed wholeheartedly.

It makes sense, I guess. Why kill me when I'm such an easy and enjoyable thing to toy with? But there was no time for reflection. It was time to go. I didn't care that other people were watching. I kissed Keith right on the lips. Then I shrieked. Oh my God, he lifted me up in his arms, carried me into Patty's bathroom, slammed the door, and we totally made out and I thought, *Holy moly, are we going to have sex in the bathroom and isn't that a little tacky and don't his shoulders feel strong and am I a freak or does it kind of feel nice with his hands brushing against the peach fuzz on my head and was it my imagination or does this bathroom look spotless and does Pigboy's true love inspire Patty to clean and can I please keep kissing Keith forever and ever and ever?* There was a gentle knock at the door.

"Time's up, sweet lovers," said Patty sensitively.

Keith left first, looking both ways before he darted out into the hall.

"He's into you big-time," said Pigboy jauntily.

He was also casually dumping all of the empty Long John Silver's trays and cups into a garbage bag while Patty gazed at him adoringly. Is Pigboy enabling Patty by cleaning up for her? And who threw away all the Mallomars and corn chips and cookies and beef jerky? Is Patty now any less "fascinated" with all of her psychological ailments? Will she now go to a psychologist instead of telling everything to her friends (a thought: Do people see psychologists so they don't have to bore their friends)? Or is the love of Pigboy a cure-all? Probably not. I don't think Keith has "cured" me of anything—I still feel semi-lousy and confused about myself—but he does make me happier and give me hope. For the first time in my life, I can see a light at the end of the tunnel, and even if I don't make it to the light, or whatever that light's supposed to be, I now know that it's there. Maybe that's love's greatest gift. Hope. That and Keith's amazing six-pack. Ha!

The hallway wasn't empty when I turned the corner to Bud's room, but it didn't matter—no one saw me step out of Patty's. Unfortunately, Bud was ready for me when I closed the door behind me. He flipped a switch, and this huge, oversize electric shaver was vibrating in his hand. He made a shushing sound, then pointed to my head. I knew what he meant. It was time to shave my head. I slumped into a chair, and I was glad that he wasn't a complete klutz about it. In fact, he was very gentle. But Bud is Bud, and for the benefit of whoever might be listening to the room surveillance, he announced, "Ooo, baby, I like it when you shave me down there. Makes it look bigger, huh? Doesn't it? Huh?"

He nudged me.

"No, it still looks tiny," I said—and loudly enough to be heard over the razor. "Like a golf pencil."

He grimaced. He was finished with the left side of my head. He turned off the razor, situated himself to my right, then flipped it back on, adding, "Mmm, that's hot. Just a nice little landing strip for you, babe. S-o-o-o-o hot."

Okay, that was enough of that. I punched him in the balls.

Hard. He yelped, dropping the razor. I snatched it back up. I could finish the front part myself. He was crumpled in pain, so he couldn't object when I kept talking, and loudly.

"Oh, Bud, I'm so glad you're doing this for me. Once we finish with your arms, let's do your legs. Then you can wear my pantyhose."

I was done. I clicked off the razor. Bud was still writhing in pain, so I made some microwave popcorn and cracked open a Dr Pepper for him, which seemed to make him feel a lot better.

It's late at night again. I really should try to get some sleep. Tomorrow morning Lindsay will somehow get me the address, and then Keith and I will be off in his Range Rover. I can't get into Meri's room or her closet on the tenth without Meri knowing unless I have a key. And the only one who has a copy of it is Mamacita.

# October 8

## Dear Diary:

Mamacita lives large. It was barely four in the morning in Oakville, a wealthy suburb two towns over from RU, when Keith and I saw what seemed to be a fantastic modified Greek temple at the end of a leafy cul-de-sac.

"Sure you got the right address?" he asked.

I looked down at the scribbled address Lindsay had passed off to Randy, who passed it on to Bud, who had given it to me. It took me a moment to focus. I was sitting shotgun next to Keith in his Range Rover, and thrilled to be with him, but I wasn't really awake, and I certainly wasn't looking forward to what I had to do.

"Yeah, that's what it says," I responded, again looking at the address.

"Maybe she works for the family there."

"Uh-uh. Lindsay says she lives here. This is her home."

It was still dark out, but Keith clicked off his headlights and drove up slowly for a closer look. What was a housemaid—one who could barely walk—doing in such a colossal home? And on what looked like three acres of property?

"I have a feeling Mamacita's not just a maid," I said with a quiver.

I'm not sure why, but my stomach began to rumble with fear. I really did not want to go into Mamacita's house, but what choice did I have? Keith is scheduled to go before the board of trustees next week, and if nothing is done to clear his name, I know in my gut that he'll be asked to leave RU. *Get a hold of yourself,* I thought, *be a heroine: See the injustice, take decisive action.*

"I'm going in," I said firmly.

The plan was simple, at least in theory: Sneak into the house while Mamacita is sleeping, find her large set of color-coded keys, and take the one for Meri's room. Since we don't want Mamacita to alert Meri, I'd have to be careful not to be seen, and if there was time, Keith wanted me to remove Meri's pink key-cap and put it on another key. That way, if Mamacita noticed a key missing, she'd think it was someone else's. Keith handed me a cell phone set on vibrate. He would remain outside and keep watch and alert me by phone if there was trouble. He held me close.

"Lindsay told me she's practically blind and can hardly walk," he said, attempting to reassure me. "And she's sleeping. She won't hear a thing."

I had to agree with that. Maybe I was getting all worked up for nothing. Keith gently kissed me—and all my fears just melted away. I've never considered myself a heroine, but I was prepared to be one for Keith.

Crickets were chirping when I stepped out of the Range Rover and stealthily made my way to the back of Mamacita's house (or mansion, or temple, or whatever it is). I stopped short. I could hear music—whiplash dance music thumping-thumping-thumping. Crouching low, I crawled up for a closer look. Through a large picture window, I saw a huge bank of video monitors, all of them tuned to various business and stock reports, and two silhouetted figures that seemed to bound up and down before them. Needless to say, I was confused. I maneuvered myself closer. What I saw nearly made me turn right back around and run for my life. There was this really huge buff guy (even bigger than Keith) who was obviously some sort of trainer, and next to him was Mamacita, furiously jogging in place and lifting immense free weights, while keeping a beady eye on the NASDAQ and S&P streams behind her. How was this possible? For gosh sakes, I carried her up the stairs to Meri's room. I probably should have turned around. I imagined a solution. I had a quick vision of myself swinging an ax at Meri's door. But I also had a quick vision of Keith behind prison bars. *Pull it together, Cindy,* I thought. Whatever the story is with Mamacita, she still has the keys, and she's obviously occupied at the moment, so it shouldn't be that big a deal to sneak inside and swipe Meri's. I saw a back door entry between two large columns to my right. If I was lucky, the door would be open and the house alarm would be off, since Mamacita had already welcomed her trainer in.

Quick as a mouse, I ran diagonally across the back lawn and swung open the back door (it wasn't locked!). I took a moment to orient myself, and I attempted to think logically. The keys were more than likely upstairs, maybe in Mamacita's bedroom. I didn't think they'd be just lying around somewhere downstairs in the kitchen or something. The disco music was still thumping-thumping, so I needed to act fast. I took off my tennis shoes, held them in my hands, and quickly tiptoed across the polished marble floor, passing the living room as inconspicuously as possible. Mamacita was now on the floor lifting her right knee to her right shoulder, grunting loudly, with her trainer crouched before her. So far so good. The grand staircase was before me. I darted up the stairs two at a time. Then I nearly screamed when I saw two Great Danes bounding forth at the top of the landing. I froze. And so did they. I didn't know what to do. No one told me I'd be fighting off Great Danes. Still, they weren't attacking (yet), they were just standing there, staring at me, standing guard. I gulped and continued up the stairs, well aware that one of the Great Danes was beginning to growl and bare its teeth. Finally, I was right before them, and I thought, *Go on, do it, put me out of my misery, kill me,* and then I felt something wet. One of them was licking my hand. They were either the lousiest guard dogs around or they were very friendly. I patted them each on the head, skirted past, and made my way to the master bedroom.

Someday I'd like to have a bedroom like Mamacita's. I took a moment to gaze at all the beautiful Greek statues, some of which were spouting water from appropriate holes, and the large Mexican mural reproductions, and the oversize bed, which seemed large enough to house a family of four. But no key chain. Nothing. I couldn't even find a closet. Frustrated, I meant to race out when I slipped on the gleaming floor and violently flew forward, slamming against a winged satyr statue and clipping its outstretched arm—which suddenly fell downward with a mechanical *ka-chink.* Behind me, Mamacita's large reproduction of José Clemente Orozco's truly dazzling ancient Mayan mural swung open, revealing what you could call a walk-in closet, but honest, that really wouldn't do it justice. *Move it, Cindy,* I told myself, *you're not here for a house tour.* I slipped into the "closet," and when I turned the corner, I saw a small office area. On a desk lay an open ledger, and hanging above the desk on the wall was the key chain!

It was done! Meri's room key was in my pocket, and I was just putting her pink key-cap on another key when I noticed that the disco music downstairs had stopped. I panicked for a moment. How long had Mamacita's workout been over? My heart was beating in my throat. I hung the key chain back up and dashed out of the closet—and I screamed. There was Mamacita at the far end of the bedroom crouched in a fierce karate pose.

"*Puta disimulada!*" she bellowed.

I meekly fumbled, "Hi, I'm just here, um, because Meri wants you to clean her room again this month. Are you busy today?"

"*Usted morirá, puta!*" she shrieked.

Obviously, she wasn't buying.

"I'm leaving now," I offered, my entire body shaking. "I'll tell Meri you'll get back to her."

Then I ran like the dickens, screaming loudly because from the corner of my eye I could see Mamacita soaring through the air, and before I knew what was happening, I was flat on my stomach, and she was on top of me, jerking my arms back in a painful hold, and I thought, *That's it, I'm dead, killed by a tiny little Mexican woman with really powerful glutes,* but then I heard a shattering crash and a savage screech, and one of Mamacita's large ceremonial Mayan bowls was shattered before me.

"You okay?" asked Keith desperately.

Since Mamacita's so tiny, Keith didn't have much of a problem fitting her into his clothes trunk when we got back to RU, but it was still difficult given that she's so powerfully squirmy—and that's despite the fact that Keith had tied her up and taped her mouth shut before leaving her house and placing her in the back of his Range Rover. He had seen her trainer leaving the house, so he knew something was up, but as he snapped the trunk closed, and it vibrated from Mamacita's fierce writhing, I couldn't help but blurt out, "What now?!"

A half hour later Mamacita was propped up in a chair in Patty's room, and Patty, Keith, and I still didn't know whether or not we should take the tape off her mouth, but Patty was worried. What if she was thirsty? What if she was hungry? I figured quick was better than slow. I ripped the tape off her mouth.

"*Usted morirá, puta!*" she howled.

"You are dead, whore," said Patty, helpfully translating.

I clamped my hand over her mouth. What if her screams could be heard outside in the hall?

"You have to be quiet," I warned. "We're not going to hurt you."

I slowly pulled my hand away, and she didn't scream. Instead, she burst into tears and began softly babbling. It was quite a performance, or at least it seemed to be. Patty's Spanish isn't that good, but she did recognize the word for "police," which made Keith chuckle.

"Yeah, let's go to the police," he said, whipping out Mamacita's ledger. Before we left the house, he had snatched it from her office. "Maybe we'll give them this."

"Don't mess with me, buddy!" roared Mamacita, who suddenly seemed to speak English remarkably well, but Keith wasn't scared by her viciousness.

Instead he lifted the phone and began to dial the Rumson River police. Given his own predicament, he knows the number by heart.

"Okay, hang up," said a suddenly resigned Mamacita, who was ready to talk deal.

Fine, we could have Meri's key, and she would agree to be held captive in Patty's room until our mission was complete, but in turn, we had to agree not to give or show her ledger to anyone. It seems Mamacita's been playing the role of a frail Mexican maid for decades, and she's worked, and continues to work, for some of the richest and most powerful families in the state. A quick study, she soon figured out how to shave a small, undetectable sum from each of their accounts every month, which she wires to her offshore accounts. But the money doesn't just sit there. After taking several night school classes and devoting herself to the work of Ben Stein, she's become a very capable investment whiz. Yes, Mamacita lives well, but she's also regarded as Santa Mamacita in several small Mexican villages, including Jalisco, Nayarit, and Sinaloa, where she provides revolving funds for education and health care, and even surreptitiously provided all of the funds necessary to rebuild several towns after the merciless Hurricane Kenna destroyed them. La Caridad de Santa Mamacita, one of her numerous charitable trusts, offers complete college scholarships and has sponsored several archaeological digs over the years. As she told us this, she couldn't help but spit at Keith, who had knocked her out with a Mayan bowl that was, in fact, not a reproduction but a priceless artifact. She also wasn't the least bit interested in hearing about Meri, or what we had planned for her, since she doubted that the loss of any funds she was still shaving from various Sugarman accounts would put that much of a dent into her ever-increasing fortune. All she wanted was our assurance that she would be given back her ledger and let go after our mission was done.

"I don't know you, you don't know me," she said. "But you mess with me, you're in big trouble."

We didn't doubt that.

"Who's got a smoke?" she snapped, which turned out to be only the first of several demands.

Still, she was thrilled when Keith gave her a cigar, and she took a moment to whisper to me, "Nice boy. Seems good for you. But grow your hair. Boys don't like girls who look like boys."

I don't know how I got through the rest of the day. It's just after dinner now and I'm so tired (I brought Mamacita Long John's for dinner and she said she'd rather eat cardboard). Bud wants to shave me again, but honest, if he comes near me with that thing again, I really will kill him.

# October 9

## Dear Diary:

All of a sudden, it felt like a thousand prickly things were poking me in the behind as I walked to my last class before lunch.

"Woof, woof."

I gulped, but I kept walking.

"Aw, don't run away."

The town car swerved up to my side. There was Meri, in her black bouffant (and blessed) wig, and an eerily bald Gloria (her eyes totally bug out now). Though they seemed very chatty, like maybe they had been doing cocaine again, they were sharing a large Negroni Sbagliato, which Meri informed me is a popular summer cocktail in Milan (with Spumante, vermouth, and Campari, which does sound kind of good). They were also popping a few pills, which Meri pointed out were Provogil, a drug intended to treat narcolepsy, though Meri swears they're the "loveliest" pick-me-up. In a way, I should have felt okay about seeing them. I mean, I do know something that they don't know (many things), I do have a safe house, I am plotting against them, but just the sound of Meri's voice was flipping me out.

"Enjoying your last semester at RU?" she asked cheerfully. "I'll miss you, Cindy. Really. You've been fun. Just remember to be a good little bow-wow these past few weeks, okay? Because if you're not . . ."

"Why does Keith have to go to jail?" I blurted, and I immediately regretted it.

"Why? Hmm. That sounds like a question for the police. He did break the law, right? Several, I think."

"One Varsity Ken bites the dust," snorted Gloria.

"Oh well. It really is a tragedy. But what's done is done. Why? Do you still have feelings for Keith?"

I knew I was on very thin ice at the moment, so I answered carefully. I shrugged.

"Not really. I mean, he's just another dumb jock when you get down to it. I was just curious."

"Don't be too curious, little bow-wow."

I was about to speak when I heard two low-flying helicopters soaring overhead. Meri smiled.

"Oops. We'll have to cut this short. We're going for a quickie to Vegas. Ever been?"

"No."

"Oh, you should. Vegas is fun. Want to come? Come on. For old times' sake. What do you think? You want to?"

Oh God. How was I going to get out of this? If I went to Vegas, all of Patty's plans would be ruined, and who knows what would happen to Keith. But I didn't want to be caught "refusing" or "disagreeing" with Meri. So I just tried to shrug it off.

"Well, you know, I'm sure I'd just bore you."

Meri exchanged a glance with Gloria, who rolled her eyes in a kind of you've-so-got-to-be-kidding way. Meri turned back to me.

"You're right," she said airily. "You're boring me now. Be good, little bow-wow. 'Cause we'll find out if you're not."

And off they went. I continued onward toward my next class and tried not to think about Meri, but I couldn't help it—it's like my mind kept cycling back to her, and she kept getting bigger and scarier and I was getting smaller and more pathetic and even more helpless. I remember hearing once that the more energy or thought you give to something, the bigger it gets, whether it's a good thing or a bad thing. I was definitely giving Meri too much thought, and she is definitely a bad thing, but I couldn't help it. It's like my whole life is on a slippery slope, and the more I try to climb to the top, and the higher I get, the more inevitable it becomes each time I slip and fall back—where Meri sits, Buddha-like, patiently waiting for me, mocking my every attempt to escape from her. It really isn't fair. My mind is a trap.

Then I remembered my Pledge Week supplies. I'd kept several of the items, including the Xanax, and I remember Patty once telling me that Xanax is a popular anti-anxiety drug. That sure sounded good to me. I am so not one for popping pills, but anti-anxiety, anti-Meri; they were one and the same in that moment. I took a detour before going to my class, rifled through my things in Bud's room, and practically wept with delight when I found that I still had the bottle. It had warnings on the label: Do not take with alcohol, do not take while operating heavy machinery. The recommended dosage was one in the morning and one in the evening, as needed, but I figured since it was late afternoon, and since I really did feel anxious, I should probably take three.

About a half hour later in class, I suddenly felt very creamy—there really is no other way to describe it. My thoughts had stopped racing, and even my arms and legs felt loose, as if I'd been clenching something really tight for years and suddenly let go of it. Before my mind was a trap. Now it was frothy and lightly whipped; it was meringue. In fact, I nodded off and awoke a few minutes later. Oops. I had slipped from my seat and right onto the floor, which didn't amuse my professor and, of course, elicited the sort of derisive giggles and snorts that I have long grown accustomed to, but the laughter didn't feel stinging like it usually does. Why? Because I truly didn't care.

Tomorrow morning is "D-day," as Patty calls it, and I think I'm more than ready for the challenge now that I'm just so completely relaxed. Meri who? Oh, yes. Her. BFD. Ha! I've set my alarm for six a.m., since I'd like to sneak into the house no later than eight. I think I'll take a few more Xanax just to make sure my mind is calm and I get a good night's sleep. I deserve it.

# October 10

## Dear Diary:

Oh my God, oh my God, oh my God, oh my God! The day began horrendously. I was awakened violently by Bud, who shook my shoulders and even slapped my face (I'll bet he enjoyed that part).

"Do you know what time it is?!" he wailed. "You don't want to be late for your first class today, do you?"

He said that last part for the benefit of whoever might be listening, but honest, I was so disoriented, I didn't know what was going on. I guess I took too much Xanax last night, because when I looked at my alarm clock, I was astounded to see that it was eleven o'clock. If Meri and the girls were already back from Vegas, I thought, then everything's ruined! I hurled the covers aside and tried to pull myself together quickly. Luckily, I don't have to bother with my hair these days, so I just tossed off my nightgown and changed into my regular clothes—realizing, as I raced to the door, that Bud had just seen me completely naked. This was not a good omen, and as I walked/ran down the dorm hall to the stairway (I didn't want to attract attention by full-out running), I couldn't get Bud's leering face out of my head; it was big, like the moon, and his mouth was luridly gaping. Eeeow! *Focus*, I told myself as I darted inconspicuously across campus toward Alpha Beta Delta. Then I panicked for a sec. Did I have everything? I reached surreptitiously into my pocket. Phew. I had Mamacita's key. What I didn't have, and what I was supposed to have, was a large gym bag. How else was I supposed to transport the stacks and stacks of DAT tapes out of Meri's closet? And what about the Hoover File? Yes, it's supposedly just a single accordion file, but given that it was started in 1919, I kind of doubted that it was all in one neat little file. That just seemed too easy.

I didn't bother looking at my watch as I turned the corner to Alpha Beta Delta. I didn't want to know how late it was, or even think about any obstacles that I might encounter while trying to complete my mission. I did pause for a moment, though, and kind of "centered" myself (as they say on *Oprah*). I thought, *No one will be suspicious if they see a bald girl strolling into Alpha Beta Delta, since all the girls who live there are bald. That's why Patty and the gang assigned me this mission. I'll walk in, get what I need, and finally save Keith!* I couldn't believe how easy it was. The street in front was fairly empty— there were only a few students strolling past. I glanced at the driveway: There were no cars and certainly no helicopters. *Relax*, I thought, *this will be a cinch.* Smooth as pie, I walked up to Alpha Beta Delta's front door, casually swung it open, stepped inside, and closed it behind me.

I've only seen *Raiders of the Lost Ark* once (on cable when I was little), but it kind of felt like I was walking into some strange cave that any minute might send a huge boulder my way, or shoot tiny little arrow-type things from the wall. I felt even more apprehensive as I climbed the stairs, even though I kept thinking, *Calm down. No one is here. No one will hurt you.* But because this was a place where I had endured so much pain and anguish, it felt like it was filled with ghosts and whispery voices. There was Meri-Ghost, screaming "Handsies-kneesies!" Gloria-Ghost was barking at me, "Woof, woof." Even Shanna-Francine-Ghost unnerved me, because she kept smiling toothsomely, as if everything were normal, when clearly it was not. As I arrived on the second-floor landing, I imagined Lindsay's room suddenly filling with bright, scalding lights, and I heard her voice, too, futilely proclaiming, "I think *Far from Heaven* is original. And deep!"

I was sweating as I climbed the staircase to Meri's room. Meri-Ghost whispered in my ear. "Katie Couric was a sorority sister."

And then she hissed, "The demands I make on myself are absolutely fantastic!"

I finally reached the third-floor landing. I was shaking, and dizzy, too. Meri's door was only a few steps away. Like a zombie, I put one foot in front of the other while slowly pulling Mamacita's key from my pocket. Then in one quick move, I thrust the key forward, turned the lock, swung open the door, and stepped inside.

*Poof.* All my fear suddenly evaporated. It was like a big balloon had been pricked, just slightly, and its air was sputtering out. Everything looked the same. The same white carpeting, the same piecrust tables, everything. Only now everything looked small. I remember going back to my elementary school playground once when I was in junior high, and I was surprised to see that it looked puny, even though it loomed large in my memory; so many wedgies, so many losing games of four square. That's kind of how it felt in Meri's room. Her room had shrunk, and everything horrific that had happened there now seemed very far away. This would be easy. I buoyantly strode up to Meri's closet door, inserted Mamacita's key, and swung it open.

Things weren't exactly how I thought they'd be (it's certainly not as big as Mamacita's). There was the digital camera, and next to it a small stack of photos, a scanner, and a large paper shredder, and farther in, a computer with several unused CD-RW discs. What I didn't see was any kind of file folder, or any loose papers, and there wasn't a single DAT tape to be found anywhere. Finally I spotted something: a small black CD case. I unzipped it. Inside were about ten CDs, each carefully marked "HF, 1919–1930," "HF, 1930–1955," and on to the present. I finally figured it out. All the incriminating papers collected for the Hoover File over the years must have been scanned onto disc and then shredded. In my hands was the entire Hoover File for Alpha Beta Delta! I thanked my lucky stars for technology. Thanks to the computer age, I didn't need to bring a big gym bag with me after all. Still, I was concerned about what might be on the computer. As I've said, I'm no computer whiz, and I had a fleeting thought that I might be running out of time, so I just scrolled with the mouse to the "Special" pull-down menu until it hit "Erase Disc," then I double-clicked it. A message popped up: "Are you sure you want to erase the entire contents of your hard drive?"

I didn't hesitate. I clicked yes, then gathered the CD case, dart-ed out of the closet, and swung open the armoire, revealing DAT surveillance central. A red light was flashing. It was recording, but there were only a few whirring tapes inside. This did not bode well at all. It meant that there was no big collection of archived DAT tapes, it meant that Meri does, in fact, erase each day's recordings, which means that there is no surveillance or evidence to clear Keith's name. I was furious! My arms madly flung out before me; it felt like I was ripping Meri's insides out as I yanked the DAT tapes out of the machine. One by one I flung them to the floor and stomped on them, then I remembered the digital cam-era. I charged into the closet, threw it on the floor, and whacked it repeatedly with a large stapler until it was a mangled pile of metal and plastic and glass shards. I was really working up a good steam, and in my anger I saw a silver lining. I had the Hoover File. Now that I could prove the far-reaching blackmailing activities of Alpha Beta Delta, would it really be much of a stretch for the police to believe that Meri had framed Keith with drugs? I was about to leave the closet when something caught my eye: a stack of printed digital photos. I swiped them—and recoiled when I flipped through them. Either Dean Pointer and I weren't worthy of the Hoover File, or no one had bothered to scan these into the computer or onto a CD yet. Or maybe they had. It didn't really matter. I now had the entire Hoover File in my hand, along with the photos, and the computer's hard disc was completely erased. Ha! And yet I was troubled for the briefest of moments. Once again I saw Meri-Ghost standing before me, ominously whispering, "Closets should be emptied four times a year. Inspect every item. Seasonal clothes should be cleaned and put into storage."

Oh God. It was starting up again (maybe I should have taken a teensy-weensy bit of Xanax before I came to the house) (then again, I suppose I should watch it with that). I quickly stepped out of the closet. There was Shanna-Francine-Ghost standing in the doorway.

"What are you doing?" she gasped.

I closed my eyes for a moment, willing myself to become less anxious, muttering out loud.

"No one can hurt me anymore. I have the Hoover File. I don't have the tapes, but somehow I'll save Keith."

I opened my eyes, calmer, but Shanna-Francine-Ghost was still there.

"Oh my God, you've just committed suicide!" she wailed.

Behind me I heard a thunderous whipping sound. I whirled around. A helicopter was diving toward the house. Then I heard a scream—from Shanna-Francine-Ghost, only she wasn't a ghost. This was really happening! I screamed in horror and ran, violently body-checking Shanna-Francine. I flew down the stairs, out of the house, and onto the front lawn, suddenly falling flat on my face. I could hear Shanna-Francine's cries from above.

"She's got the Hoover File! She's got pictures!"

Before me was the first of the landing helicopters—and the stunned face of Gloria, who was just stepping out. My heart was exploding. I ran and ran, and I had no idea where I was going and my legs were moving so fast that it felt like the wind was thrashing my face and tears were streaking from my eyes, but not down my cheeks, they were streaking horizontally to my ears. Then I heard screams and hollering threats. I glanced over my shoulder. Gloria, Meri, and Shanna-Francine were running after me! Where to now? I ran across the Great Lawn, completely oblivious to the gaping stares. Where to now? I darted down an alleyway, whipped around the corner. They were still on me. I could hear them. They were gaining. They were closer. Where to now? I ran around another corner and pushed myself through a building front entrance, roughly knocked past a crowd of students. Where to now? I ran up a stairwell, faster and faster, and I could hear the echoey cries of Meri, Gloria, and Shanna-Francine below. Oh my God, where was I going, what was I doing? Would anyone come to my funeral? Will I be buried bald? Even if I'm dead, is there any way to stop Lisa from singing at my burial (she'll do it, I know she will, and she'll get lots of publicity and maybe even write me a tribute song)? I blindly ran down a hallway and into an empty classroom. Oh my God, what a mistake!

The door slammed behind me. I was in some sort of RU shop room. I know this because I suddenly heard the whirring of a chainsaw—a chainsaw being wielded by Gloria! Meri delicately whispered, "Don't fuck with us, little bow-wow. You might not mind missing a leg, but missing your head will be such a trial."

Gloria lunged forward. I yelped, leaping back. Meri hissed.

"Drop the CD case. Drop the pictures."

"Do what she says, Cindy. Like, this is so not worth losing your head over," wailed Shanna-Francine, who looked genuinely concerned for the first time ever. (Is this what it takes for Shanna-Francine to pay attention? A beheading?)

Where did I get the nerve? I screamed, "Drop the charges against Keith!"

"I don't think you're in a position to negotiate, little bow-wow."
She moved closer, her voice becoming newly acid and singsongy.

"Oh, it was awful. She broke into the house, she took some drugs. Everyone saw her running like a maniac across the Great Lawn. Then she came in here and we tried to pull the chainsaw from her hands, but she wouldn't let go, and it suddenly flipped back up and—oh God. An open casket is definitely out of the question. The Alpha Beta Delta Drug Rehabilitation Fund will surge with new donations. You won't die in vain."

"Go to hell," I roared.

But Meri wasn't going anywhere—and neither was Gloria. My life passed before me (that really does happen), and she lifted the chainsaw in a wide arc before me, ready to strike. Then I heard a sudden mechanical coughing—or burping, really—and in a flash, everyone knew what it meant. The chainsaw was out of gas. This was my moment. I leaped forth, knocking down Shanna-Francine, determined to race out the door to freedom. I had escaped death. I would not be beheaded. But maybe I would be fried. A blinding flash stopped me cold. Meri had lit a butane torch and she was running right toward me, screaming like a psycho (okay, not "like"; I'll go out on a limb here and just call her plain old psycho). I was trapped, there was nowhere to go, I was cornered. The torch swung right at my face and I screamed, holding up the CD case to protect myself—only to realize suddenly that I was now holding a large, fiery blob of melting plastic, and Meri's screams were more piercing than ever when she forcefully slammed into me. My body fell back, my arms went flying, and the fiery blob and pictures flew from my hands. I heard a crash behind me. Gloria screamed, "No fucking way!"

I was later told that it was quite a sight to see a large blob of burning plastic as it soared out of a sixth-story window. Students quickly dispersed. No one had any idea what it was. By the time the blob hit the ground, the fire was out, and it flattened like a pancake. Everything from the Hoover File, from 1919 to the present, was now reduced to a large, hot, bubbling plastic pancake. And tumbling from the sky after it, a bit slower, were a few eight-by-ten pictures of Dean Pointer and me. They fluttered down, finally landing on the ground before a demure pair of patent leather heels. Delicate, feminine hands picked them up. Oh my God, it was Louella Pointer, Dean Pointer's wife. She looked at the photos carefully, and seemed to have a small moment of shocked comprehension, but it didn't last very long. Seemingly out of nowhere, she was beamed by a football—*ka-pow*, right in the head—a football thrown by Keith Ryder! Talk about great aim! She tottered for a moment, then fell backward to the ground. She was out cold. Patty ran up to her and called for an ambulance on her cell phone, while Bud, of all people, quickly retrieved the photos, ripped them into shreds, and later burned them in a trash can.

But like I said, I didn't learn about all this till later. The crash from the window and Gloria's earsplitting scream gave me my moment. I ducked my head and ran, and if I'm not mistaken, even though she was standing near the doorway and could have blocked me, Shanna-Francine didn't move (what's that all about?). I flew down the stairs and ran outside and felt strong arms and hands as they engulfed my trembling body and stroked my bald head, which was thankfully still connected to my shoulders. I also saw Dean Pointer escorting a very rattled Louella to a waiting ambulance. She was babbling, "I saw a picture. I saw a dirty picture."

Everyone was in a grim mood back at the safe house. Yes, the Hoover File was now a thing of the past, but without the DAT tapes, proving Keith's innocence was looking next to impossible. Still, I did suggest that maybe I could finally move out of Bud's room, but Patty warned against it. I hadn't destroyed the DAT recording equipment, and even though I wasn't supposed to do that (I was just supposed to get all the tapes), the fact that Meri's surveillance was still active meant that we needed to keep our respective covers in place.

"You guys are screwed," chuckled Mamacita, who was smoking the last of Keith's cigars and wanted more.

Even worse, Meri still had a firm hold on the campus. Lindsay had gotten word to Patty. Meri does, in fact, keep DAT tapes of each day's surveillance (but where?), and she's put the word out to Dean Pointer, the board, and most of the professors: Alpha Beta Delta still has plenty of ammunition.

"She's bluffing," scoffed Pigboy.

He may be right, but everyone agreed that it was best to assume she wasn't.

"So now what?" I wailed.

I was so angry and exhausted. Everything we had done was for nothing. Keith gave me a kiss on the cheek and insisted I return to Bud's room to sleep while he and Patty and the rest of the group continued. Poor Keith. Valiant Keith. Even though his future is so bleak, he was thinking of me.

I'm in Bud's bed now. I can't think straight anymore. I did, however, get an e-mail from Lisa. She told me that Dad had tried to call me more than once at Alpha Beta Delta, but every time, someone laughed and hung up. I don't have the energy to respond to her right now.

# October 11

## Dear Diary:

It was a day of ups and downs. Mostly downs. I had a test in one of my classes, and after I completed it, Professor Macinhouser quietly told me that he'd be grading it "normally," which means that he won't automatically fail me. To my relief, it seemed like most of the professors were unimpressed with Meri's claim that she was still in power. Still, if they doubted it this morning, they were convinced this afternoon.

After lunch I was strolling past the Great Lawn when I saw Professor Hollingsworth being handcuffed and led into a squad car. He was later booked on a felony for selling cocaine. It took me a moment, but then I remembered that it was Bethany and Shanna-Francine who had gotten the goods on Professor Hollingsworth during Pledge Week—but not on paper, on tape, when they wore wires and posed as customers. Meri had sent the tape anonymously to the RRPD, and like a well-oiled PR machine, her words spread throughout the campus: The Hoover File had contained items of mostly historical interest, and while she was deeply saddened to see them go (and was especially dismayed to lose the first entry from Miss Anita Woolrich, Alpha Beta Delta's first president, who had started the file at the height of Prohibition), current information, on tape, was still very active and very useable.

I returned to Bud's room in the late afternoon. I had a notice waiting for me from the office of Dean Pointer. I am now officially on academic probation. Should my grades not significantly improve by the end of the semester, I will be barred from returning to RU. I sat there reading and rereading the notice. The walls started to close in. I had to get out of there.

I stepped outside, and I thanked my lucky stars that I still had two good legs to use, given yesterday's fiasco. I also saw a number of girls from Alpha Beta Delta, all of whom were wearing official "Captain & Tennille" Captain hats and passing out flyers. The Oktoberfest Dance tomorrow night is still a go (of course), only now the proceeds will be going toward the newly created "Alpha Beta Delta Historical Society." It was Shanna-Francine who handed me a flyer and explained.

"Meri wants Alpha Beta Delta to go, like, completely high-tech," she babbled. Then her face scrunched up. "Oh God, I really shouldn't be telling you this."

"You don't have to tell me anything," I wearily intoned, but of course she couldn't help herself.

Now, information collected from surveillance and future Hoover File contributions will be carefully catalogued and backed up to several master computers at three "undisclosed" bunker locations.

"It'll be, like, our own Library of Congress," she merrily chirped.

Naturally, such an effort will be expensive, and this year's Oktoberfest Dance will have the distinction of being the first Alpha Beta Delta event to contribute to this noble cause.

"You're coming, aren't you?" she urgently queried. "Toni Tennille's gonna be there. It's gonna be, like, s-o-o-o completely awesome."

I stared at her intently for a moment—at her wide-open pinwheel eyes, her toothsome smile. Ever since I'd joined Alpha Beta Delta, I'd wondered: Is she really this dumb? Or is it an act?

"Meri wants you to come. She said that we have you to thank

for our, um, oh God, how did she put it? Oh, okay, I remember. Our 'upgrading.'"

Upgrading is a three-syllable word, but it tumbled with great difficulty from Shanna-Francine's lips, as if it contained at least five. That sort of clinched it for me. She is, in fact, as dumb as I've always thought. Off she went, cheerfully passing out more flyers. It was a cloudy afternoon, but the sun shone brightly on Shanna-Francine, as I suppose it must on all people who are too dumb to know better and yet are somehow better off for it.

"Hey ya, girlfriend."

Bud abruptly embraced me from behind, and I nearly jerked around to slap him across the face when he leaned in and whispered in my ear, "Meeting at the safe house tonight, but Keith doesn't want you to come. Too risky. But he wanted me to tell you that we're still trying to figure something out."

I guess that should have cheered me up, but it didn't. It's two a.m. now and Bud is snoring (loudly), and here I am, once more unable to sleep. Should I go to the dance tomorrow night? Am I a glutton for punishment? Do I really want to see Toni Tennille performing live?

# October 12

## Dear Diary:

Oh my God! It's been a day of explosions—literal explosions! Early this evening, I heard a huge *ka-boom* inside RU's three-story Parking Garage East. Luckily, no one was hurt, and a few minutes later, when I stepped into the Captain & Tennille–themed Oktoberfest Dance (Lindsay was manning the door and comped me in), I did a double-take when I looked up at the DJ booth and saw DJ Mo Ghee with Pigboy and Patty—and Keith and Bud, too. What was going on? What were they doing there?

"Oh God, I really shouldn't be telling you this," blurted Shanna-Francine when she poured me a cocktail later.

Lindsay assured her that she could, in fact, tell me absolutely anything she wanted now. They both could. The dance was over. It was all over.

"Okay, well, let's put it this way," she said, leaning in to whisper. "Let's just say that Dean Pointer didn't give a shit anymore."

Why? Because someone made an anonymous call to him early this morning, saying, "Meri's got nothing on you."

Then whoever it was hung up. It dawned on Dean Pointer that the caller could be right. Meri no longer had the damning pictures of him in bed with me, and even better, all the "goods" that she previously had on him were from 1998—when an industrious pledge gathered evidence that proved he had deliberately passed two failing football players in order to keep them playing for RU's team. Dean Pointer is a gambling man, and he decided to operate on the assumption that this evidence, which has long kept him under the thumb of Alpha Beta Delta, had been destroyed in that flying plastic pancake. The more he thought about it, the angrier he got. In fact, he got so angry that he tore through his house, hurled his couch covers, pulled up the carpeting, and soon found several hidden mics. In his office on campus, he found several more after he unscrewed his phone receiver and tore apart the lamp shades. Was this enough, he wondered? Did he really have enough to make a very special phone call?

He had more than enough. Or so it seemed. Later that afternoon, RRPD swarmed into Alpha Beta Delta with a search warrant and quite literally ripped the house apart. Meri wasn't there, and neither was Shanna-Francine. The only ones there were Lindsay, who anxiously stepped aside, and Gloria, who was loudly protesting. She had no idea what the police were talking about. This was an outrage. What mics? What recordings? Surely they had the wrong house. She didn't even blink when they swung open Meri's armoire, revealing her DAT recording equipment.

"So?" shrugged Gloria.

This proved nothing. There was nothing being recorded. There were no incoming signal antennas. There were no tapes. What "tapes" were they talking about? There was nothing anywhere in the house to connect the mics to Alpha Beta Delta. Wiretapping charges? Please. What were they talking about? Frustrated, the police continued to rip apart the house and even pulled up the floorboards in both Meri's room and the living room. By that time Gloria had called Meri on her cell phone, who in turn called the Sugarman family attorney. Quicker than you can say "harassment," "illegal search and seizure," and "defamation," the police received orders from their superiors to immediately vacate the premises.

"Bye," said Gloria, giving a wave. "And remember, boys, Alpha Beta Delta is a contributor to the Rumson River Police Department's Benevolent Society."

A few hours later Meri got the all-clear from Gloria and returned to the house. She shared a good, hearty laugh with Gloria and a somewhat jittery Lindsay. Talk about luck. Only yesterday, as part of Alpha Beta Delta's surveillance modernization, and in anticipation of its new, "undisclosed" bunker surveillance and data storage headquarters, the current DAT surveillance system had been shut down, and all the incoming antennas and wiring in the house had been removed. Meri smiled, smartly adjusting her black bouffant wig.

"Whoever did this will pay. Big-time. Good job, guys. What did you do with the tapes?"

"They're gone," said Gloria proudly.

Meri raised an eyebrow.

"What do you mean, 'gone'?"

It seems there was more good luck for Meri. The DAT tapes have long been archived in Shanna-Francine's room (I never would have thought to look there), and this morning, fearful that they might somehow be discovered and used against the house, Shanna-Francine gathered all of them in one large box and took off. Meri bolted up.

"What do you mean, 'took off'?"

Lindsay noticed that Gloria seemed to visibly shrink. She had thought she was being prudent. She had approved of Shanna-Francine's plan. The mishap with the Hoover File could have proved disastrous. It could even have brought down the house for good. By now, she submissively intoned, Shanna-Francine had more than likely destroyed the box and all of the DAT tapes inside of it.

The sun was setting at RU's Parking Garage East, and Shanna-

Francine was on the roof when she heard several bloodcurdling, high-pitched screams in the distance. Was someone calling her name? Setting aside the large plastic gasoline can that she had brought along with her, she stepped to the edge of the roof and looked down. Below, Meri and Gloria were running to the garage— and Gloria pointed straight up at her, calling out, "Don't move!"

Meri was having a lot of luck today. She and Gloria ran up to the rooftop and were flat-out astonished to see that they had arrived just in the nick of time. Before them was the box of tapes, a plastic can of gasoline, and Shanna-Francine, who stood dumb-struck holding a matchbook in her hands.

"Don't burn them!" howled Meri. "Those tapes are my history. My oral history."

She greedily hefted the box and charged angrily down the stairs.

"This could have been a catastrophe," she said, her anger rising. "I'll be punishing you both. I don't know how yet, but I will— and it won't be pleasant."

Stepping out of the garage, she barked orders. "Cigarette."

Gloria gulped, gently placing a cigarette to Meri's lips.

"What? I'm supposed to light it myself?"

Shaking, Shanna-Francine lit a match, brought it to the tip of Meri's cigarette, then hurled it over her shoulder. Oops. It seems Shanna-Francine was holding the plastic can at a slight angle; it had dribbled a trail of gasoline when they walked from the rooftop to the ground below. Behind them, they heard a violent *ka-boom*. Meri spotted the ignited trail.

"Run!" she cried.

The girls ran for their lives, then leaped in the air and crashed to the ground. Behind them, there was a series of violent explosions from inside the parking garage—*boom-boom-boom*—one after another, until the entire complex was engulfed in flames and blackening smoke. With a sigh, Meri stood up, dusted herself off, and shrugged.

"My car's not parked there."

Then her eyes popped out of her head.

"Wait a minute," she bellowed, looking down at the felled box and all of the tapes that had tumbled out of it.

"Those are 8-track tapes. Where are my tapes?"

Then she laughed, and Gloria joined in. Thank God for Shanna-Francine's ineptitude. To think, the real tapes might have been burned. Then, as if she were talking to an especially dense third grader, Meri turned to Shanna-Francine and very slowly spoke.

"Everything's okay now. You did good. But we don't want those tapes. We want the other tapes. Where are they?"

Shanna-Francine was awfully confused.

"Well, um, let's see," she said, trying to figure it out. She pointed to the 8-tracks. "I thought this box had the other tapes and the other box had these tapes. Right?"

"Good, you're doing good," said Meri encouragingly. "Where's the other box?"

"Okay. Um. Okay, let me think. See, those are the 8-tracks. And they're all Captain & Tennille. Which means I must have given the other box to the DJ this morning. You know, for the dance? Oh my God, like DJ Mo Ghee is s-o-o-o cute."

I should have known something was up when Lindsay blithely comped me into the dance tonight, but I was still so depressed, and I was a bit shaken by the sight of that very strange explosion I saw on my way over. And it made no sense at all when I saw everyone up in the booth with DJ Mo Ghee. I practically leaped out of my skin when I heard bellowing screams and hollers behind me.

Meri and Gloria angrily pushed forth.

"Where is he?" bellowed Meri, but the music was so loud ("You Better Shop Around," which is one of the few songs I like from the

Captain & Tennille songbook), that I could barely make out what she was saying. She stepped closer, seething. "Where is he?"

"Where's who?" I asked.

"The fucking DJ."

Was this a trick question? "Uh, why don't you try the DJ booth?" I pointed. Meri jerked her head up—and DJ Mo Ghee blew her a kiss. And so did Patty and Pigboy and Bud. Suddenly, blaring from the speakers, and mixed perfectly to the house beat that DJ Mo Ghee had added to "You Better Shop Around," was an unmistakable voice. It was Meri's voice, chopped up and staccato.

> *You're my little bow-wow. Bow-wow.*
> *You're my little bow-wow. Bow-wow.*

Meri stood at the center of the dance floor, rooted to the spot, the color draining from her face. The song's beat hit double-time, and the voices intermingled (beautifully, I might add; he is a good DJ), adding more words and phrases.

> *Never told you to do anything illegal.*
> *Never told you. Never told you. Never told you.*
> *Plant drugs in Keith's locker.*
> *Keith's locker. Keith's locker.*
> *We can do a hit on Rags.*
> *Rags. Rags. Rags.*

By now the crowd was catching on, and so were the professors, all of whom had been too afraid not to attend. But they weren't afraid now. They were euphoric. An unhinged giddiness was spreading. You could tell that Meri wanted to run. But where? The crowd was closing in on her and the music was getting louder, and the voices were increasing in both beat and variety. It was a sort of "Best of Meri" house mix, with each clip more damning than the next.

> Blackmail. Woof-woof.
> Let's make crystal.
> Bow-wow. I run this school.
> Woof-woof. Fuck the dean.
> Bow-wow. Run this school.
> Run this school. Run this school.

And then the most fantastic sight; it's almost impossible to describe. It was as if everyone decided to move at once, including Nester and Randy, who had previously placed countless digital cameras in a strategic circle all throughout the hall. Now I understood what everyone was talking about in the safe house when they mentioned *The Matrix*. At just the right moment—in tandem with the suddenly surging crowd—Randy gave the signal, and Nester hit a remote switch, igniting the cameras to take flash pictures one second after another. The result was a cacophony of blinding flashes that swirled over and over in a whiplash-fast circle around the entire crowd. But no one noticed. They were diving for Meri. I covered my mouth in horror. She screamed, then vanished, consumed by the maddening throng, and then she was flung violently into the air, her hands reaching vainly for the heavens, while others clawed at her body, her face. She screamed like a hellcat. This was power destroyed, a monster vanquished! Then the flashes were extinguished, the song abruptly ended, and the crowd, as if jointly awakening from some sort of supernatural reverie, slowly stepped back. Meri was gone. Was the nightmare really over? How could it be? Meri always wins. A sudden, familiar musical vamp blasted from the speakers, and a spotlight whipped to the stage where a performer cheerfully began singing.

*Love, love will keep us together*
*Think of me, babe, whenever*
*Some sweet-talking guy comes along, singing his song . . .*

It was like a dream. Keith's arms engulfed me, and then he whirled me to the dance floor. We were the only ones dancing, and as he held me close, I looked up. It was really her! Oh my God, Toni Tennille was really here—and in darn good voice, I might add.

*When the others turn you off*
*who'll be turning you on*
*I will, I will, I will, I will*
*Be there to share forever*
*Love will keep us together . . .*

One by one, we were joined by more couples, including Patty and Pigboy, and a large group of giggling Abercrombie & Fitch boys too—you know, the clean-cut guys with really short haircuts (okay, I finally "get" them now; boy, am I slow or what)? Soon everyone was dancing, but this was no ordinary college dance. It was a freedom dance! Now I have everything I've ever wanted—a supergreat boyfriend, great friends—but I have something else, too. I have me. And the best part is, I don't have to "pretend" to be something that I'm not anymore. I'll probably always have moments of loneliness, along with times when I feel like a complete loser, but at least I'll know that's not the whole picture.

When the song was over, I allowed Keith to lead me outside. The fresh air was intoxicating. Everything was twinkling; the stars, the lights, and of course, Keith's eyes.

"It's all over," he sweetly enthused, kissing my cheek. "She's gone."

That's when Patty stepped outside with Pigboy. She was

screaming and laughing, and I was laughing too, but the laughter kind of got stuck in the back of my throat. "It's all over." That's what Keith just said. But was it? Everyone around me was ready to celebrate, and yet I felt strangely unsatisfied. Yes, Meri was gone, and the nightmare was over for Alpha Beta Delta and Rumson U., but was that enough?

"What's up?" asked Keith, who could tell that I was distressed (he's so sensitive that way!).

I stood silently for a moment, formulating my thoughts, and then I stated my case as plainly as I knew how to Keith, Patty, and Pigboy, and Lindsay and Shanna-Francine, too, who had just stepped outside to join us. Was it really enough, I asked, that Meri was gone? That she'd been driven away? Shouldn't she be held accountable? Shouldn't she be punished? Weren't we being selfish by thinking only of ourselves? Sure, we were safe, but was the world safe from Meri?

"She's probably halfway to Bosnia by now," chuckled Lindsay. "It's the only place that'll have her."

Everyone joined in, laughing and giggling. They were all so exhausted and so giddy and relieved, and given all their hard work, it probably wasn't fair to expect them to immediately take the long view. But it was different for me. All my anxieties that had lessened only moments before due to Meri's momentous downfall were almost immediately replaced with a newly goosey apprehension. Meri was free, she was out there, ready to strike whenever and however she wanted. Trembling, I took Keith's hand and told him I needed to take a walk—alone, just for a bit.

"Are you sure?" he whispered, leaning in close. "Are you okay? Do you need anything? Should I follow behind you in my Range Rover?"

Oh my God, he's so amazing! But no, this was one walk I need-ed to take alone. Leaving Keith to explain my quick departure to the rest of the group, I strolled silently through the campus. *It's not over, it's not over.* That's what I kept telling myself. It was time to nail Meri—once and for all, permanently—and somehow I felt only I could do it. A simple plan began formulating in my mind. Was it too simple? Would it work? Still, I knew I would need some help, but did I dare ask for it? I had her number. Her superprivate cell phone number. My body leaped into action before my mind did. I pulled my cell phone from my purse and took a big breath. Then I dialed Mom.

# October 13

## Dear Diary:

Chicago's O'Hare Airport is a complete nightmare (some hotshot urban planner really needs to be slapped, and how!). It was two o'clock in the morning, and there I was, overwhelmed, overtired, yet overjoyed that Mom took my call and my plea for help seriously. In fact, I'd barely finished explaining my plan of action when she said, very tersely, "Hang up, dear. Wait ten minutes. Then call me back."

*Click*, and she was gone. When I called back, she coolly rattled off our itinerary.

"You're booked on a flight to Chicago in one hour. I'll meet you at the Skycap Lounge. Our connecting flight leaves Chicago thirty minutes after, so don't dawdle, go directly to the lounge."

"Mom, do you think it'll work?" I nervously asked. "Do you think . . ."

"Cindy, listen to me. Don't tell anyone what you're doing, don't tell anyone where you're going. You're right. It's not over. And whether your plan will work or not is irrelevant until it's relevant, so until that time, just relax. Have a cocktail on the flight. And remember, as the former president of Alpha Beta Delta, Mommy knows exactly how to help."

Then she giggled—I swear, it was high-pitched and everything—and hung up. I took Mom's advice. I had a lovely Brandy Alexander on the plane and even managed to close my eyes, only to bolt up with a gasp of panic when I saw a vision of Meri, her face looming like a full moon behind a stack of fast-moving clouds, abruptly screaming, "Handsies-kneesies!"

The plane landed hard. In the airport I found the Skycap Lounge, a semi-annoyingly designed faux Art Deco diner that charged me three fifty for a syrupy glass of Diet Coke. But Mom was nowhere to be found. Was her flight late? Did she miss it? Then I heard breathy giggles in the distance. I nearly shrieked. Meri was coming! She was here! But looking out, I saw that it was Mom, several feet away, smiling and tittering, dressed impeccably (as always), accompanied by two women. One of them was tall and rail-thin, dressed just as nicely as Mom, with flawlessly coiffed auburn hair. The other was short and plumpish, dressed in frumpy, layered, slightly mannish clothes that were probably all the rage in their Diane Keaton/Annie Hall day. Mom gave a wave and they strode up to me. The short, plump one leaned in close. She seemed stunned, awestruck even.

"So you're the one," she blurted ecstatically. "Can I shake your hand?"

"Oh, Debi, dial it back," scolded Mom playfully. Then she proceeded with introductions, gesturing first to the tall, thin woman. "Cindy, this is Julianna Slipovitch, former vice president of Alpha Beta Delta."

"I'm honored," said Julianna, firmly shaking my hand.

"And this," continued Mom, gesturing to the plump woman. "This is Deborah Pinga, who was, well . . ."

"Oh, I was the all-around get-it-done gal for the house," she whimsically exclaimed, shaking my hand. "And please, won't you call me Debi?"

I was enthralled. There's no other word for it. I guess traditions hold fast at Alpha Beta Delta. Mom was president of Alpha Beta Delta, and she certainly has the assurance of Meri; Julianna, Mom's second in command, was a dead ringer for Gloria Daily; and I guess every year has its Shanna-Francine, whose future may be brighter than I thought, given the life of Debi Pinga. Though Debi was known during her college years as "Deborah-the-Dilettante," I'm happy to report that she subsequently spent a decade with the Peace Corps in Vietnam and Thailand and is now a much-beloved high school drama teacher and guidance counselor, as well as the happy single mother of three boys (via artificial insemination, she cheerfully told me, from carefully screened donors with PhDs). She whipped out a picture, which told more then a thousand words. It was a formal portrait, with Debi smiling, eyes twinkling, hair askew, her chubby cheeks flush with pride, surrounded by three handsome teenage boys who towered over her like giant oaks and gazed down on her not just lovingly, but protectively, as if to say, yes, their mom is total wacko-city (of course), but also very precious.

"Rhea Nichols will be joining us when we land," Mom informed me, getting down to business. She glanced at her watch and tsked. "We'd better get to the gate. Lead the way, Cindy. You're in charge."

I had to laugh. Mom and her friends were ready and willing to take orders from me. From me! As we boarded the plane and took our seats, I explained my plan of action to Julianna and Debi. It was simple, really. Upon landing, we'd meet up with Rhea—yet another alumna of Alpha Beta Delta, and crucial to my strategy—locate Meri, and finally put a stop to her. I leaned back in my seat. This must have cost Mom a pretty penny. On both flights I was traveling first class.

"I'll pay you back," I assured her. "I swear."

"Don't be ridiculous, dear," she said with a mischievous glint in her eye. "Our air travel comes courtesy of my management fees deducted from Lisa's trust, which has been fattening quite a bit lately due to that disgusting little song. I told her she doesn't have to be dirty, but does she listen to me? I don't know what it is with you girls. You're both so stubbornly independent. God forbid anyone should ever listen to their mother. Do you honestly believe I came into this world fully formed just like I am? Don't either of you believe I was ever your age?"

I was trying not to smile. Behind her Debi was impishly mouthing, "Blah blah blah."

"I may not be as smart as you, or as plugged into pop culture like Lisa, but I do know a few things. So remember, Mommy's here for you. She knows things, and she's made of very high moral fiber."

"Yeah, one hundred percent nylon," cracked Julianna.

Debi and Julianna chuckled, ribbing Mom, who finally broke, laughing along with them. I don't believe I've ever seen her laugh in quite that way—so openly, so freely—and for the first time ever, it was actually possible to imagine that she was once my age. Oh my God, Mom is a real person! I know that sounds like I'm stating the obvious, but jeez, there she was being ribbed and deflated for her pretensions by friends who not only knew how to do it, they were used to it. She turned back to me, composing herself, attempting to finish her thought.

"All I'm trying to say . . ."

Julianna cut her off.

"She's trying to say she loves you, Cindy, even though she has no idea what she's doing. Okay?"

"Oh, but does anyone?" blurted Debi. "My boys—they're such sweet boys, all three of them—and, well, anyway, the oldest, Timmy, he has such pretty brown hair, and he told me the other day that he's interested in studying diachronic linguistics and comparative philology, and I said, 'Oh, Timmy, sweetheart, that's just wonderful.' Now I ask you, what the heck do I know from diachronic linguistics and comparative philology?"

"Nothing!" exclaimed Mom and Julianna simultaneously. Then Julianna ordered everyone a round of Chambord martinis and toasted to our mission and to my plan. I couldn't believe it. There I was, having girlfriend-cocktails with Mom and her friends! Still, one thought was nagging at me.

"Why didn't you warn me about Alpha Beta Delta?" I asked her.

"I didn't think I'd have to," she said. "I thought you'd go through one day of pledging and realize, 'I'm above this,' because you are. And remember, Alpha Beta Delta wasn't quite as bad in our day."

Julianna and Debi snorted, but Mom protested. Yes, their pledging rituals were harsh, and yes, they did have the Hoover File, that's tradition, but no one ever did anything with the information; there was no grade manipulation, for instance, and all the house outings were social and mostly involved shopping excursions or dances. But, as Mom pointed out, her tone darkening, things changed a few years ago when Meri Sugarman was elected president of Alpha Beta Delta at the beginning of her freshman year. Suddenly, the Hoover File was being used in a variety of ways, and not just against people about whom incoming pledges had gathered information. Selected Alpha Beta Delta alumni began receiving cryptic notices from the house, which informed them that "certain embarrassing details" about their past contained in the Hoover File would be immediately and publicly disseminated unless a "nominal" fee of one hundred and fifty dollars was sent to the house on a bimonthly basis.

"I thought it was a joke," said Julianna.

"So did I," added Mom, her eyes narrowing.

But then they received copies of their Hoover File entries. It was no joke. My mind was reeling. There was dirt on Mom?!

"See? You really are a hero," Debi squealed. "More than you knew. You're a hero to me, and to Julianna."

"And to me," said Mom, gazing at me, her eyes momentarily welling with tears. Then she quickly looked away, composed herself, and cleared her throat.

"Your mom detests cheap sentiment," Debi merrily pointed out.

The plane landed. We had arrived. My mission was about to

unfold. From the airport, we took a cab into town and arrived at the main strip. The sun had already risen, but the city was far from sleepy. We were in Las Vegas, where Alpha Beta Delta presidents traditionally maintain a year-round retreat. I was betting that Meri was here right now, and Mom, Julianna, and Debi agreed.

"You're right. Whatever her next move is, she'll make it from here," observed Julianna.

All I had to do was direct everyone to the right hotel and we could begin. Uh-oh. I suddenly realized that there was a little chink in my plan. Okay, a major chink. I had never actually accompanied Meri to Las Vegas (even though I'd been invited once), a fact that left everyone a bit stunned.

"We're fucked," blurted Debi.

But we weren't. We all had cell phones. Quickly retreating to the Tiki Stardust Lounge at the Lady Luck Casino and Hotel, we called every single hotel in Vegas and asked to be connected to both Meri Sugarman and Gloria Daily. No luck.

"She's under a false name," said Mom, gritting her teeth.

"Like I said. We're fucked," observed Debi.

It kind of seemed like we were, but then I remembered Jackie O., Meri's idol. Surely Meri wouldn't be silly enough to register under the name of Jackie or Jacqueline Onassis or Kennedy, though this might be the key to the name she was using. But where to start? I'd only glanced at a few of Meri's many Jackie O. tomes, and while I was fairly confident that I knew a few facts about "America's Queen," would they be enough?

"So we're looking for something similar to a code," said Debi intently, her brow creasing. "Something easy to remember. Like a password. Like all those dumb passwords and reminders I have to remember for all those stupid Internet sites and my e-mail."

"That's it!" I shrieked.

I was ecstatic. This had to be it. We called each and every hotel in Vegas once more, but this time we used a different name. It wasn't a site code we needed to prompt us, but the reminder, like the reminders that Internet sites use when they want you to prove that it's you if you've forgotten your password—specifically, "What is the name of your first pet?" It might be obscure, but I happen to remember from one of Meri's books that Jackie O.'s first and most cherished pet was a little Scottie dog named Hootchie. Score! Mom practically shot to the ceiling. "Hootchie Bouvier" was staying at the Venetian Resort Hotel and Casino. We leaped into a cab. Mom dialed frantically on her cell phone and contacted Rhea Nichols, who agreed to meet us at the Venezia, the new "exclusive" Venetian Hotel Tower, which apparently offers unparalleled amenities and where "Hootchie Bouvier" was currently registered as a guest. The back of my throat was drying up. Would this really be the end of Meri? And did I really have the nerve to go through with this? Mom's hand gently curved into mine and gave a reassuring squeeze. I squeezed back. Meri might be a formidable foe, but I wasn't alone. I had Mom!

At the Venezia, we scrambled from the cab and raced into the elevator, which whisked us up to the "exclusive" fifth-floor registration lobby. Everything, I noted, was "exclusive" at the Venezia, and good lord, "gaudy" is a word that can't even begin to describe the wildly overwrought rococo design scheme; it was like a schoolboy's idea of Old World opulence. The lobby itself was this totally witless riot of gold-leaf paint and baroque nude statuary, but so scrubby clean and sterilized that you couldn't even enjoy the sheer tackiness of it. Julianna snorted.

"Now this is class, with a capital *K*."

The elevator pinged. Out stepped Rhea Nichols, formerly of Alpha Beta Delta, but jeez, she could have been a movie star. I'm not normally daunted or impressed by beauty—since everyone knows that all the beautiful girls in *People* and *Vogue* are created by

PhotoShop. (It's true. The worst offender has got to be *TV Guide*, which had the nerve to put Oprah's head on top of Courtney Cox's body.) But this was the real thing. With her dark olive skin, piercing green eyes, and shiny-shiny shoulder-length black hair, along with a curvy figure that seemed to be setting off cymbal crashes, Rhea instantaneously caused every man, woman, and child within eyeshot to crane their necks. But she didn't seem to notice. She strode right up to Mom, gave her a kiss on each cheek (so European!), lit a Benson & Hedges Ultra Light, and throatily intoned, "Okee-doke. Let's bag the bitch."

Would it really be that simple? After exchanging a few whispers and a wink with the registration clerk, Rhea directed Mom, Debi, Julianna, and me down a long corridor toward Meri's room.

"What number are we looking for?" I asked, my heart racing.

"Ten twenty-two," answered Rhea.

"Why don't you lead the way, dear," said Mom sweetly.

Rhea gestured magnanimously and stepped aside, allowing me to charge confidently (or at least I thought so) into the main elevator, which whisked us all up to the tenth floor. I had barely taken two steps out of the elevator when I heard a very tiny high-pitched screech. My eyes popped. At the end of the hall Gloria stood startled, holding an ice bucket, momentarily frozen in place, outfitted with a new and saucy black bouffant wig. Then she hurled the bucket, which scattered dozens of little round ice cubes ("exclusive" ice cubes, no doubt), and ran. I honestly don't know what came over me. All rational thought seemed to vanish. In what seemed like a split second, I was off. I raced after her, whipping down the hotel corridor, and suddenly felt a truly frightening roar blast from my wide-open mouth. I roared! I actually roared. And before I knew it, I took a full-out flying leap (gracefully, I thought), with my arms extended as far as they could go. I was airborne! Gloria whipped around. She looked up. Her face was gnarled in terror. *Ka-boom!* I flattened her,

practically squashing her like a bug when my body landed on top of
her and forcefully slammed her to the lime green carpeted floor.

"Cindy!" exclaimed Mom, who raced around the corner with
Rhea, Julianna, and Debi.

Then they burst out laughing, having discovered that I had
everything very much under control. Mom leaned in and whispered
threateningly to Gloria, "Card key. Now."

"Good job, Cindy," said Debi, giving me a wink.

This was it. We knew the room number, we had the card key, and
Gloria was safely detained in an exclusive Venezia utility closet,
snugly bound with a vacuum cleaner cord and gagged with the back
belt of Debi's pea jacket. She didn't look too happy about it. Aw.
Toughie-wuffy. I harbored no sympathy for Gloria. Instead I led the
way to Hootchie Bouvier's room and firmly slashed the card key in
the entry slot. The door softly clicked open. Mom pressed her finger to her lips. "Shh."

I glanced back at her nervously. She encouraged me with a res-
olute expression. Julianna looked equally determined, Rhea was
grinning with anticipation, and Debi's jaw was flopped open, her
eyes wide as saucers. We padded gingerly into the suite foyer. It was
darkened, though I could see beyond the foyer to the sunken living
room below and out to the large garden terrace where the morning
sun was beginning to shine brightly. Rhea motioned me forward and
we stepped into the living room. From the bedroom we heard faint
breathy moans: "Lower. Little lower. Oh God, that's it. Work it.
Really work it. Harder."

I glanced at Mom, horror-struck. Yes, I wanted to bring Meri
down, but I really didn't feel like interrupting some smutty game of
slap-and-tickle (even the thought of it made me feel so scuzzed out).
Mom must have read my mind, because she shook her head and
elaborately motioned with her hands and fingers, miming the move-
ments of a massage therapist.

"Don't you have magnolia oil?" purred Meri from the bedroom. "I just love magnolia oil."

Uh-oh. Sashaying out from the bedroom was a Venezia "massage technician," but honest, he looked just like a lifeguard from *Baywatch* with his big Nautelized chest and fleshy lips, along with a certain brain-free gleam in his eyes that seemed to be saying, *I am s-o-o-o proud of my vintage Barbie collection. Wanna see? Motown Midge is my fave.* And he was humming. Oh my God, I recognized the tune.

*Tune my motor up!*
*Oh, baby, tune it, tune it, tune it, make me purr!*
*Tune my motor up!*

He stopped short, staring confusedly at me, Mom, Debi, and Julianna, and he was just about to say something when Rhea popped up from behind, slapped her hand over his mouth, and yanked him down to the couch.

In the bedroom, Meri was wrapped in a plush towel and lying flat on a massage table, her head protruding through the hollow opening in the tabletop, her black bouffant wig slightly askew. She was blissfully unaware when a new pair of hands began lightly massaging her back. Then another pair. And another. Startled, she jerked her head up, and that's when she saw me, standing just a foot before her, my hands on my hips, my expression really fierce (I thought). The end of Meri had arrived, though she wasn't quite ready to accept that. She whipped around, gazed open-eyed at Julianna, Mom, and Debi, leaped furiously off the massage table, swiped a robe, and firmly tightened the sash. Meri was in control once more—or so she thought. For an eensy-weensy moment, I felt sorry for her. It kind of reminded me of the time I found this really huge and disgusting water bug in the bathtub and stomped on it, then gathered it in a paper towel, hurled it into the toilet, and flushed it down, thinking in those brief final moments as it swirled in the bowl, *Yes, it had to happen, but it is sad to see any life end.* And yet, after it was all flushed away, my sympathy evaporated. *Poof.* Just like that. After all, no one really likes water bugs.

"Well, well, well," Meri acidly intoned. "Is this a reunion?" She glanced at Mom. "I know you. I know all of you. Gee, it's so nice that we're all here together. Let's have a party. Drinks, anyone? Mimosas?"

She reached for the phone—and Julianna's hand slapped down hard on the receiver.

"End of the road, Meri," I stated plainly.

"Tsk, you're cute. Be a little ring ding and order drinks, would you? And coffee, too. The caffeine will bring me up; the booze will bring me down. In other words, it'll make you bearable. Now, where's that Tony?"

She made to step to the living room, but I blocked her, swiftly stepping in front of the door.

"I told you, Meri. End of the road."

She smirked. "What are going to do? Jump me? Aw. Let me guess. You've just seen *Kill Bill.* And you're feeling empowered. As a woman. Which is really very sad. Do you honestly believe that movie's any different from any other mass entertainment? It's not. It's exactly the same. It's just more jolts for jocks."

Debi seemed completely bewildered. "Would someone please tell me what the hell she's going on about?"

"Nice try, guys," Meri continued, triumphantly whipping out her cell phone from her robe pocket. "Now move or I'll call security. This is my party. And you're not invited. Get it? You've got five seconds. Ready? By the time I reach five, you'll all be gone. You too, Cindy. Don't be a weenie. You know I mean what I say."

I had to interrupt her. Now was the time. "Meri, before you start counting, I'd like to introduce you to another alumna of Alpha Beta Delta."

I swept aside from the door and in sauntered Rhea, grinning complacently.

"Meri Sugarman, meet Rhea Nichols."

Rhea didn't wait for her response. She pulled out a pair of handcuffs and said, very coolly, "Meri Sugarman, you have the right to remain silent—"

Meri exploded. "Are you out of your mind?!"

"Oops, I guess I forgot to say," I gleefully interjected. "See, Rhea's a detective with the Las Vegas Police Department. Isn't that cool?"

Meri snickered. "You're all just itching for a lawsuit. I've done nothing in Vegas. Nothing."

She was right, she hadn't, but as Rhea calmly explained, she was arresting Meri on behalf of the Rumson River Police Department on charges of extortion and illegal wiretapping, along with a myriad of other charges big and small (they'll even be hitting her with animal cruelty charges, given her hit on Rags!). For the first time since I've known her, Meri stood stifled and nearly motionless, since she surely knew that there was nothing she could do. After listening to Rhea recite the Miranda rights, she abruptly gasped, like she was choking for air. Then she spoke out loud, more to herself than to us. She was reassuring herself. If she was going to be arrested, or if she had to serve time, then okay, fine, at least it was in Vegas. But she was out of luck there, too.

"Sorry, kid. What happens in Vegas stays in Vegas," Rhea informed her. "What happened to you happened in Rumson River. And that's exactly where you'll be going."

Then she held out the handcuffs and motioned to Meri. "Now give me your hands. Let's do this calmly."

Meri shuddered, meekly held out her hands—then violently shoved Rhea, who tumbled backward. It all happened in a flash: Rhea hit the floor hard, Mom screamed, Debi brought her hands to her face, crying out, "No-o-o-o way!", Julianna lunged for the phone.

And me? I ran out of the suite as fast as lightning. Did Meri really think she could get away? Not if I could help it. I leaped out into the hallway. My adrenaline was pumping. Which way did she go? I heard a *ping* from the elevator and the breathless voice of Rhea behind me.

"She's in the elevator! Quick, the stairs. We'll catch her at the registration lobby."

I bolted ahead, practically leapfrogging down the stairs, and behind me I could hear the violent banging of Mom's and Debi's and Julianna's and Rhea's shoes against the hard metal stairs—rat-a-tat-tat, like machine guns. Then I heard a gasping scream. Uh-oh. Poor Debi. She must have lost her footing. Before I knew what was happening, she was tumbling head over heels down the stairs ahead of me, her frizzy hair flying, her eyes wide with shock. *Boom-boom-boom*, down she went, one flight after another.

"Keep going!" cried Julianna, who decided to stay behind and tend to Debi, whose fall was luckily stalled three floors below when a hotel guest abruptly swung open a stairwell door, making painful contact with Debi's head.

I kept running, and my hands thrust out before me when I reached the door to the registration lobby. I pushed it open with all my might, and I guess I must have looked horrible, or maybe threatening, because the lobby attendant jerked his head in my direction and let out a gasping girly squeal. But I didn't care. Before me, I could see the bank of elevators. One of them was opening, and running out of it was Meri. She soared across the lobby to the adjoining bank of elevators that would take her to the ground level. I howled inhumanly and charged right toward her, and in a quick and elegant whirl, she switched directions and ran the opposite way down the adjacent hallway.

Could I really keep running? Could I really catch her? *And more to the point,* I thought, *doesn't Meri know when enough is enough?* I mean, jeez, even Godzilla goes down at some point. I purged these thoughts from my mind and ran faster. I became a machine, a running, screaming Robo-Cindy, whose tiny computer chip had been programmed with just one objective: Bring down Meri. It worked! I was gaining on her, and there was nowhere for Meri to go at the end of the hall unless she decided to take a flying leap out the window, which seemed wildly unlikely since it would have been deadly (true, some war criminals and psychos opt for suicide when they're cornered and have no way out, but oddly enough, I think Meri is made of much stronger stuff, and like James Cagney in that old movie *White Heat*, which Dad loves so much, I think Meri would much prefer to go down in flames). I flung my hands out, my fingers greedily reaching. If I pushed myself just a bit more, I could smash her against the wall and finally wrangle her to the floor.

Then the unthinkable happened. As I thrust myself toward her, a maniacal glint appeared in her eye, and quick like a bunny, she darted to her left—and poof!—she was gone. I stood there dumbfounded. *What the heck just happened? Is Meri supernatural now?* I thought. *Oh my God, that is just so unfair if it's true.* Screams and hollers from Rhea and Mom shook me out of my reverie, along with a sudden jolting metallic *bang*. I whipped around. The hard metal door to the large Venezia garbage chute slammed shut. My jaw dropped, though I'll bet not as fast as Meri was dropping right at that moment down the chute, which I'm sure is absolutely filthy no matter how "exclusive" it may be. I guess I could have just flung my arms up at that moment and said, "I give, she wins," but I didn't. While Rhea was frantically calling for backup, I grabbed Mom's hand and ran. She was wailing, "Cindy, let's leave it to the professionals!"

But really, who could be more professional than me at this point in terms of bringing down Meri? Foregoing the elevators, Mom and I ran down the stairs to the ground level and sprinted to the back alley, where a seemingly endless line of gargantuan Dumpsters were lined up, each with a large chute and flap before them.

"Cindy, stop," commanded Mom.

She was right. Meri was in one of the Dumpsters. It was over. I could relax now. Finally. Twenty minutes later Rhea and several LVPD officers had cordoned off the alley and begun the arduous task of tipping over each Dumpster, one after another, all of which spilled out really rank and disgusting piles of garbage. Yuck. As Rhea informed Mom and me, Meri was surely inside one of the Dumpsters, and probably knocked out cold from the fall and in need of medical attention. But as each Dumpster was tipped over, and the officers poked through the piles, there was no Meri. There was nothing.

"This is the one," said Rhea, gesturing to the final Dumpster.

The officers tipped it over, and the garbage cascaded out. I held my breath in anticipation; the garbage seemed to tumble forth in slow motion. Then it settled, and I nearly gasped. There it was. Right on top of the heap. Meri's black bouffant wig.

I already knew that Meri was long gone as the officers began poking through the pile, and I guess I looked pretty defeated, because Mom put her arm around me and gave me a kiss on the cheek.

"You did good, honey," she said.

It was Rhea who actually made me feel better. There would be an APB out for Meri now. She was a wanted criminal (a bald wanted criminal). Yes, Meri could run, as they say, but she couldn't hide. Her downfall was assured. Did I feel sorry for her? Maybe. Just a bit. Then I smiled inwardly, and I thought about that awful icky water bug. *Flush.*

"Close your eyes and hold out your hands," said Mom.

I held them out. I felt something soft and plushy. When Mom told me I could open my eyes, I stared down at my hands. There it was—Meri's wig. For a moment it felt like I was holding a hunting trophy, like a stuffed moose head or a tiger pelt.

"Maybe you'd like to burn it," offered Mom.

"Or nail it to a cross," chuckled Rhea.

Neither one appealed to me. The wig needed to go somewhere, yes, but not with me. I flung my arm out, forcefully hurling it. It seemed to magically pause in midair—would it suddenly sprout wings and fly away?—and then it landed with a moist plop in the large pile of "exclusive" Venezia garbage. Right were it belonged.

"This is your time, Cindy," Mom said, and I was kind of disappointed when she did. We were back on a plane headed to Chicago, and I really wanted Mom, Julianna, and Debi to continue on with me to Rumson U. and join in the celebration, since I knew that Patty, Pigboy, Keith, and Lindsay (and okay, Bud), would be thrilled to hear the news, if they hadn't already. But Mom insisted that this was my time, though Julianna was quick to say, "Really, Cindy, the last thing your mom wants to do is hang out with a bunch of perky sorority girls and feel her age."

They giggled. Mom pinched her. Then they all thanked me again for being their hero and for having the strength to have fought so hard against Meri for so long. Debi suddenly gasped in shock.

"Gloria!" she squealed.

Oh no! We forgot about Gloria! Oops! After we said our good-byes to Rhea (we said our good-byes to Tony Spinoza, too, the Venezia massage technician, who turned out to be this really nice guy with a very high-pitched voice who unfortunately told us his nickname was "Tony Pepperoni." Gross!), we headed straight to the airport.

"Fine, I'll call Rhea," said Mom, lazily reaching for the plane's airphone.

But Julianna stopped her. Couldn't we call Rhea after we landed? Or maybe later in the day?

"Like much later," she chuckled.

At O'Hare Airport, Mom, Julianna, and Debi walked me to the departure gate for Rumson River, and they got a little teary-eyed, and I guess I did too, especially when I looked up at Mom's smiling face. No, I don't have a new mom now, but I do have more of a mom—a more complete mom, with all sides in view to me now—and while it's true that we don't have much in common on the surface, I don't think we'll be seeing that as much of an obstacle from now on. In fact, I have a feeling we're going to be really great girlfriends. Ha! How many people can say that about their mom and actually mean it?

"I nominate Cindy as our new house president!" cried Lindsay as she raised her cocktail glass. I turned beet red back at Alpha Beta Delta when Lindsay offered this cheer. Everyone was gathered at the house for cocktails, and you should have heard the shrieks of joy when we got a phone call from Dean Pointer telling us that all charges are being dropped against Keith. Keith held me close.

"You rock," he said sweetly, kissing my cheek.

"Oh my God, she so rocks," squealed Shanna-Francine.

"Posttraumatic Stress Disorder," observed Patty. "It's the next stage for our Meri."

"I completely disagree," said Shanna-Francine, who suddenly became alarmingly lucid. "Her demeanor will never significantly change. More than likely, it will harden with age. I believe it was Jack the Ripper who said, 'I need to repeat the acts which bring me pleasure as soon as possible.' In this light, we can see the choice that Meri has made, and indeed must have made, perhaps unconsciously, from her very earliest days. Erich Fromm tells us, 'The ultimate choice for a man is to create or to destroy, to love or to hate,' and I think we can safely say which side of the fence Meri falls on in that somewhat empirical equation. Don't you agree?"

My jaw dropped. I was flabbergasted. I was stunned. I was way, way beyond shocked. Shanna-Francine is not a dim bulb!

"No, but I play it well, don'tcha think?" she drily asked.

It all became clear. Ever since joining Alpha Beta Delta and learning of Meri's true nature, Shanna-Francine decided to protect herself by playing stupid—really stupid—while also desperately looking for a way to bring her down. She credited me with giving her the opportunity. "Oh God, I really shouldn't be telling you this," was, in fact, Shanna-Francine's way of keeping me informed every step of the way—letting me know right from the start, for instance, about Meri's surveillance, to cite just one example. Now I know why she told me to take Meri her breakfast that very first day ("You needed to get the lay of the lair," she informed me), and why she commanded me to retrieve my notebook from my room after Mamacita arrived to clean Meri's room ("You didn't know her room had separate locks and keys"), and guess who placed that anonymous call to Dean Pointer the other morning ("He still didn't realize Meri had nothing on him anymore; someone had to tell him")? But perhaps her riskiest gambit was her "big oopsie," when she gave DJ Mo Ghee the DAT tapes instead of the 8-track tapes, a plan that had long been in the works from the moment she'd convinced Meri to let Alpha Beta Delta take over the Oktoberfest Dance. I couldn't help myself. I nearly screamed, "I nominate Shanna-Francine as our new house president!"

Happily, everyone agreed. Shanna-Francine also agreed to help Randy with valuable background information about Meri for his school newspaper article, "Meri: The Sociopath Among Us," as well as details regarding her juvenile court records, including her most embarrassing crime: her junior high school arrest for stealing Jaclyn Smith matchables at Kmart. Everyone wants to help. Patty's going to be interviewed for a psychological sidebar, and Keith and Pigboy and Bud and I will be interviewed too. But what about all those pictures Nester took at the dance?

"For the yearbook," he proudly announced. "In the corner there'll be a flip book. Flip the pages and you'll see Meri brought down. Pretty cool, huh?"

As for Mamacita, Patty and Pigboy had given her the ledger and let her go once DJ Mo Ghee was given the DAT tapes by Shanna-Francine. She had seemed indifferent to the fact that Meri was about to be brought down, though she wished them well. Obviously, Mamacita has bigger fish to fry.

It was past midnight when the party finally broke up.

"I'll miss sleeping with you, Cyn," said Bud with a leer. Then he cleared his throat and suddenly became very serious and pulled me aside. I braced myself. Would he try to kiss me? Didn't he know to wear a cup by now? He spoke, his voice barely above a whisper.

"I guess I gotta come clean with you, Cyn. And, you know, kinda 'come out,' so to speak."

No! Please God, say it isn't so. Bud Finger is gay? I suddenly got an image of Bud in a very tight-fitting Abercombie & Fitch T-shirt and matching earth-tone capri pants. No, no, it just didn't compute! Bud can't be gay. And yet, I realized, he does love-love Kylie Minogue. Oh my God. And he loves "Lissa," too—and so does Tony Spinoza, aka "Tony Pepperoni." Oh my God, oh my God, oh my God. Poor Bud. His life was now guaranteed to be complete hell. Given that he's had such difficulty navigating the straight world (to put it charitably), he was sure to need my friendship now. I mean, there's no way the gay world will very easily welcome the likes of Bud Finger, if at all. I was about to tell him that I was happy for him, and that I'd be there for him through this difficult time (even if it meant hanging out with him and listening to Kylie, though I would draw the line at "Lissa"), when he smiled goofily.

"I mean, we were just pretending at first—you know, like it was me and you making out in my room—but after a while, we really hit it off. And now that everything is over, we're not going to be kissing in the shadows anymore. Are we, punkin?"

What? Did he mean . . . Was he saying . . . Lindsay demurely stepped forth, put her arm around his waist, and kissed him sweetly on the cheek. Whoa. This. Was. Too. Much. Bud Finger and Lindsay? Together? All this time I had been worried about Lindsay and felt bad that I was leaving her in Bud's clutches in his dorm room in order to help our cause, but there they were right in front of me, arm in arm, gazing into each other's eyes.

"But you two are so different," I sputtered.

"Oh, c'mon. Don't you listen to Paula Abdul?" said Bud with a lopsided grin. "Opposites attract."

Then they chuckled and strode out, but not before thanking me profusely for bringing them together. I numbly said, "You're welcome," but I'd actually prefer not to take credit for this one.

Patty and Pigboy were off too, though Patty did have some parting advice. I forgot, but I had once told her about my nightmare—you know, the one about Dad and the strip club and the cigar? She was concerned about Keith and me.

"I'm happy for you," she said. "But you know, you really do need to get past your Elektra Complex. And remember, sometimes a cigar is much more . . ."

I laughed, grabbed a Grand Torpedo Magnum from Keith, and happily puffed away.

"Patty, stop worrying. Sometimes a cigar is just a really good smoke. Okay?"

I'm in my old room now at Alpha Beta Delta. Keith is next to me in bed. He's sleeping (he doesn't snore). Rags is curled at the foot of the bed (he does snore). Tonight I'll sleep without fear or worry. Maybe I'll even have nice dreams.